ALL GODS
DEAD

Maureen O'Neill

Marian O Neill was brought up in Dublin. She graduated from UCD in 1987 with a degree in Art History and English Literature. Since graduating she has worked in publishing, book retail and advertising. She currently teaches Creative Writing and Academic Writing Skills. Marian lives in Thomastown, Co Kilkenny with her husband Stephen Buck.

Also by the same author:

Miss Harrie Elliott
Daddy's Girl
Seeforge

ALL GODS DEAD

Marian O Neill

NEW ISLAND

ALL GODS DEAD
First published 2012
by New Island
2 Brookside
Dundrum Road
Dublin 14

www.newisland.ie

P/B   ISBN   978-1-84840-174-7
ePub   ISBN   978-1-84840-175-4
mobi   ISBN   978-1-84840-176-1

Cover design by Nina Lyons
Typeset by xxxxxxxxxxxxx.
Printed by ScandBook AB, Sweden 2012

New Island received financial assistance from
The Arts Council (An Comhairle Ealaíon), Dublin, Ireland

10 9 8 7 6 5 4 3 2 1

For Stephen and Patricia

ACKNOWLEDGEMENTS

I would like to thank Prizeman and Kinsella for their support, Cecily O Neill for her editorial input and Stephen Buck for his encouragement and professional help with the research of this book.

'… all Gods dead, all wars fought, all faiths in man shaken.'

F. Scott Fitzgerald

CHAPTER 1

I am old now. Some days I recognise the fact; some days the face in the mirror mirrors my own. And some days I can negotiate my limitations; some days my hands connect my intentions to actions and my speech conveys my thoughts to others. They tell me here that these are the good days, but then there are the other ones. The nurses don't tell me too much about them, but I can read the reserve on their faces.

I don't quite know how long I've been here; I suppose about a year. There was a tree for Christmas and now someone has, quite thoughtlessly, decorated the day-room with pumpkin heads and streamers dangling skeletal forms and witches' hats! I ask you, twenty-five wizened old crones and five shrivelled up old men sitting under that; it's far too close to the bone but, pun aside, it is rather funny. There's no one to share the joke with though. I tried with Nurse Ryan, 'Imelda Ryan' in large red letters pinned to her bulging bust.

'Graveyard humour,' I said, trying to smile with the half of my face that works. I should have known better. I should remember that words tend to drool out of my mouth these days and that my smile catches on a snarl.

'It's only a bit of fun,' she snapped back, bringing me to a stop by the window, clanking the breaks on my chair. I snarled properly then; she had parked me too far to the left, I couldn't see the road at all and the neatly tended shrubs lining the car park offer no amusement.

I tried again when the family came to visit. I have two daughters, four grandchildren, three great-grandchildren. The daughters take it in turns to come, about every third day. The grandchildren, the ones who live locally, turn up when their mothers can't and the great grandchildren they keep for special occasions. They don't know that I know this, that I can still keep track; that I carried the burden of duty for far too long not to recognise it in others. They sit, they say

'Cold for this time of year.'

'What did you have for lunch?'

'Do you want to watch the telly?'

'Warm today.'

In an attempt to reply I struggle with words and they drool down my chin, and I snarl, even when I'm trying to charm, and I always forget that I look so much worse than I am. Ruth, my youngest daughter, came today and I tried again with the Halloween decorations.

'What?' she asked, three times, and then just let it go. She told me slowly and loudly about how her family was, what they were doing, where they were going. All good things. I know they protect me from the day-to-day disasters that must punctuate their lives; I just don't know why. Don't I look battle-scarred enough? At ninety odd, don't they know that I must have survived worse?

'Brian sends his best,' she said as she was going. I nodded, not even attempting a smile. I wonder if she ever knew how disappointed I was in her choice of husband, and how surprised I am by how long she has stayed with him. Herself and Deirdre too, married to some kind of replica of their father. The both of them choosing what I was forced to settle for; what I refused Phil for: family, security and sweet, soft luxury.

She patted my hand as she left and tears gathered in the folds of her middle-aged, almost elderly, eyes.

'Ah, Mam,' she said and kissed my cheek.

Nurse Ryan got to her before she left the room, drew her aside, by the door to the day-room, and started muttering her litany of concern. I couldn't hear much, more the tone than anything else. It was low, worried but caring. Every now and again Ruth would interject with an 'I can't believe it!' or an 'It's so unlike her!' And then old Mrs Doyle started on with her singing and everything else was drowned out.

'Daisy, Daisy give me your answer do, I'm half crazy…' That's funny too, come to think of it.

But I didn't have to hear any specific words to know what ol' Imelda Ryan was saying. She was telling Ruth about the day before. The day when I came to in my room, in my bed with Doctor Delaney bent over me and young Nurse Kerr hovering behind him. I remembered nothing since lunch, nothing since over-set jelly and canned cream.

Doctor Delaney was very kind about the whole affair. Brushed it off with a wave of his pudgy little manicured hands.

'Just a little disorientated?' he asked. 'You got a wee bit agitated at lunch; do you remember?'

I shook my head, trying with all my might to pull my face up into an expression of rueful regret. Would that be the right emotion to show? I could guess at what had happened. Would abject mortification be more apt? Does it matter?

'Maybe you should stay in bed now that you're all settled. Nurse Kerr here will look after you.'

And Nurse Kerr shuffled forward. I could see by her expression that she had obviously been involved in my 'agitation'.

It's strange to admit that at my age, at ninety plus, I've just recently felt the chill of death. Cancer has been eating at my bowels for years now and the fall that smashed my hip curtailed all but minimal movement – but it was the stroke that did it. I woke up in hospital with the clutter of my past hovering in the shadows and the chill of death seeping into my bones. Since then I've been waiting for it. It rasps about my conscious self, blurs my waking hours with long-dreamt dreams, long-forgotten memories, daily these shades gain in substance. Soon, as they claim me, as they will, my death breath will bloat them into flesh-filled forms. Soon they will be my reality and this chintz-frilled bedroom will fade entirely. On my bad days, like yesterday, these ghostly memories cluster so close they block out all else and force an interaction.

Goodness knows who I thought poor Nurse Kerr was, but I can imagine the sort of things I said to her, all those words that were screaming in my head when I first woke up from the stroke. I couldn't speak them then, but I can now. All those words I spent a lifetime suppressing, all those secrets.

And what of them now? They are insisting on some form of acknowledgement. A long death, a life slowly inching past, a story untold, half remembered. If my misshapen mouth righted itself for long enough for me to howl out clear and loud a litany of all the sins of my youth, would anyone listen? Would the trust and love that glisten behind Ruth's tears diminish? Would the security I've built a life on crumble? Would it matter?

CHAPTER 2

Ruth Mahon sat in her car in Superquinn's car park and, in case anyone was looking in, made a show of rooting in her bag. She was crying. That place always did it to her, the guilt. But full-time care? Her own family? Brian? She had had no choice, but still the guilt. It was always upsetting, but this was worse. Shopping could wait. She pulled herself together as best she could and drove down the blindly familiar road to her childhood home.

They, her sister Deirdre and herself, had agreed that the time had come to clear it out. It was to be sold. Initially it had been an easy decision to make – sell the Dublin house and keep the small holiday cottage in Kerry – but then that decision had triggered a thousand more. Who was to take what? What could they sell and what should they take down to Kerry? What was of sentimental value and what was charity-shop junk? Who could tell the difference? The last time Ruth had tried to box things up she had found herself crying over a biscuit tin.

'The blue one?' Deirdre had asked and Ruth had laughed.

'Of course the sodding blue one.' The blue one was the one that they had kept the chocolate biscuits in, the brown one had the Mariettas.

Ruth drove up the short avenue to the house and parked right by the porch. It was raining now. In the south-city suburbs of Dublin, an avenue, no matter how short, and a porch denote serious comfort if not serious wealth. Ruth's parents had bought the place when the former was more applicable. Her mother, then Brigit Simpson, had sold some property before the marriage and her father, William Egan, had been a barrister. But still, despite its suburban grandeur, and its present shut-down, shrouded state, it was still primarily a family home, tousled and scuffed and slightly smelly in corners from incontinent pets.

Ruth ran in, straight down the hall, straight to the phone. Deirdre was at work, a small solicitor's office. Her tone was clipped, but that was because others were within earshot. Ruth didn't mind; she only really wanted someone to listen. She spoke about the visit, the state of their mother's hair, how she looked frailer than before and then she said it.

'She told one of the nurses to go fuck herself.'

'She did what?'

'Yeah, and worse I think. They didn't really say, but it was something very sexual.'

'Like what?'

'The nurse said that mother was talking about a sexual act, I don't know. But she told one of the nurses she shouldn't do it for less than a guinea.'

'Mam?'

Yes, their sweet mother. Who never raised her voice. Who never cursed. The doyenne of the tea trolley and the porter cake. Their sweet mother.

'Are they sure? You know she is very hard to make out at times?'

'They're sure and quite upset. She tried to throw a teapot but she couldn't lift it.'

'What do they say? What are they going to do?'

'Well, monitor her. They say it's a sign of senility, foul language, personality changes. And they say that they may have to keep her more separate, that she could start upsetting the others.'

'Sure that lot wouldn't notice or hear or care.' Deirdre's voice was rising in a swell of indignation. Her mother! Their money! Services required! It was a voice that Ruth could never bear; one that, over the years, she had heard echoed around hotel foyers, restaurant tables, subdued boutiques. Ruth thought it common to have to insist on a quality of service. She thought that those who truly deserve it never have to demand it. She never said that to Deirdre though; instead, she began her usual placating.

'It's not so bad,' she said. 'It just means that she'll spend more time in her room. She isn't up to much anyway and that crowd in there are far too depressing to be doing her any good.' It worked. Once Deirdre was convinced that no corner-shirking was going on, she concentrated on the real horror of the information.

Their mother. Their sweet, dear mother.

Ruth felt better once she had hung up. Felt well enough to bring some boxes up to the room they had always, rather pretentiously, called the library. The box bedroom, shelved floor to ceiling, crammed full of books, comics, photo albums, cards, in fact anything at all that was flat or stackable.

She would box the books by type – fiction, biography, history – and, as she went, she could separate anything that obviously belonged to Deirdre. Starting at the far corner she pulled down one of the dust-sheets.

After the fall, which broke her hip and limited her access to just three rooms on the ground floor, Brigit Egan had insisted on covering the rest of the house in these sheets. Her daughters had laughed at her.

'What for, Mam?' they asked, while carrying out her instructions.

'To protect our valuables from the harsh Irish sun?' But still, even though Brigit never saw the upstairs of her house again it was arranged exactly as she had wanted.

The sheet fell with a dusty thud and Ruth reached up to the top shelf. As always she slowed almost as soon as she started. The smell of school books, illustrations that floated her six-year-old self before her. Achingly familiar editions of childhood classics. She moved on to her father's books; dry, outdated law tomes were easier to dispose of. Shelves were cleared. She had done enough.

Although it was only half four it was getting late – late for October, late for shopping and cooking and presenting a proper evening meal for Brian. Ruth stood up and her legs creaked. She stayed still for a moment feeling the tingle of trickling circulation. Money and time could keep her slim and groomed, but she was still fifty-six, almost sixty, and ludicrously, in this context, still a child. The house always did it to her; too many memories. She stretched her hand out and ran it over the spines of the books that had always been known as 'Mam's collection'. A selection of the great writers of the early twentieth century: F. Scott Fitzgerald, Hemingway,

Anaïs Nin, Dorothy Parker and some of the lesser-known ones, such as Mina Loy and Robert McAlmon. Some were in French, from the young Brigit Simpson's teaching days, and some in German. Then there were the biographies – an obsessive amount on Picasso, but all the main writers and artists of the time were well represented.

The time being between the wars when the young Brigit Simpson must have been thrilled by the artistic and academic movements taking place. Ruth smiled; it charmed her that her mother's girlish passion had survived the cynicism and apathy of adulthood. As a child Ruth could remember her mother leafing through collections of Picasso plates, still rapt, still eager to talk about form and detail. But now that she thought about it she realised that that hadn't happened for years, decades even. Maybe the cynicism and apathy of middle age had finally quenched her mother's youthful enthusiasm.

Ruth closed the door and, out of habit, turned left down the hall to her old bedroom. She creaked open the door – it had always creaked – and stood staring into its white, lumpen emptiness. It had long since been stripped of all her childhood possessions. But still, especially in the cold, grey winter's dusk, it was cluttered with emotion. All those hours, all those dramas, camomile lotion on rashes, cold stethoscopes on fevered chests, birthday treats of breakfast in bed, doors slamming, insults flying, screaming laughter, soothed nightmares, guilty two-o'-clock-in-the-morning shufflings. And through it all her mother's face, calm and kind. Was it really that idyllic? It felt so to Ruth, even though she was well aware of Deirdre's version: that their mother had controlled the household, battering them all into guilty submission with her passive-aggressive martyrdom. Did she? Ruth didn't really know.

How can unconditional love maintain a balance between victimhood and control? It must swing one way or the other – a good question to put to Deirdre.

It was almost dark now. She creaked the bedroom door closed behind her, locked the front door and drove back to Superquinn.

CHAPTER 3

I notice that I'm being fed my breakfast in my room these days. Later on in the morning they wheel me into the day-room but Imelda Ryan, with her bulging bust, always hovers close. I don't like it; don't like her. I prefer that pretty little Kerr girl with her dark hair and round, brown eyes. But then I always was a sucker for a pretty face, a pretty form – on girl or boy, pretty helps.

And I've noticed that in the evenings I'm wheeled back to my room a little earlier than any of the others. More tablets on the tray, deeper sleep. I don't mind that, it's the waking confuses me. It's the waking and the drugs; that's not my mind going. I know the difference, like this morning when I grabbed a hold of Imelda's thick forearm and spat at her,

'You were always some bitch.' The minute I did it I knew she wasn't Mother, that she had just merged with my dream. I tried explaining but I got nowhere. Just a few 'there, there's, and a worried hover as I ate my porridge.

Not that I ever would have said such a thing to Mother. But oh I wanted to. That and so much more. I haven't spoken about her, about them, in years. My children never really asked. Well, never asked enough to probe the veneer or tumble the lies. Of course I've told them the bones.

My childhood was spent in Dún Laoghaire, a satellite, port town of Dublin. I was born there in 1904. Then it was known as Kingstown. My father, James Simpson, was a doctor who ran quite a lucrative practice. My mother, Emily Malone, was the only child of a well-connected but quite impoverished family.

But the flesh? They never asked for that and I never volunteered it.

After all these years is it possible to describe a person accurately? After all these years are memories honed to fit a subjective preconception? Maybe, but I think some facts do remain. Some things I think I do know, rather than think.

I do know that during the early part of my childhood we were comfortably off but that Emily Simpson had not been reared to equate marriage with mere 'comfort'. Oh no.

'Standards!' I remember her shouting at my father. 'You are only ever as good as the standards you set yourself.' It was her excuse for insisting on Egyptian cotton bedding, linen shirts, silk underclothes and cashmere wraps.

She always spent more than my father earned and, for years, that never mattered. He would just work a little harder to catch up. He seemed happy to; I think he was proud of maintaining my mother's 'standards'. But then, after the First World War, the years seemed to speed into another age: a brassy, commercial age that was suited only to new money. Old stocks and old bonds faded into the dust of old houses and overly trimmed hats.

Of course we never admitted to any of this, not even to each other, but we took to eating cheap cuts of meat, we never lit the fire in the parlour unless we had callers and we used our electricity so sparingly that, during the winter, we were forced into each other's continuous company, sitting together all evening close by the one lamp and retiring at the same time.

I can still see my mother sitting stiff in the dusky shadows of the back kitchen, her shoulders rigid with cold, her eyes squinting over a book or some needlework. She took pride in flaunting her discomfort in front of my father who, in contrast, sat under the lamp, feet square on the fender. Words were used sparingly but to great effect.

'We have had to change butcher again.'

'Maybe now I might look forward to a decent meal.'

'The coalman has called twice this week and Mitchell once.'

'Do you need to be at home to every tradesman in town?'

'I thought it common knowledge that I am no longer at home to anyone.'

'So if you're not entertaining where does all the coal go?' My mother would stare past my father at the fire she had removed herself from.

'I have no idea,' she would answer finally, after leaving so long a pause my father would assume another topic had been raised.

'Of what?' he'd ask, but mother would be done talking for the evening. Her book would rustle, the fire settle and we three would sit on.

Those evenings sparked with a static tension that I couldn't understand. Both my parents obviously blamed each other for the situation but I, being a child and unaware of the causes behind our cosy brand of bristling politeness, blamed myself. I thought that I wasn't charming enough, wasn't

wanted or loved enough to generate the familial warmth I
had witnessed in neighbouring homes. Then, when I grew
up enough to realise that I couldn't be held responsible for
my parents' humours or failures, I began blaming them for
the years of self-imposed guilt I had suffered. Families can be
strange, fragmented things.

From quite early on we – my mother and I – stopped
buying clothes. Instead, as an excuse for her limited
wardrobe my mother took to lamenting the closure of old
establishments and the loss of the 'standards' that went with
them. She swore that she just could not abide the slipshod
cut of modern fashions and so she continued to wear her
old clothes; gowns that had been made by the best and were
now proving themselves durable. Durable if not fashionable,
but nuances of taste rarely touched on someone of mother's
social standing. If she wore mutton sleeves, or even a bustle,
her peers in Kingstown would follow suit rather than laugh.
And as for me? Well I just had to learn to adapt what I had
to my changing figure.

So, I suppose for a while my family managed to maintain
a visible standard that paralleled the opulence of our
parlour and the situation of our house. My, but it was an
ugly house. Large and imposing, it had been built for the
Victorian professional class and its ridiculous collection of
fussy chimneystacks carved a silhouette of superiority on the
landscape of that small-minded town.

But of course we couldn't hide the extent of our genteel
poverty forever. By the time I was sixteen I could hear the
whispers that rustled after mother and me. I knew that
I would not be introduced into society as mother had
been; that I would have to limit my expectations to suit
my prospects. I had already left school. The fees were too

expensive, and there seemed to be nothing left for me to do but to slide into the background of my mother's life. Filling the role that, before our troubles began, had been occupied by a well-presented upstairs maid. Perhaps it is a role that suits some girls, but not me. I wanted something more and I knew that there was something more out there for me. I could smell it on the salt sea air that drenched that port town. I could hear it in the roar of the age.

This much I know and this much I could have told if asked but it's here I get confused. And the telling of it would just confuse me more. Mother said I taught English and etiquette in a convent in Lyons. Father said nothing, damned me for a fallen woman and thought no more about it. Black and white. And me? What do I say? For almost sixty years I've said little enough, nothing of consequence. Now I think the honest explanation of my actions would be to say that I had no choice, I was just answering the call of the times.

And that call, that roar, was the roar of the Twenties, born out of the scream of the trenches and carried far and wild on the pulse of jazz. It tore the previous generation's world apart, ripped its conventions and spat on its god. The roar of the Twenties was a roar of youth and it generated its own rules, its own religion, its own wealth, all three founded on the promise of the future, all three offered as an apology for the past. In time both the promise and the apology were broken. But we weren't to know that, not in the beginning, not when the intention was still intact.

But even then, back when the world was promising reparation, our world, our little Irish world, was retreating into divisive, religious negativity. I remember my country at that time as being a mean place. It was grey and monotone, dull and self-obsessed. Its people all pawed at just the one god, dismissing all others. They bowed and scraped through their lives of negation, lives of dishonesty – a cruel existence to offer their young. And I was young. The people around me, especially my parents, had other words to describe me. They called me fast, bold, cheeky, ungrateful, unnatural, but I think that all I was was young. My mother's lectures and my father's fast, furious and often violent punishments did nothing to quieten me. Wrapped tight in corsets, and stockings, and buttons and bows. Weighed heavy in cotton, and serge, and navy gabardine, I was still young.

In Kingstown, in the spring of 1920, a motorcar could still pull children running and shouting in its wake. It could quiet conversations and turn heads and, one day, the sound of a motorcar's horn drew me down my father's garden path and through his garden gate. I was wearing a clumsy brown suit that buttoned high under my chin and fell low over the tops of my boots. But my skin was pink and white, my hair was a dark, rich chestnut and my lips were wide and full. I closed the gate behind me and leaned against it, watching the glint of sun-lit chrome glide slowly past the still bare, black shrubbery.

I remember doing that and I remember thinking, as that car slowed to a halt beside me, that I was willing to go all the way. And that was the only thought I entertained. If I had tried to put motives on my actions, if I had tried to reason with my guilt, I wouldn't have followed my instinct. I wouldn't have pushed my hip to one side and arched my back a little. I wouldn't have lowered my eyelashes as I smiled, and that car would have driven on by.

'You wanna ride?' he asked.

All it took was two steps. Two steps and I was standing beside him, my hand stretched out for the door handle.

Two more and I was sitting beside him on soft, cream leather. I didn't speak, but when I smiled at that young man he nodded at me. I never asked him, but I think he understood what he was agreeing to.

'What do they call you?' he asked, and I paused before answering. Brigit no longer seemed suitable so I picked my middle name.

'Jane,' I said, and he laughed. Laughed at the pause rather than the name.

'Have it your way,' he said, 'but you don't look like any Jane I ever met.'

We drove on in silence after that. Drove on out of my small town and into the larger countryside. Later on, much later on, he stood looking down on me, buttoning his shirt, nervously dragging a hand through his hair.

'How old are you?' he asked.

'Old enough,' I said.

'You OK?' I shrugged. 'This OK?' My eyes followed the sweep of his hand, taking in the tumble of bedclothes, the deep glow of mahogany furniture, the half-pulled curtains blocking out the diminishing, liquid trail of dusk. I shrugged again.

'You don't talk much,' he said, and I just shook my head.

I hadn't yet structured a new vocabulary to suit this oh-so-recent reinvention of myself and I was afraid that if I opened my mouth too wide all the old words would come spilling out. All the Hail Marys and the Our Fathers, all the greetings wrapped around a listing of god and his saints, all the dirty-girl guilt that was battling a path from my heart to my mouth. I didn't want to say any of that and so I said nothing at all.

We went to London first, me and my man, Phil Anderson Junior. Two days, and all those little two steps later, and we were standing on board the *Minniwaska*, a tiered liner, all glass and gloss, sailing from the New World and carrying us even further. I wrote to my parents, a purposefully adolescently muddled note, that led them to believe I was following my heart around Ireland, on the trail of the travelling salesman I had been discovered with a couple of months previously.

With my parents otherwise occupied and with enough money in Phil's pocket to smooth over any untoward questions, it was surprisingly easy to escape. We sailed from Cork. We stood watching the Atlantic etched coastline ebb away and I yawned. Stretching my young body forward cat-like, I licked the salt from my lips slowly, watching Phil from the corner of my eye. I was learning my new language.

'You and me are gonna get along just fine,' he said, and for a long time, we did.

Phil Anderson Junior was a young man. He must have still been in his early twenties, but he seemed old to me. I confused the trappings and confidence of wealth with those of age, and Mr Phil Anderson Junior was nothing if not wealthy. He never explained the origins of his wealth to me, but I doubt that much of it lasted beyond 1929. It seemed too new to be founded on anything tangible.

Everything about Phil was new. His car still purred with perfection, his luggage still squeaked with novelty, and his clothes still clung to their intended shapes and creases.

He was a conventional man really. In another time he would have been conservative, but he had chosen bohemia as his convention and so he bought me gin and promised me promiscuity. He prided himself on my youth and he constantly referred to his refusal to offer me the proposal he assumed I was waiting for. And maybe he was right. It seems a long time ago, a different head dispensing thoughts, but I do think that maybe, back then, still coddled in the romance of childhood, I may have interpreted a kiss as a promise of commitment. 'Don't get me wrong, babe,' he'd say, as he lay over me or as he grabbed a hold of me. 'It ain't that I don't wanna marry you – it's jus' I don't wanna marry at all.'

And then, a little to please him, a little to play the part I had been reared to play, I'd pull my mouth down on a sulk. He liked the challenge of cheering me up; he liked the power of feeling in control.

'But hey, babe, who's gonna treat you like I do?' he'd whisper. 'Think a husband could do any better than this? Or this? Think if we got hitched I'd roll you any better? Come on, you're still my babe. Say it, babe, say it.' And by then all I could do was moan 'And you're still my man.'

And I was proud to call him that. Proud to link my arm in his, to look up into his handsome, tousled, vibrant expression. Eyes wide, hair glowing bright in the sun, swept wild in the wind and mouth split open with the joy of it all. Proud to match my step to his as he strode through the world he enjoyed so much. Proud to wear the clothes he had bought for me, to feel the delicate fabrics skim and compliment my figure rather than restrain it. And proud to fold myself into his arms at night and allow myself be soothed by his hands and reassured by his confidence.

'You and me, we get along just fine,' he'd whisper, and for a long time we did.

CHAPTER 4

Three weeks after their mother's 'episode', Dr Delaney called Ruth and Deirdre in for a consultation.

They sat side by side in his overheated office, two middle-aged children trying to calmly swallow the inevitability of what he had to tell them. He had seen it all before, for so many 'a good innings' was no consolation. He shook hands, rustled files, spoke a little about the weather and, by then, he could see that the two women understood the situation.

'She seems quite lucid,' Ruth said, but without the confidence of defiance.

'And hopefully she will retain a degree of lucidity,' Dr Delaney replied. And then, before that achievement could be read as any form of hope, he moved on to the reality of the matter at hand. 'Though I am afraid that, to combat the pain, we will have to maintain quite a high level of medication. As you know we do offer hospice care on the premises. We will do everything we can to keep your mother as comfortable as possible.'

And there it was.

Deirdre and Ruth allowed themselves be shepherded
out of the office. The door closed behind them and they
walked slowly, and in silence, down the long corridor to
their mother's room. It was lunch-time, the air was clogged
with the weighty stench of overcooked vegetables, and Ruth
thought that the smell alone was enough to bring tears to
your eyes. She took a sidelong look at her sister and decided
to say nothing. Deirdre's shoulders were hunched, arms
folded tight across her spreading, middle-aged bulk, mouth
drawn, greying eyebrows furrowed together, an expression
Ruth knew well. There would be lists, and rotas, legal
issues, undertakers, letters written, medical staff to monitor.
Deirdre's coping mechanism had its benefits.

Their mam, their dear, sweet mam lay flat on her back, eyes
open, mouth drooling, her covered body raising barely a ripple
under the weight of blankets. Ruth sat on the bed beside that
wisp that was Brigit Egan, combed her hand gently through
her mother's hair and bent her ear over the mouth that was
working frantically, urgently trying to spill out something.

'Look at you with your hair so trim and your mouth so
tight!' it hissed. 'I know what your man does at night.' It
was slow, hoarse, rasped, but it was clear. Ruth jumped back.
Deirdre froze by the bedside locker, water jug in hand.

'Judge me, would you? Husband or John, we all whore to
someone.'

Later Ruth told Brian that it was the tone, the tone more
than the words.

'Who would have thought the old bird had it in her?'
he had laughed and, in that moment, Ruth had really, truly
hated him.

Deirdre left the room. She said she was going to talk to
someone about it, as if such a thing could be fixed. Ruth

stayed on, stayed on until her mother relaxed into some kind of ease. And then she stayed on, transfixed by the odd word, the murmured segments.

Ladies in hats, London was full of them, bustle and bows and nowhere to go, cluttering up everywhere, even the air with their la-di-dahs. They were here too. I heard them, all simpery smooth, and then I saw them and the pity oozing out of them. Pity for me! I pity them and their tight-lipped morals, they know nothing. Pity and scorn, two sides of a coin.

God I hated London.

It was nothing like what I had expected it to be. I had always thought of it as the city that's mere reflection was my home. I had expected a negation of Ireland. I had expected something superficially bright. A quality that shimmered over thighs and breasts while women heaved through the opera, a haze over the Thames that could catch the light from dawn to dusk and diffuse the harshness of a raw day. But all I saw on our first morning in London, on the way from the station to the hotel, was a war-weary, grey roll of guilt and depression.

We were in a cab and I was sitting forward. I saw it all: the set expressions on pinched faces, the dull overcoats and bland hats, the heightened colour on some men's cheeks and the painfully uneven gait of others. There was something old in the air. Something as age old as the raw grief that had been left in the wake of all those wasted young men blown so recently to their graves. It scared me, nearly scared me straight back home. I sat back and pushed my hand into Phil's. He squeezed it. I had no idea how he interpreted the view from that cab, but I could see that he was looking at something I couldn't see. Something that flushed up his cheeks and kindled a spark in his eyes.

'We'll get ourselves settled in and washed up and then you and me, babe; we're going to take this town,' he said and I smiled.

During our weeks in London I grew to realise that it did indeed overshadow Dublin, but only because of its size. Every vice I associated with Dublin was augmented in London; every petty social grievance, every closed-minded condemnation, all those ladies, all those hats. But it wasn't just them; the staff in the hotels we stayed in sneered at me when they caught me alone and ignored me when I was with Phil.

To outwit my parents we changed hotels a lot and would always register as Mr and Mrs Haliday. We thought it such a joke because it sounded so much like 'holiday'. No one believed us, though. I never looked the part. Even when I wore my big brass wedding ring and my best tea dress, I didn't look the part. Waiters in restaurants, doormen in hotels, drivers in cabs, shop girls behind counters all took the time to silently let me know that much, and when I opened my mouth on what F. Scott Fitzgerald would later call the 'melody of my accent' they'd go so far as to sneer straight in my face. They were probably right; I must have given them plenty to sneer at.

I did everything wrong. I didn't know what to wear or where to shop. I didn't know that women of a certain class were bound by an unspoken rule of curfew. I didn't know that certain places could never be arrived at on foot and that certain streets could never be visited at all. No one told me that a woman could drink a glass of wine at dinner, maybe an aperitif before, and whatever else she needed only in the privacy of her bedroom. No one told me that a young, handsome American was not considered a suitable chaperon.

When I pointed out my ignorance, and the reactions it provoked, Phil just laughed. His sex, youth, nationality and wealth all protected him from the more understated niceties of social etiquette. Charmed as he was by the British veneer of manners, he was blind to their subtle insults.

'Laughing at you! Hell girl, let the guy smile once in a while.'

'Talking about you! You'll end up like my Aunt Stacy – swore the cat was plottin' to do away with her.'

And still we stayed on. Days settled into weeks and the weeks passed like years. Phil was kept busy, though, with a load of social engagements and he was eagerly waiting for the arrival of a much talked-about friend of a friend: a writer called Robert McAlmon.

Ruth heard the name mumbled, remembered it from the collection of books she had been brought up with. A writer, someone she had never bothered to read.

'Robert McAlmon?' she prompted.

'Such a fucking fairy. Wish we'd never met him.'

'You met him?'

'Fucking fairy.'

'Where did you meet?' Little, shrivelled Brigit Egan tried to focus, tried to lock eyes on the blur by the bed, a large shadow. Substantial, the look of Mother.

'I'm sorry, Mother,' she said, slow, quiet, rheumy eyes floating tears. 'I should never have gone to London. It all started there.'

That evening Ruth was late home, twenty to seven. The television was on but the hall and kitchen were in darkness.

'Only me,' she called out, as she always did. She had long since forgotten that she had started using that greeting as a parody of inanity. No answer. Brian would be watching the news, and the girls were gone. Three of them grown and gone. The youngest, Isabel, only recently left for college and the house seemed dead without her. The eldest, Catherine, at thirty-one, was married with two children and a home and a husband and a pained expression whenever Ruth opened her mouth. Ellen was twenty-six, living in London and offering no details. The empty house, the stilted phone calls, the silent meals, all roared a reproach at Ruth. She had done something wrong.

Growing up, growing old, herself and Deirdre had always run home to their mam. Phone calls had always gone on too long, dinners had always stretched to the third bottle of wine. Their father silent, slightly withdrawn, looking on benevolently as his girls, later his women, laughed, just laughed. Stood in the kitchen, automatically reaching for the makings of a meal, Ruth found that she couldn't remember any of the jokes. She heard the hiss of profanity, saw the slack-jawed crone and couldn't remember the jokes.

She made carbonara, quick and tasty, pretty with a salad, bulked up with garlic bread. Brian came when she called him. It was still their habit to sit at either end of the family-sized table and make some attempt at conversation.

Ruth tried not to bring it up but it came anyway.

'It was the tone of voice more than anything else,' she explained, and that was when Brian had laughed.

They were married thirty-two years. Thirty-two years of work and children. Of family holidays, Sunday roasts, monthly dinner parties, slamming doors, flying insults, camomile lotion on rashes, birthday treats of breakfast in bed. Thirty-two years and she still hadn't got it right. And he was a good man. Open and accepting, more involved than her father had ever been, and still she couldn't get it right. She tried hard not to clatter the dishes together, but they clattered anyway. Brian either didn't notice or didn't care. He poured himself another glass of wine and went back to the television.

And this was it then. Another Tuesday, settling into another week. Maybe it would be different if she worked, but the thought of returning to teaching filled her with horror. She had heard all the stories about modern kids, violent, abusive. Something else maybe? Something as satisfying as Brian's career in insurance?

She would ring Deirdre. She would go for a brisk walk, she would find a book, one of the classics, she would take a long soak, light candles. She poured herself another glass of wine.

CHAPTER 5

Phil was here earlier, Phil and Claudette; they stood right by me, him holding on to my wrist, her right behind his shoulder and the two of them laughing, laughing like spring in Paris the two of them were. Her round brown eyes were all crinkled up and her thick brown hair flitting about her face. She was flirting. I tried talking to him but he didn't listen, just patted my hand and wrote something down on his big clipboard. Today's a good day. Today started with a spring-bright laugh and a handsome man, I remember him so well now. The contours of his body, the dimple of his smile. And I remember more too – all of it, I think – it's coming back thick and fast, seems to seep from the outside in. I remember the streets of Berlin, the cold of the road, the warmth of a Parisian café. I remember Pablo, haven't allowed myself that luxury in a long time.

And I remember London. Phil in London.

Phil made everything so much brighter. Time with Phil always came cushioned by charm and money. While we were in London we only ever stayed in the best accommodation, ate in the best restaurants and shopped at the best stores, and my but we shopped. I had come to Phil with nothing, but that was how he liked it.

'Came to me with nothing but your innocence,' he would say, 'and boy don't you Catholic girls put some price on innocence.' And he would sign another cheque.

Phil had so much money that his spending it on me barely counted as generosity, but he was a generous man; generous with his time, his conversation and his enthusiasms, and I loved him for that. I loved waking up beside him. I loved watching him fall into the day as greedily as exhausted people fall into sleep. No matter how much he had drunk the night before, no matter how late he had tumbled into his bed, he would always wake bright-eyed and burning, always with some plan spinning in his head.

'You wanna see a movie? Ever been in an aeroplane? Let's take the car an' hit the coast. You know anything 'bout horse riding? You want champagne for breakfast?'

And I would agree to everything, follow him everywhere, because wherever he was was always the brightest place to be. His perceptions seemed to actually distort his surroundings. He could walk through the grey drum of tedious rain, down mean, dirty streets striped with terraces and washing lines, and all he would see was a soft mist settling over the friendly warmth of community. He could push open the door of dust-filled corner shops, whose softened corners were rotting with mould; he would breathe in deep the spores of neglect and declare himself delighted by the cosy customs of family-run businesses.

'Too much glitz and the heart goes out of it, eh babe?' he'd say and I'd agree.

So, during all the time we were in London I stuck as close to Phil as I could. I was desperate to see things the way he saw them and, as long as he was there to describe his world to me, I could, almost. But as soon as I was alone all I saw was the grim reality of the place, and that scared me. The memory of it still does.

And I was very often alone. I was too afraid of being tracked down by my parents to venture into any 'decent' social circle, and socialising was what Phil had come to London to do. He was very serious about it.

'You don't go visiting your Aunt Mabel just to sit all by yourself in her parlour do you?' he'd ask. 'Same as you don't go visiting a country just to have a look in its museums. No sir, you come calling to spend time with people an' that's just what I intend doing. I'm goin' to find this here town's kitchen and set myself a place at that table.'

And 'by heck' that's what he did. Almost every evening he'd have someplace to go. Some reason to leave me alone, kissed and crumpled on some dishevelled bed. I would hold him tight as he struggled to get dressed, teasing him, pleading with him, declaring my love for him. That always made him feel a little uneasy, for him love still went with marriage.

'That's a big word for such a little girl,' he'd tell me. 'Hell, you're only old enough to love your doll's doll face.' But I think that I did truly love him in a way. I certainly hated him leaving me, but maybe that's not the same thing.

Phil had come to Europe as socially well prepared as a man in his position could be, and that was very well prepared indeed. He had letters of introduction to almost everyone, and almost everyone was glad to meet him. Handsome, rich, young Americans were very highly prized back then.

You see, back then, young British men were scarred. Faces drawn tight over the horror of too-recent memories; morals and expectations loosened by war; distorted limbs trailing reminders of mortality, and worse. But young British girls still wanted to dance, still cooked up picnics, went bluebell picking in May. They still dressed in white, still dreamed of scented conservatories rustling with whispered words of innocent commitment. And their mothers still had an obligation to provide this for them.

So those same mothers queued up to invite and charm my Phil. He put up with it for a while, was flattered for a while, but he wanted nothing from those young girls, not even their tears, and so he began to tire of the game. And aside from the game, British society had little enough to offer him; tough beef in cold dining rooms, cheap port and redundant politics, too many cocktails at the Ritz and too many games of billiards played on ripped baize. Soon even Phil began itching for something more.

'Don't get me wrong now, babe; they're all good people,' he said to me coming in late one night, after yet another supper party, 'but by heck after a while they all get to sounding just the same.'

'Sounds that way to me,' I agreed. I was sitting up in bed, surrounded by a clutter of magazines, sucking on the dregs of a bottle of wine. I was miserable and I knew just who to blame. I hated Phil's friends by description. Their clothes sounded shabby and ill-fitting, generation-old tweeds shaped to long dead figures, their houses sounded gloomy and cold and their conversations always seemed to sap some of poor Phil's vitality.

And I was jealous. Jealous and bored and more than ready to move on, but Phil refused to go anywhere until he had met Robert McAlmon. We had a row about it. I was so desperate to leave London that I threatened to go home, started flinging my stack of new dresses into my trunk, but

Marian O Neill

Phil just laughed and said, 'Why you bothering to take them? Where you gonna wear 'em?'

He had a point.

'Out, I don't know…' I was holding an ivory silk evening gown and had a sudden mental image of it hanging, faded in the back bedroom. 'Nowhere.' I stopped what I was doing and sat down heavily on the bed, suddenly overwhelmed by the horror of my parents' house. I realised then that returning wasn't an option. I was completely reliant on Phil. He was talking; I looked up at him, scared, knowing that I had to hide the neediness I suddenly felt.

'There you go, babe; you got more sense than pride. You stick around, things'll pick up, you'll see,' he said, and he kissed me. 'So that's all settled up then, eh babe? We give this town another chance, we stay an' wait for this Mr McAlmon. I got me a letter from a real good personal friend of his and I figure it would be just plain rude not to use it.' He tried to sound casual, but his eyes were all lit up with enthusiasm and so I felt duty bound to ask.

'What's so great about this guy?'

'Oh I jus' figure he'll be interesting,' Phil answered, and then he winked at me. 'And trust me, it'll be some education for you meetin' him. Bet you've never met any of his type before. He's a bit … you know…' he said, nodding. I didn't know, so Phil was forced to be more precise.

'The man's a fruit,' he said, and I still shook my head.

'A queen, a cherry, a daisy picker…' I just kept on shaking my head and so, finally, Phil had to swallow hard and tell it to me straight, and I laughed like anything at the joke of it. But Phil wasn't joking and then, after he had finally convinced me that homosexual men did exist, he had to start all over again with Robert's wife-to-be.

Winifred Ellerman was a very wealthy woman, the daughter of Sir John Ellerman. She was also a very independent-minded lesbian, so she was planning on marrying Bob the following year.

'It's all here in black and white,' Phil told me, patting his breast pocket. 'My friend got it from someone right bang slap in the know.'

The arrangement was that Winifred would provide Bob with access to her fortune and, in return, he would provide her with the freedom to escape from her family. Considering the times it was a practical – probably even a necessary – arrangement, but it sounded outlandish to me and just plain titillating to Phil. He talked about it continuously, dwelling on the sexual preferences that dictated it. He put such great, passionate words on the whole affair that even I began to feel some excitement at the thought of meeting the players. But still Robert stayed away. Word was he was in New York, and still we stayed in London. Waiting.

We stayed on for another three weeks, hellish weeks. Aside from being left lonely most days and every night, I was beginning to become very paranoid about my freedom. As it turned out I had no reason to be.

My parents had tracked me to London all right, and they also knew that I was with a Mr Phil Anderson, but that's where their search stopped. Years later I found out that they had held a family meeting about the situation. They, my parents, a couple of aunts and an elderly, wealthy cousin, had reasoned that their choices were to bring me home in disgrace, to bring me home married, or not to bring me home at all.

They rightly deduced that if I was to be dragged home against my will I would only run away again, and they hadn't the finances or the social imagination to deal with such a prospect. They assumed that as I had nothing to offer, other than what I had presumably already given away, the man I was with would never marry me. And so they opted for their third option. They told their wider circle that I was studying in France with a view to teaching there and, in time, I think they began to believe their story themselves. I wrote to them sporadically. Upbeat letters that skirted any specifics but hinted at a myriad of successes, so I suppose any fears they may have had were allayed, but still, I've often wondered at how easy it was for them to dismiss me so completely, so quickly. Maybe I had been right all along. Maybe I had never been charming, wanted or loved enough after all.

I remember that right. I'm sure I do, it's how it always stayed in my head, but time, perceptions and death seem to have distorted that absolute. Mother visits now. She sits by my bed, combs her hand so gentle through my hair and sighs her kindly questions. She never did that before. Never wanted to know.

But, back in London, I knew nothing of her decision. If I had I could have been saved some heartache. Three weeks! So long to the mind of a child. Ninety-three years so quick to the mind of a woman. And then, finally, Robert McAlmon came calling.

Back then, way back in 1920, Robert was still nothing much more than a social adventurer. Later he became a poet, a writer and a discerning publisher, and later still he became bitter. But, when Phil and I first met him, he was still young enough to be more closely associated with potential than achievement and so he was potent company.

The first time we went out with him he brought us to the Tour Eiffel. He met us at our hotel and I met him when he was already on his second drink, his second one with Phil. I walked in on them, on him and Phil, just as they were lighting a couple of cigarettes. They both looked up and I remember thinking that, through the haze of their smoke, I would have to look as beautiful as I felt. I was wearing a new dress, one of the many new ones that Phil had bought for me. It was blue silk, sky blue, calf length with a low-cut back, and it was as soft and as fine as a young woman's gown should be, a world away from navy gabardine. 'You coming with us?' Robert asked, and I nodded.

'You're a bit dressed up,' he said, and I was.

The Tour Eiffel was a dingy, drab, poke of a place, but Robert didn't apologise for it, instead he apologised for London.

'It's all there is,' he said, shrugging.

That first night though I was too totally captivated by Robert to notice the shabbiness of my surroundings. His long, sharp features may have helped, but his eyes were what held me, so startlingly blue they caught in my throat and tangled my tongue and then, once they had noted their effect, they just settled somewhere over my head. I was dismissed as a silly girl, too young to bother with. It took a little longer for Robert to dismiss Phil, took a few years, but by then Phil was past caring.

That night, the first night, we all drank far too much. I don't know about the others, but I was drinking to keep up. Didn't know what with though, some mood maybe or some kind of expectation. I started drinking champagne and then moved on to beer, the two drinks were bubbly and I thought that that was tremendously funny. Then, sometime during the evening, I got lost, sat down at the wrong table, my arm around the wrong man. Phil finally found me and roared his approval. I remember him standing over me bellowing.

'Seeing double, eh? No excuse for infidelity though. Eh Bob? Eh Bobby boy? Get it? Seeing double.' Robert was gone but I laughed enough for two.

He turned up again though, the very next afternoon, and then again that evening and the next one.

'London is sooo boring,' he would say over and over. Draped across our settee, toying with yet another unwanted meal or hunched over a drink at the bar. 'I'm so stiff with tedium I can't stretch to a yawn. Aren't you sooo bored?' he would ask, and Phil would shake his head in confusion and launch into all he had seen that day that had amused him.

'Bored! Hell I'm tired fit to want a little boredom. Bored! I tell ya me and babe have spent the last few hours jus' having the most English of all teas. Hell the trip over's been worth it just for a taste of those whatya-call-'ems?'

'Scones,' I prompted.

'Yeah, scownes. They're some cakes. Light but with a good bite to them and they come with…I dunno, it's not butter.'

'Clotted cream,' I prompted.

'Never heard of the stuff back home. And then we had us a bit of a stroll right down Oxford Street. Man we've had a time of it all right.'

'Really?' Robert would ask and I'd see the glint of amusement lighting up his dead bored expression. Phil never did though. Phil was too straight up not to expect honesty in others. All he ever saw in Robert was a man lit up with interest, 'a good pal', 'a guy he could really talk to'.

In the beginning, for the first few nights, it was just me, Phil and Robert, but that didn't last long. Robert soon realised that he couldn't contain Phil's boundless enthusiasm alone, or maybe he just felt selfish not sharing the joke, and my inarticulate style of drunken company was no use to him at all, so he called in the troops. On our fourth night out together we were joined by Tom, a friend of his who he described as a brilliant poet.

'Well this cer-tain-ly is the life!' Phil declared, slapping his palm down on the table in front of him, causing both Robert and Tom to flinch slightly. 'Can't beat the company of poets when you're out looking to learn a bit about culture.' And then he sat back waiting to be enlightened. I could see Robert look to his friend and I could see the answering smile skirt Tom's polite enquiry.

'So what is it you would like to know?'

'Well, heck, everythin' I suppose. Like say for instance where you get your ideas an' all from? Like I seen my share of sunsets, but all I can ever think of sayin' is isn't that grand.'

'So would you like some pointers?' Tom asked while Robert, coughing a little, excused himself.

The next night Tom brought some of his friends. In time they brought some of theirs, a collection of self-termed intellectuals: poets, writers, models, artists, all well down-trodden but all bursting with the integrity of their disciplines. Nightly our table swelled and roared with the loud, brash noise of fun I was to get to know so well. Sometimes I loved it, but often I felt uncomfortable, a little for the sake of my ignorance and gaucheness, but mostly on Phil's behalf. I was always aware of him, could always hear him no matter where he was sitting.

'So you, like, don't eat any meat? Not even a goose at Christmas?'

'So if a word don't rhyme but it like says how you feel, you just leave it in anyways?'

'So, like, even when you were a kid you thought painting – was what didya say? – obsolete?'

'An' you do it with no clothes on at all?'

I suppose I couldn't blame them, Phil was too easy a target and he did provide them with far too much drink to allow for any sense of moderation.

And still all those weary weeks wore by, and still Phil bought most of the drinks, and still we stayed on in London.

CHAPTER 6

It was just one more night. I was getting ready, trying to pin my curls into shape. Behind me Phil was pouring another drink and beyond him, through the open window, the evening was stretching on out into full summer. Beyond that I could see it stretching into the change of seasons, the turn of years, the time when Phil's life would call him home, would leave me alone.

'What are your plans?' I asked as prettily as I could. I knew to temper my demands into requests. I had no wish to appear tiresome.

'A few drinks, might take in a show.'

'Not for tonight, for...well... for the next while.'

'A few drinks, might take in a show.'

'And are we staying here?'

'It ain't a bad spot, central enough; you wanna change, babe?'

'I mean London; are we staying in London?'

'Don't see why not. Hell, this town's just gettin' interesting,' Phil said, swinging his arm into an expansive arc, splashing his drink. 'We're just beginning to make ourselves some friends.'

'Friends!' Despite myself I spat the word back at him and my tone cut right through his self-assurance. 'With friends like them...'

'You don't like them?' he asked slowly, drawing his arm back in, cradling his glass close to his chest. 'Why...' But he didn't finish his question. I could see that he had started looking for an answer himself and I didn't want him to find one. If he didn't know by now how he was slighted or teased, I figured he didn't need to know at all.

'It's just that they're your friends, really, aren't they?' I said, but Phil didn't answer, he was still thinking and so I talked on, talked over all his gathering suspicions. 'You know they never talk about things that interest me. Of course you like them and I know how fond they all are of you, but I'm not that knowledgeable about art and all. Sometimes I feel a little left out.'

I moved over to him, pulled him down on the bed and curled onto his knee.

'But babe, don't you wanna learn? You gotta put in the time to find out what it's all about.'

I didn't answer – just sat playing and pulling at his clothes, breathing close to his working mouth, whispering little moans of dissent in his ear. Soon he lost the thread of his argument and, later on, he began weaving the thread of mine into a definite plan of action.

'Tell you what,' he said, 'we'll have ourselves a few more good nights out on this town. Give us a chance to make ourselves some memories, and then we'll go see what Paris is up to.' And that sounded like such a good idea I climbed right back onto his knee to thank him.

We went to Rector's that night. I think it was Rector's, not that it matters. I remember a low, dark, sleazy, little place that was dimly lit by candles covered over with crimson glass bowls. The furniture was heavy and ornate, the wine thick and strong and the walls dull with dirt and dusty with frayed hangings. The place may have managed a certain cosiness in winter, but in summer all it was was dingy, which was pathetic because I suspect it was aiming at decadent.

It should have been a good night, though. Me and Phil started out in grand, fine humour and there was an interesting crowd in the place. Robert was there as always, and Tom was there with his usual companion, a tall girl who seldom talked but smoked continuously. It was a look a lot of the girls adopted. And there were others: the dramatically beautiful, the just plain dramatic and the just plain. All crowded around their drinks, shoulders hunched, ideas flying. One girl was leaning in towards Phil, her argument thrusting her face forward,

'But how can words portray anything as nebulous, as subjective, as feeling? Once translated isn't the feeling objectified? And once objectified it loses its personalised import, its soul. All poetry is soulless.'

'But doesn't every thought we have come dressed in language?' It was Phil answering. I looked up and he winked at me. 'Figure I put in enough time,' he whispered before turning back to his argument. 'You think therefore you are. You wanna tell me you think therefore you got no soul?'

I winked right back and Robert, hovering within earshot, hooted out his approval. For the first time he smiled genuinely at Phil and for the first time I genuinely liked him.

It all started out as a good night but, as it progressed, as the crowd relaxed into their drinks, their arguments and their flirtations seemed to pass me by. I felt their mood as a palpable thing and it passed me by. As the hours drifted on I could feel the place drag on me and nothing could lift my spirits, not the effects of the alcohol, or the happy, tinny music, or the elegance of the young artist's model folded into the chair beside me.

'You look too blue,' she purred, and I just nodded. 'I know just the thing,' she said, and she took a hold of my hand. 'It's good stuff, you can pay me back sometime, it's no trouble at all, I don't like getting all snowed up alone anyway.'

We were in the bathroom and she had a razor. She was cutting some powder on her compact mirror and I still didn't know what she was talking about. I did what she did though without questioning her. Put my nose to the rolled up bank note, ran it along the length of white powder and then rubbed the residue on my gums.

'There,' she said. 'Now nothing nor nobody can touch you.' And she left. I stayed staring into the mirror. I felt language drain from my mind and remembered Phil's words.

I remember walking back to the table, seeing the crowd with everyone talking and no one listening. I could see the redundant words swirling high, screaming blue and, over in the corner, barely discernible in the candlelight, I saw a young man. I see him now, in the corner, staring. He was staring at me then too, and the side of his face was pulled down on a deep red scar. It pierced his eye, puckered his cheek and stretched his mouth back, splitting it skull like open on a permanent smile. I stared back, stared into the pulse of his thoughts, felt them pound through my brain. For a moment, or a lifetime, my reality melted into the substance that supported it. A hell-broken structure of mean-minded hate. But still those words describe nothing, come nowhere near to settling a meaning on the images that began crowding my thoughts.

I turned to a passing waitress, tried to tell her, but no words came – my ideas were flying far beyond the trappings of language.

Outside, where it was cool, I saw a man who looked like he might know and I asked him how we could all still function, still drink and laugh knowing what men are capable of? He shrugged me off, and so I turned to another, and another. Some answered, some laughed, but I couldn't hear either response because the blood was ringing too loud in my ears. I followed them though, those wordless men, and they led me down strange roads, past all knowledge I had of that city, or of humanity. I was lost, clawing for the charity of strangers; I found they had none.

Later, in some hotel-room mirror, I saw my eyes rimmed with black. They held all the horror of London and I cried for what they had become. A man escorted me into the morning. He wasn't Phil and my eyes that morning looked worse, deeper and blacker. I left that place with my thoughts still hanging on to the previous night and I didn't know anything. Could make no sense of time and place. Couldn't bear to think of it. All I knew was that the clamour was still there, ringing high in my ears, and that I could not have slept through it.

A man bought me a drink. All the kind men. All the drinks, and every glass rang with that ring of truth, because they told me I was beautiful. And I was and so was the powder. Seemed when I opened my eyes to it, it was everywhere; it blurred my senses but focussed the present and I was too lost in time to risk losing that focus. And so I took what I was offered, and when it wasn't offered to me I got it any way I could.

Down steps, steps out of the night, down into some place warmer, some place darker where men gather. I found what I was looking for there.

Sometimes it was light and I would walk through the ghosts of that city, gaunt young men with holes for souls, limping past me staring. I stared back and I stopped to laugh at the ladies out shopping.

With their hair so trim and their mouths so tight.

I knew what their men did at night.

It took Phil days to find me. He found me in some bar, swaying on my own to whatever music was playing, my clothes torn and my hair wild. He caught me as you would a bird. He crept up on me and threw his coat around me, then wrapped me tight into his arms. He held me fast until I stopped fluttering and all the time he whispered and whispered, sweet sounds, soft words. Slowly the ringing in my head was silenced and the world was returned to me. It was a more complex world but a more honest one, stripped of all pretence. In that first quiet, I understood that I had been born into a honed, new reality, and that I fully appreciated, and feared, its potential.

Later I often got to wondering if that lost spell in London facilitated my future behaviour or inured me against the inevitability of my path. If I don't know now, I suppose, I never will, but I do know that the girl who left her parents' house by the garden gate, the same girl who equated a kiss with a promise of commitment, died somewhere on the streets of London. So I guess from then on I must have started walking in someone else's shoes.

Those shoes took some breaking in though. I remember trying to claw my way back to the familiarity of past securities.

All Gods Dead

I remember looking up at Phil, so hungry, searching for something in the light of his eyes.

He whispered, 'You were lost.'

I had the words ready. I was going to answer, 'Until you found me,' and if I had then everything might still have been all right. But looking into his trusting, honest face I felt the pain of my loss of innocence. I saw the clarity of Phil's expression and thought to myself, *never again, never again.* In a howl of grief I cried, 'You lost me!' And then, too late, realised what I had said and all I could do was watch Phil's eyes dim a little.

'I'm so sorry,' he sighed. 'Oh my sweet, I am so sorry,' he murmured.

We walked on to Phil's car where Robert was sitting waiting for us. He must have finally recognised the fact that he owed Phil something and so he had offered to help him look for me, but he looked away as Phil settled me into my seat. He kept his eyes fixed on a spot over my head and muttered something about it being good to see me again. But I knew that there was nothing good in it. Nothing good in the state of my clothes or the filth of my flesh. Nothing good to see in any of it, not in me and not in the grind of life that that car was pulling us through.

'You all talk of art all the time, but why bother recording this?' I asked and, after a moment, Robert lowered his eyes to mine.

'What?' he asked.

'Well this…all of this…' I said gesturing roughly out the window. I meant it all. All the weary plod through another summer, all the death, all the suffering, and all for what? The Great War had wasted the winners just as surely as it had the loser. It had wasted a generation's spark, a race's youth, a nation's pride. It had wasted an Empire. I tried to explain this to Robert but I found that I couldn't express myself properly. Finally I just shrugged and gave up.

'I mean this fragmentation of life,' I said. 'I can't put it into words; it runs so deep it pulls language apart.'

We were silent for the rest of the journey but Robert maintained eye contact, kept on looking at me straight, and I took comfort from the fact that he didn't wince at my condition. From then on we became friends, and we stayed that way for a while.

We, myself and Phil, left London almost immediately after that and headed straight for Paris. We never spoke about my lost days, but the fact of it tore us apart. I resented Phil for staying too long in London, for letting me sink into its depths, and he resented me for slipping, slipping right away. His babe was gone, his bright-eyed, decorative doll who giggled at the outlandish idea of men kissing men, she was gone for good and both of us were in mourning for her.

CHAPTER 7

'I took the mirror out of her room.' Ruth was on the phone to Deirdre. She was sitting in the kitchen of the old family home, boxes of silverware and dinner services piled high on the table. 'She got terribly upset when she saw herself.'

'Well, that makes sense; we should have thought of that sooner. I didn't think her eyes were that good, though, or that she'd even know who it was.'

'Well I don't know if she did. She seemed to think it was a man in the corner, staring at her. God it was awful, Deirdre, the worst she's been. She was saying all sorts, like talking about taking cocaine, or heroin, I think, and sleeping with men, and still she's going on and on about Robert McAlmon.'

'Weird, isn't it? And he's nobody really, you'd think she'd have got fixated on Fitzgerald or Hemingway or someone, she must know their books by heart.'

'Maybe she never met them.'

'And you honestly think she was shooting up with McAlmon?' Ruth laughed.

'You have a point there, see you later so.' She hung up and went back to sealing boxes.

It had been this way for weeks now. Their mother drifting in and out of consciousness – lost somewhere, in some past. Deirdre deadening the process with practicalities, and Ruth listening so hard, trying to make sense of the fragments she caught and, all the while, trying to comfort.

'Who knows what thread's the last to unravel?' That's what Deirdre said over and over. 'Could be as simple as some movie she saw that left an impression.'

Ruth conceded that her sister had a viable point, but she still couldn't dismiss the details, the emotional responses, the real sense of terror that she had witnessed earlier that day. Could such things just exist in a haze of drugs and confusion? And if her mother's reaction to such fabrications was so heartfelt, did it matter if they ever happened or not?

Her sweet mam. Her dear, sweet mam, lost in some past, on some forgotten or fictitious London street.

The kitchen was almost empty now. It looked shabby and cold, the walls patterned with the shapes of removed pictures, shelves, plates. Who would have thought the place was so dirty? But still it wore the form of a bustling Brigit Egan. The scrubbed pine table, the aga, the scuffed, tiled floor, so many meals. Food used as a bribe, a celebration, a consolation. The look of happy acceptance when news was good, the look of forgiving resignation when things went wrong. Never a cross word, just that weight of loving expectancy.

Ruth had had enough. Something close to anger was welling up. She felt, cold, dry mouthed, angry. She picked a cup out of an over-packed box and poured herself a cup of water from the tap.

In front of her the back garden stretched out. Her mother's view, her mother's work, but not any more. Now a weed-speckled lawn bled into overgrown beds; the once-sharp contours of bushes were frayed with neglect and the sodden mulch of unraked leaves blurred every corner, stained every path. Her mother's work unravelling.

Ruth left her cup by the sink, went upstairs to the library and began flinging her mother's collection into a box. She put McAlmon's autobiographical work, *Being Geniuses Together*, to one side. She would read that one first; she would start it tonight, as soon as she got back from Deirdre's, as soon as she had cooked for Brian, fed him, cleared up after him and suffered her stilted weekly phone call with Ellen. She would definitely start it then.

Deirdre hadn't moved far from the family home. A twenty-minute drive away, a similar house, slightly smaller. Ruth had never thought much about it before, but now, as she parked and waved to Mark, her brother-in-law, she felt an overwhelming sense of claustrophobia. In his early sixties, bent over a pile of leaves, thin grey hair flopping too long at the sides, a lawyer, he could have been their father. Add a few pounds he could be Brian.

She picked up one of the boxes she had come to deliver and, laughing over at Mark, used her nose to ring the doorbell.

'Home delivery,' she called out as soon as she heard Deirdre behind the door. 'Anyone order a dinner service?' It wasn't funny. Deirdre didn't laugh and Ruth didn't mind. At times she even irritated herself.

They sat together for a while in Deirdre's sitting-room. Even though she was driving Ruth said that one glass of wine wouldn't hurt. And it wasn't hurting. The room wasn't doing any harm either, soft lighting, a spitting fire, a deep couch. Deirdre's one child, James, lived in Sydney with his partner Geraldine and their daughter Matilda. Pictures of them smiled out from various corners of the room, blonde, bright, foreign-looking.

'They escaped,' Ruth thought, and that was the first time she had framed emigration in those terms. She realised that, up until now, she had seen them, Deirdre's James and her Ellen, as exiled, to be pitied.

'So they're not coming home for Christmas?' she asked, and Deirdre shook her head.

'You know, time and the expense, and Matilda's three now. The flight would be a nightmare.'

'Yeah,' Ruth agreed, but they both knew that that meant James wouldn't be coming to say goodbye to his grandmother, that he wouldn't be here to help bury her. 'It won't be much of a Christmas anyway.'

Ruth couldn't help it; she tried not to say it, but it came anyway.

'Ellen says she'll be over and Catherine's coming for dinner with her lot.' She sounded smug and she knew it. A coup in the contest for best mother, the contest that Deirdre had never really entered into.

'That'll be nice,' was all she said in reply.

They talked on, talked about nothing until Ruth was ready to leave, and then she brought it up again. She knew Deirdre wouldn't understand, she would have to have been there, and even then it mightn't have affected her as strongly, or at all.

'Mam really was awful today, she was so distressed about the mirror, really scared.'

'Did you tell anyone? It must be the drugs.'

'I suppose. But it seemed so real to her. She keeps thinking I'm her mother now.'

'Well that's understandable. Everyone used to say you have the look of her.'

'Yeah, that's true. I took her books, they're in the car. Do you want any of them? You can go through them if you want.'

'No, I've read what I want of them. They're all yours. Just don't…'

'Don't what?'

'Ah, you will anyway. But don't go making too much of this. Don't go upsetting yourself too much.' Deirdre spoke hesitantly, but both sisters knew exactly what she meant.

'Don't go upsetting myself over my mother's death you mean?' Ruth's voice was pitched high, fast routed into a familiar argument.

'Ah Ruth, you know what I mean. She's dead already really, our mam is gone and all that's left is a shadow. We'll make sure she's as comfortable as possible, but don't go investing in all this rubbish she's saying now. Like don't go spending the next ten years reading those books looking for an answer. She's dying, she's old and confused, that's all there is.'

'That's how you put it? "That's all there is"?'

'Yes, that's all there is.'

Both their voices had settled in tone, neither of them had the energy for this argument that had never been settled. Over the years it had erupted over every decision concerning their mother. Ruth's emotional reaction always sparked against Deirdre's reserved control.

'In the house today I was remembering the stories,' Ruth said, and then, in unison, sing-song wise both women chimed out, 'Once upon a time there were two little girls, both very beautiful, both very kind.'

Then they laughed, all tension broken. It was a family tradition: every night the sisters used to curl up, either side of their mother who rested an arm across both pairs of bony shoulders.

'Once upon a time there were two little girls, both very beautiful and both very kind.' Over the years those two little girls had battled ogres and giants, witches and worse. And then, as they grew into their early teens, they battled moral issues, false friends and forward boys and always they made the right choices.

Ruth remembered one specific instance, in one specific story. She was to go to a ball with the prince of her dreams and she was to wear, and here her mother paused to allow Ruth the time to say, 'A dress of sky blue.'

In these stories Ruth always wore a dress of sky blue. But this time, the nine-year-old Ruth had answered, 'A dress of moss green.'

'Really?' her mother had asked, a question settling on her brow. 'That sounds lovely, but I don't think it will match your silver tiara. Gold goes better with green.'

'All right,' Ruth said, still confident in her choice. 'I'll wear a gold tiara.'

'And what about your sparkling sapphire shoes? And the shawl the fairies made for you woven from the finest spider filaments? And the moonstone ring to light you home? I don't think they match green so well.'

Ruth listened, enchanted. She could never have dreamed of such accessories.

Driving home from Deirdre's house she followed the memory forward and forced a laugh as she admitted to herself that the one formal gown she still owned, hanging musty in Catherine's old wardrobe, was sky blue.

CHAPTER 8

The man in the corner is gone now. Mother took him away, simply crossed over and folded him away. She's being so kind now. She brushes my hair, smoothes my pillow, holds my head when I drink. Was she ever this kind in life? Or do I remember her wrong? Was it my selfish fault? I don't think so, not all of it. She did shout. I remember the shrill sound of that, so I must have heard it. She did shout and boss and sulk and pout and poor old Father, and poor, poor me. Stuck in the dark with him in the corner. But he's gone now.

'There,' Mother said when she came back to me. 'It's gone now.' But it isn't, not really. He isn't. I haven't thought about him in decades – that shattered, sneering smile – but I carried him inside me all these years. So he's not gone, never was. Never will be. He's there, lying still under the folds of life. I tried telling Mother this and I told her that the first folded tier was Paris. She didn't understand though, she thought I was crying for Paris, and then remembering it. Remembering all the faces, all the nights, all the parties, the rowdy, raunchy laughs, the vibrant bounce of flesh on flesh, the pulse of excitement that pounded us through those early years. Remembering it all, I did cry, who wouldn't? I ask you, Mother dearest, wouldn't you?

The texture of one Parisian night should be enough to well you up. One isolated scent, one smiling concierge, one squeak of a street organ, the pop of one champagne cork, the shine of one young beauty's hair. It took a little time but in the end all these details, all of these and so many more, grew to fill my world.

But my lost days had done a damage, one I couldn't easily trace. Physically my body seemed to be in order. My mind ran along its usual tracks, it just seemed to me that the world no longer flowed by my side. I saw a few doctors and they all recommended rest and so that was what I did. For months I rested and slowly, slowly I slipped back into the material. Staying in Claridges Hotel helped.

Phil booked us in there on our arrival and we stayed for over two months while he looked around for just the right apartment for us. He wanted something comfortable but aesthetic, a home that displayed taste rather than wealth. But for those weeks all I wanted was our room in Claridges.

I can still see that room. I can still almost touch and smell it, it was that opulent. It had a huge bed centred on a pure white rug, with a coverlet of gold satin embroidered with a deep, violet peacock motif. For days I would stay in that bed, naked, wrapped in the cool of that coverlet, moving only to let it kiss a new patch of skin, letting its gentleness erase all those memories I hadn't the strength to recall. In the evenings Phil would come home and, before dinner, he would trail his lips, wet with wine, behind the movement of the gold.

It was a light, bright room with a ceiling that reached far above me and windows that seemed to stretch my boundaries beyond my control. There were two full-length windows that opened on to a balcony, that opened on to the world. In safety I could observe that flow that no longer included me.

And there was a yellow divan with the softest cushions and the deepest seat. And every three days the flowers were changed, and they were always white, and every third day the room was heavy with scent. And my feet disappeared into the depth of the pale blue carpet when I walked, and when I lay the warm, scented air of the city would breathe on my face. And there was a bath, a marble bath that juxtaposed the heat of the water with the cool of the stone so beautifully as to elevate a common wash into such a sensual experience.

I ate well and plainly, fresh bread and ripe cheese, juice-filled fruits and butter-based sauces. I put on weight and I developed an educated taste for wine. I was being healed in the most perfect way.

After just two weeks I felt strong enough to venture out. I started touring the streets, and I went alone. I had grown far beyond the confines of Phil's optimistic perception of the world. He'd watch me go, wave me away.

'A girl's gotta see things for herself, I guess,' he would say and I'd agree.

'I can't call a place home until I know where to buy my stockings, cigarettes and chocolate,' I'd say and he'd nod.

'You go and take your own sweet time, babe,' he'd say and I would, and I always pretended not to notice how happy he was to see me leave.

I knew why he wanted me gone. It was because when I was around him his innate happiness became shadowed by guilt and sordid imaginings. That was why he avoided looking at me, why he buried his face in my flesh or in the trail of my gold coverlet. I didn't blame him, not for a minute, he just couldn't cope with what he couldn't understand, and he couldn't understand what had happened to me. He was good and brave enough to admit responsibility for it, though. He would even have married me if I had ever encouraged him in that direction. But of course I never did: what kind of union would we have made by then? With me stripped of any illusion of innocence? All we could have achieved was a marriage laden with suspicion, guilt and duty, all the emotions we were both running so hard to escape from.

From the start I loved the streets of Paris. I suppose I associated my first explorations of that city with my first real explorations of myself. From the start it was a deeply personal place. At first I took my walks when the streets were quiet. I still felt too fragile to deal with people; I was just learning to deal with myself.

The smell of Paris, at its extremities, during the early morning or the late night, became like a drug to me. It was the smell of possibility, of youth and opportunity. I began walking the streets obsessively, my nostrils dilating, collecting the stench of the city, the perfume of grass and flowers, the heavy scent of bread and garlic, of alcohol and tobacco, the fumes from cars and the stale country odour of animals. It was all there, and at night it was blanketed by the death of the day and in the morning it was dampened by the sweetness of dew.

My walks started, under Phil's direction, along the Faubourg Saint-Honoré, but its lavish shop windows towering their beauties over the heads of the masses soon ceased to enthral me and began to merely irritate. I walked on. I crossed the Seine and once I reached the left bank I slowed down and strolled up to and through the Luxembourg Gardens. I preferred them to the Tuileries, but I loved to sit on the terrace of the Tuileries that overlooked the Place de la Concorde. And I loved so much more as well.

I loved the quayside stalls that would be just opening up as I passed on the way to or from my gold coverlet. I loved to listen to the silent hum of work, and I loved to watch the slow structuring of goods as the vendors carefully laid out their prints and books under the gaze of the day.

And I began to love the people I saw stagger through those nights and mornings. All of them blind to me, lost in their condition, lost in the night still ongoing, or lost to the night just passed. They all flowed past me and I watched them go, happy for their enthusiasm, even if it was only for alcohol.

And sometimes I would run. I ran through two seasons that first year, from autumn into winter. I ran with the heat of the sun driving me, and later I ran into the damp fog of my own breath. I would run to catch the night, or run to outstrip the day. I ran down the Rue de Rivoli and I ran across the Avenue de l'Opéra. I ran along Montparnasse and down the Boulevard Raspail and my heart sang with those names that still ring like poetry in my veins. By the time Phil had found us the apartment he thought would suit us, I was ready to be moved.

For all the time I lived with Phil we lived on the Rue de Fleurus, a few doors down from Gertrude Stein. I think that was what must have swayed Phil because, although our apartment was very nice indeed, it was nothing more. Of course at the time I loved it. At the time it was presented to me as a gift to be played in and with. At the time it came wrapped in a gold coverlet heavily embroidered with a deep violet peacock motif. Phil had negotiated a price with the management at Claridges.

It was a two-bedroomed apartment spread over two floors. Two bedrooms and one large sitting-room on the first floor, the bathroom and kitchen were on the floor above and the whole of the place was open and bright, ready to become as bourgeois or as bohemian as we saw fit. But, although we tried so hard for the latter, we succeeded beautifully in attaining the former. We knew no better. It was a few years later that a friend, who knew the rules of life, took me aside and told me how to manage my money.

'Cut your own hair,' she told me. 'Buy no more clothes but buy Miró and Léger.'

But by then it was too late, by then I had become poor.

Myself and Phil chose the decor for our new home together. We polished up the blocks of furniture that were already there, added a few more bits to clutter up the corners, covered everything over with frills and flowers and filled the walls with sweet prints of Parisian views. We made our little nest as cosy as possible, wrapped ourselves all up in fleshy comfort and told ourselves that that meant we were happy together.

'My, but you Catholic girls sure know how to sin,' Phil would say and I would climb up on his knee, just like in the old days, to whisper in his ear, 'It's the nuns. They have to tell us all about sins, just to make sure we're not doing any of them by mistake.' And Phil would laugh and look away. We both knew that I hadn't learned my tricks in the convent.

It was cold that winter, though I didn't really notice it, and I was almost happy, though I barely noticed that either. I was too busy searching for the Paris I could see but couldn't access. Sometimes I felt brave enough to sit outside the Dôme. I would sit by the brazier they burned there and watch the people walking hurriedly by, kicking up little sprays of water as they went. I would listen to the snippets of conversation that reached me and wonder what I had to do before I would be allowed to join in.

Then, late one afternoon, Robert McAlmon came calling and sneering at our oh-so-sweet little apartment. He always called it Main Street, number 22 Main Street. It took me years to track his reference to Sinclair Lewis's book and to the insult he intended. I never took offence though, he was right. Our home was just about as avant-garde as apple pie, just about as risqué as some visiting uncle saucing up the ham with the suggestion of a blue joke.

'Jus' come by to see what you two folks are up to in this 'ere big city,' Robert said standing in our doorway, grinning, confident of the welcome he knew would be his. Confident enough to draw his words out in an exaggeration of Phil's accent and, as usual, Phil didn't notice a thing.

'Well isn't this just the greatest thing?' he declared, reaching for Robert's hand, slapping him on the shoulder, nodding his head emphatically. 'Well heck, isn't it? Isn't it just mighty fine, eh?' And, because there was no one else around, Robert looked to me to share the joke of Phil's enthusiasm. I looked away and started mixing the drinks. It was early still, barely past noon, but a visitor was always cause for celebration, and so we celebrated, first with gin and later with the bottle of absinthe that Robert had brought with him. It turned into one of those days, one of those days that got lost somewhere after the fifth drink.

I hadn't known that Phil was still in touch with Robert and, I suppose, I was a little naïve not to wonder why he was so delighted to see him. At the time I just thought it was because he was relieved at not having to spend yet another evening with just me, and so I sulked. Sulked my way down most of a bottle of gin and I was drinking a lot slower than the men. By early evening I was asleep and they were singing. I heard them in my dreams calling me and laughing, stumbling about and then whispering and giggling.

When I finally woke up the room was quiet, gently quiet. Both men were sitting close together, arm about shoulder, head to head. It looked to me like they were talking, just talking. It was night now, night and cold. The fire hadn't been lit and the blinds hadn't been drawn. Outside the street lights were curtained by the oily slick of city rain and I felt rotten. I tried to get up, tried to haul myself back onto the sofa I had slid off but nothing worked. My hands got tangled in cloth, my body felt heavy, cumbersome and my feet kept slipping and bumping.

'Hey!' I heard Phil call. 'Hey, look, babe's up and at 'em.' And then the light was switched on and the room was filled with noise and laughter, mine as much as anyone's.

'You swine!' I shouted, but just for form, I was thrilled by the attention. While I had been sleeping Phil and Robert had dressed me up as what Robert called 'the uncut undergraduate! The revelling, rebelling gentile.'

I was wearing Phil's shirt and Robert's trousers and jacket. Robert was in his underpants, shirt ends flapping over pale, winter legs. Phil was bare-chested.

'Let's go out then,' Robert shouted jumping to his feet. 'Fetch me a suit, cane and selection of watercolours, let us go forth and paint this town.'

Phil did as he was told, found Robert a suit and himself a shirt, and that's how we set out on the town, the three of us linked arm in arm, two of us swimming in clothes three sizes too big for us.

'You'll set a trend!' Phil shouted as we sang our way down the rue de Fleurus, intent on doing just that.

That was the first night of far too many. That was the first night I joined the staggering young people I had grown used to passing in the early morning, the first time I was included in the conversations circling the Dôme.

As soon as we swung through the door of the Dôme we were hailed by a large, welcoming woman. Above the elbow her arm wobbled loosely as she waved it wild and high, and her red hair fell dank against her forehead, sticking to her sweat, as she tossed her head back to yell.

'Bob! Bob you bastard, come here and buy me a drink and then get your friends to do the same.'

'Florence Martin,' Robert explained before leading us over to her.

Florence *was* the Quarter. She was as loud and as blowsy as its life, and she was as generous and as sentimental as its spirit. She had been a Ziegfield girl and, under a thickening layer of alcohol-sodden flesh, the shape of a dancer was still discernible. She called herself the Dowager of the Dôme, Queen of Montmartre and Montparnasse, the empress of imbibing. I called her the spirit of the age and she loved me so loudly she dragged me into recognition. A lot of her respect for me was based on that first night, on our first meeting. Me, swaying in shoes that were stuffed with socks and still I had to curl my feet to keep them on. Me, loose in clothes that merely accentuated my femininity.

That first night, though, Florence was drunk enough to accept me on face value and I was drunk enough to try to live up to the part I was dressed for. Much to Phil's and Robert's delight, I twirled a cigar in my mouth, ordered a whisky and cursed loudly.

'Fuck it, but I need a drink. Give the girls what they want but give me a stiff one.'

'And that's just what I want,' Flossie drooled in my ear. 'So, what's your name then?'

'Hell, don't you know?' Phil was incredulous. 'Why this is none other than...' Robert blew a fanfare and, as I bowed, Phil formally recited my title. 'May I present Mr Archibald Smithsonian the second, the scourge of his college, the pride of his mother, the uncut undergraduate, the revelling, rebelling gentile.'

Flossie clapped and howled with laugher.

'And here's to fair fucks!' she shouted and emptied her glass.

Flossie was known for her language, she prided herself on it. On that and her drinking. She said that she could drink anyone under the table, that that was the one talent she had inherited from her father, and we all had no choice but to believe her as, night after night, she proved her claim. At times though she would crumple under the strain and one of her friends would have to tow her away to some bed and some sleep. I remember one evening it was my turn and I had to steer her stumbling and screaming out of the Dingo, another of our haunts.

'What's all this talk of home?' she shouted at me. 'Your pussy tired of the men? You want to warm your hands in some sweet Flossie muff?' We were outside now and a sleek, black car was purring to a stop in front of us.

'Come on,' I was muttering, trying to quieten her down. 'You've had too much.' And then I tried pulling her and that did for me. No one pulled Flossie in any direction other than where she was going.

'Right then!' she screamed full in my face. 'If you think I'm too low with the booze give me some fucking cocaine, or maybe, baby, you could just give me some fucking.'

The car door opened and a beautifully groomed lady stepped delicately out. She seemed satisfied.

'Yes,' she said to her chauffeur. 'Yes, this must be the place.'

Beaming delightedly, she tripped happily past myself and Flossie. We fell against each other laughing, and Jimmy the barman, who had been watching, making sure we were leaving, winked at us. The wink said it all, one more tourist come to visit with bohemia. Years later Jimmy was to write a book about it all and that's what he called it: *This Must Be the Place*.

There were others there too on that, my first night, and later all through all those years made up of so many nights: Yvonne, Rita, Florianne, Nina, Helene and, of course, the famous Kiki de Montparnasse, and that's just the girls. There were also the writers like Djuna Barnes, the rich like Peggy Guggenheim and the little, bold girls like the shipping heiress Nancy Cunard who took a black lover just to send some photos home to her mother. I knew them more by rumour though. Us girls of the Quarter, laughing, drinking and sleeping our way through our youth, were fun to watch but were seen as little more than the house entertainment. The good parties, the expensive dinners, the friendships formed on shared backgrounds and academic or artistic achievements were closed to us. Bohemia has its own brand of social etiquette. I suppose that's just human nature, even anarchists have their own set of unwritten, unruly laws of conduct.

The men were, understandably, more welcoming. In the early days Robert McAlmon led that group and the artistic socialite Laurence Vail led him. Before she married him Peggy Guggenheim called him the King of Bohemia. Afterwards she called him a lot worse, but, when I knew him, he was definitely a king, with bright, flowing clothes, long, golden hair and the assumption that the world was his to play with.

I spent my best years with those people. I drank, danced, whored and travelled with them ageing badly by my side.

Yeah, Mother, I can see your face, puckered kind just 'cos I'm sick, but I know what you're thinking. That's right, I whored. I whored and I got no shame. There's nothing more honest than a hooker on her patch. There's no room for any pretence there.

No room for genteel living either, though. So we all aged badly, those of us that lasted to age that is. Age took us all unawares, you see we were the first youth-driven generation. We expected to live hard and die young. We had grown into adulthood with too much death around us to respect, or anticipate, age. It was a time to live and live well. We thought that the old values had gone for good, that they lay buried with the generation they had killed.

Certainly those values had no bearing on our moral choices, and our moral choices were not to be questioned. No one questioned partnerships. No one questioned drinking or drug habits, what you wore or where you lived, how money was made or why it changed hands.

Most of the money originated in the fabricated markets of America. Most of it was finally filtered down to the Dôme and the Dingo passing through the hands of restaurateurs, hoteliers, drug traffickers, barmen, prostitutes, lenders, borrowers and thieves. No one questioned any of this; there was enough money to go around and that was all that mattered. Florianne got her money from a champagne manufacturer, Yvonne got hers from visiting dignitaries, a lot got theirs from passing trade and, in the beginning, I got mine from Phil. No better than you, Mother, sucking Father dry. No better but no worse either.

CHAPTER 9

I remember that first night out on the town very well. I was so happy, so ready and open to be impressed, so willing to appreciate everything. I suppose that night I was seeing the world through Phil's eyes and it was a fine place, all bright and sharp.

I remember Kiki coming into the Dôme, tottering over to Flossie and I, breaking up our drunken flirts. Her geometric bob cut her face into a dramatic square, her bow-painted lips were tight and pursed. Her eyelids were painted a deep jade and her eyebrows were arched high in distress. In my new role as a man about town I stepped forward to protect her against whatever her eyebrows were running from. Squaring my hollow shoulder pads and shaking my tiny, ineffectual fists I kept asking, 'Whassup? Whaswrong widdya? Whosafta ya?'

And she tried to tell me but, seeing as she was just about as drunk as a girl can get, I couldn't understand a word she was saying. And I couldn't understand Robert when he stepped in to explain to me that Kiki lived with Man Ray, that he made her up in different moods. That he shaved her eyebrows, applied her make-up, dressed her and photographed her and, on that day, he must have been studying alarm. Nor did I understand Phil when he explained to me that Man Ray was a photographer, an artist. By then I was almost as drunk as Kiki herself, I was past understanding anything.

Robert and Flossie found me later, sitting on the curb outside the Dôme facing the thinly populated terrace of the Rotonde. My head was slung low between my legs, my hat had slipped far enough to the side to reveal my long hair and a pool of vomit was neatly deposited in front of me. I was concentrating on not letting it touch the shoes that swamped my feet; they seemed to me to be too fine to stain.

'Didn't muck up your shoes, not one bit,' I said to Robert, who casually asked, 'Was it something you ate? Do you suffer from that South American malady? Are you of a delicate constitution?'

'Why we're all bitches together,' Flossie screamed, grabbing a fistful of my hair, 'a dreadful lot of bitches!' And so we were.

'Phil?' I asked, and Robert shrugged.

'Ours is not to question why or with whom.' I felt a twinge and was dismayed to recognise it as relief rather than jealousy. I did think that for form's sake I should threaten to go search and question but, truth was, I was too drunk to put on that much of a show. Instead I just reached my two arms out, childlike. Robert and Flossie levered me up and we were off, arms linked, heads back, screaming out:

'Amen means so be it, half a crown a thrupenny bit –

Three men six feet walking down sunny street singing bully beef tuppence a pound.'

Somewhere along the way we lost Flossie, and further on in to the night, somewhere off the Boul'Mich, we found the Gypsy bar.

'You'll be a man for a night,' Robert said, 'and it will stand you in good stead when one day you find yourself worrying your husband about the length of his shortcomings.'

Robert knew the patron of the Gypsy bar and the patron seemed happy to serve us for as long as we were happy to be served. So, we ordered our drinks and, without me seeing him, Robert organised that we be joined by a couple of girls.

They played jazz in the Gypsy bar, and they were playing some good stuff that night. Real, raw jazz with a low, throbbing beat and a twinkle of movement running up and down its spine. Just like the pulse of sex with a suggestion of tease rippling over it. We sat near the band and our girls, Jeanette and Alys, came with our drinks. Jeanette was far taller than the fashions of the time allowed for. Over six foot with her body proportioned to her height, she seemed to burst out of her clothes. She bounced about with all the enthusiasm and vibrancy of a young horse, cantering around the floor, stopping every now and then to boom out some earthy advice. Passing a table of sedate-looking young men sitting huddled and serious together, she shouted, 'If you want to shit solid, stay off the beer.'

She scared me. I think she even scared Robert but, faced with the choice of us she wrapped her arms around him. She must have known that a hug from her would break me, so she left me for Alys. Sweet, little blonde Alys whose whispered obscenities were barely noticed, dropping as they did from such pretty, pouting lips. She slotted herself close to my side and immediately went to work so, in an attempt to distract her wandering fingers, I led her up to dance.

We danced awkwardly at first. I was waiting for her to lead and she was clawing at me, assuming my invitation to dance was merely an invitation to foreplay. It didn't take long though before the alcohol and the dim lights, the soft warmth of my partner's shoulders and the deep, jungle pulse of the music worked on me, thawed me into movement.

I held Alys tight to me and she immediately sensed her role. Her dainty, slippered feet slipped in between my heavy, loose shoes. Her arms lay soft on the cloth of my jacket, her pretty little curls traced the line of my jaw and I whisked her away. Twirled both of us away into the heart of the night and the warm, dark soul of the music.

It may have been the drink, but I honestly think that I danced better that night than I ever did afterwards. Of course it was just the drink, this was before I'd had any training at all. But that night I got an intimation what real movement was and, ever after, I mainly just copied that emotion. Luckily most people don't know enough to tell the difference between an original and a good copy, but the true dancers of the time, Isadora Duncan and Josephine Baker, they knew. They knew enough to pity the likes of me, those bound by mediocrity. They knew what I felt that night in the Gypsy bar. They knew that a good dancer moves to the beat of the music, but that a great dancer uses the music as a foothold to a higher rhythm. A great dancer will dance in time with your mood, she can dance a season, a city or a memory for you.

That night, with pretty little Alys posturing by my side, I started off moving slow and sensual. I held her close and ran my hand down her bare back. I worked our bodies over and around the night, through the bars and the whores, the drinking and the loving. I danced a slow, hard street dance, a call to the urban wild. When we stopped, Robert was looking at me with something like respect. He was looking at me over Jeanette's broad shoulders. They were both quite drunk and Jeanette was doing her best to seduce. She ran a hand through Robert's hair and he pushed it away, leaned her head on his shoulder and he shifted position, slid her hand under the table and he grabbed it and slammed it right back on view.

'You just haven't met the right woman yet,' she purred.

'And you're a right one are you?' And then he laughed at her confusion over the idiom.

I took up my hat, which had fallen close to his chair, and left to walk through the Paris I was already familiar with. The early morning city populated with the ghosts of the night before and the seeds of the day to come.

I went to the Gypsy quite frequently after that. Sometimes with Robert and Phil, but mostly alone. Fact is, from then on, I started doing most things alone. I didn't see too much of Phil any more. Sometimes he'd crawl into bed beside me, some nights I'd wake him with drunken, maudlin caresses and after every encounter we'd hold each other close, asking no questions, making no promises.

I wasn't lonely though. Following some rare advice from Robert I started taking dance classes, classical and jazz, taught by a trim, elderly French lady and a blousy middle-aged gay man respectively. I never learnt much though, just the rudiments, but that's all I ever needed. My real skills were my youth and my fine, full chest.

And I was busy with my new friends. I had found girls enough to frill up my days with and eager young boys to liven up my nights. The proprietor of the Gypsy sometimes paid me to dance and I took the money proudly, thinking it elevated me into the position of professional artist. I was very young back then, too young to know that I could have charged a lot more for a lot less effort. All the clientele were interested in was how naked my breasts looked sculpted against my sweat-soaked clothes, or whether my top would stay on for the whole performance.

Life was fine then for a while. I had friends enough to fill my world with noise and I had come to depend on noise; it deadened the forebodings that that those lost days in London had planted in my brain. Drink drowned them and bright lights bleached them out but, sometimes, a night thick enough to blanket all activity would fall and then, curled up in Phil's arms, or more often, curled up alone, I'd be forced to lie awake listening to the whispers of time.

'*We've stretched the earth too tight over corpses*,' they'd hiss. '*The bulge will rupture and our man-made hell will be spat back on us.*'

But still, mostly, life was fine and then, clichéd though it sounds, I fell fully, physically, passionately in love and, for a moment, life was wonderful. The clamour of noise and the horror of quiet were both silenced by the roar of my happiness.

CHAPTER 10

I had a lot of visitors today. The room was all cluttered up with them, they even brought some great-grandchildren. Must be a special occasion. There was a tree when I came here first so I suppose this is Christmas, it certainly feels as if I've been here for weeks.

They came, they sat, they all asked questions: *How was I feeling? Was I hungry?*

A lot of silences. I tried to answer, tried to drool some words down my chin, but the banality of it all froze me. I want to go back to where I was, all wrapped up in the warmth of a Parisian night, clinging to the hard urgent flesh of my lover. I closed my eyes and they left. I stayed still for a while waiting, I knew she'd come and she did. Mother sat lightly on the side of my bed, her hand cooling my forehead, her ear hovering over my mumbled words.

'Tell me more about Paris,' she said and I did.

Outside, in the corridor, under the dismal streams of tinsel the family waited, and waited. Catherine shifted baby Jack on her hip, gestured to Simon, her husband, to catch a hold of Leah, their three-year-old, and sighed up at her father.

'Is she going to be much longer?' Deirdre answered for him.

'God knows, she's spending all her time in there now really. Isn't she, Brian?'

'Yeah, day and night it seems.' Brian groaned, but the response was automatic, triggered by his sister-in-law's tone. He hadn't really taken much notice of how much time his wife was spending with her mother.

'Night and day is right. I keep telling her to let me take over but she won't hear of it.' Isabel and Ellen exchanged glances again. Deirdre had a well-earned reputation for imposing on their mother's more docile nature. 'But still, Christmas day! We have to get back to eat.'

'Yeah, this is ridiculous,' Catherine agreed. Red-faced, tired and sensing a tantrum, she opened the door. 'We're going now, Mam,' she called in. 'I have to get Jack down in the next half hour.'

Ruth stood up. She was well used to responding immediately to her family's demands. She kissed her mother and left.

'She seems well, considering,' Ellen said from the back seat of the car.

'Yeah, that's the best she's been in a while,' Ruth agreed. 'She knew us all, she hasn't recognised anyone properly in weeks.'

'Maybe they did it on purpose.' Brian said, half-listening to the conversation, totally disconnected to the quaver of hope his wife was expressing.

'What do you mean? Who's "they"?'

'Well, the doctors; you know, for the day that's in it.'

'What do you mean?' In the back seat Isabel and Ellen exchanged glances. Their mother was never known to raise her voice at their father. Brian was startled enough to glance over, away from the road, something he very rarely did.

'I mean they may have lessened her medication so that she could appreciate her family visiting,' he explained. Ruth merely nodded. The fact that her mother had been lucid made her further revelations all that more disturbing; disturbing and fascinating.

And then they were home. Catherine and Simon were there before them. Deirdre had gone back to her house to collect Mark; they were joining the Mahons for dinner.

Ruth hadn't expected to celebrate Christmas this year. Her mother was lasting far longer than any of the predictions. As Brian had said the previous evening, 'She's a tough old bird.'

He had meant it kindly. He had put his arm around Ruth, holding her from behind as she stuffed the turkey, and he didn't even think enough of what he had said to laugh. It would have made it easier if he had laughed. The doorbell rang then, so Ruth was saved from responding to the ridiculous insult he had presented her with.

It was Catherine. Catherine, Simon, Leah, Jack, a buggy, a baby carrier, two suitcases, a box of presents, a box of wine, a bundle of coats, a changing bag – enough confusion, bustle and noise to smother any gathering tension.

As usual, automatically, Ruth cooed open-armed over to Leah.

'Who's my favourite granddaughter?' she asked, high pitched. No one laughed; even Leah, at just three years old, was tired of the joke. But for form's sake she answered, 'I'm your *only* granddaughter.'

Ruth forced a laugh and then turned to Catherine balancing the baby and a bag, 'And can I have a cuddle?' she asked and mentally kicked herself when she saw Catherine's answering expression. *Why oh why can I not just say I'll hold the baby?* she thought as she led the way into the kitchen.

At home, long, long ago, with their mam and dad, Christmas Eve was stomach-churningly beautiful. Dad would ice the cake then fix the plastic Santa, sleigh and reindeer around the edge. Mam would bake and joke, she'd dance around the room swinging child by child, humming out Christmas songs – not the hymns, the ones the crooners sang in the movies. Ruth always lit the candle in the window – she was the youngest, that was her job – and Deirdre would place the baby Jesus in the crib, but she didn't get to hold a lit match.

All these years later and Ruth tried but couldn't stop herself. She was baking buns that wouldn't be eaten, she was humming 'A White Christmas' and she was reaching down to Leah, trying to catch her hands to swing her into the approximation of a dance. Isabel and Ellen were smoking and drinking beers in the garden, Brian and Simon were watching television.

'You'll get her overexcited, Mam,' Catherine said and so Ruth stopped. Stopped and looked at her now grown daughter and she tried so hard to say something apt.

'You look tired,' was all she could come up with and that, obviously, wasn't the right something.

'Yeah,' Catherine agreed, and without another word took Leah by the hand and led her out of the room. Ruth could see her comment had been read as a judgement. The same as when she looked at the cigarettes Isabel had produced, the same as when she handed Ellen her third bottle of beer. It wasn't fair of them, she was their mother; this element of caring was her job, wasn't it? A lifelong position, wasn't it?

She left the buns to cool, poured herself a glass of wine and joined the men.

Christmas day was easier. Everyone trying to live up to the expectations of their good clothes. Leah bounding with excitement and the wizened old woman they'd visited earlier reminding them of the transience of it all. The house was full, loud and warm. The tree twinkled, the table groaned with food, candles flickered: every cliché of perfection. Usually Ruth would have been proud, but today she felt uneasy.

She looked about her blooming family, on their best behaviour, even Simon gallantly helping to lift and carry. She watched Brian tighten the bolts of a new tricycle in the back garden, heard her daughters squeal together from the upstairs bathroom and she felt uneasy. A lurking doubt dragged guiltily at her capacity for enjoyment.

Just the gravy to go – her secret, a dash of soy and tabasco – and then it hit her. *This wasn't enough.*

She thought of her mother floating down some past of hers or her creation and she felt jealous. Jealous! Deirdre was working behind her, straining vegetables, tossing the potatoes in butter.

'You were right,' Ruth said as lightly as she could. 'Mam's got herself fixated with the greats now. She thinks she had an affair with Picasso.'

CHAPTER 11

'Did you love Father?' I asked my new, kind mother, a question I had never associated with their union before.

'Yes,' she said, and that was all she said, so that means she couldn't have, that she didn't even understand the question. The question I was asking was did he boil your blood, did your stomach lurch and your senses sting? Did every breath taste, every word sustain and every touch burn? Does the memory of your sex with him still shoot bolts of desire down your spine? 'Yes,' is no answer. I tried to explain this to her, I tried to tell her about Picasso.

I met him in the early summer of 1921. Of course, by then I knew almost all there was to know about him. Every conversation about art, love, genius, sex and passion revolved around him. And for us lot, snuggled securely in the self-centred earnestness of youth, there was no other topic worth discussing. Robert especially held him in an almost obsessional regard. He used to speak about him continuously. Him and Braque and Derain and Duchamp, all the great men who had worked so hard to tear the visual arts apart. But I don't know if Robert ever met him. After his association with Braque dissolved, Picasso always held himself artistically apart. He belonged to the generation before us and had little time for the gaggling cliques that were filling up the bars. We had nothing new to tell him.

It was partly because of this, his superior, artistic reputation, but mostly because of the adolescent crush I had for the man, that I made it my business to attend *Quadro Flamenco*, which opened in Paris in May in La Gaîté Lyrique.

Isn't it amazing what the mind throws up? That just slid off my tongue, well-oiled and confident, so I will believe in it, but I don't know. My family were here today, all of them, great grandchildren and all. Is it the panto I'm thinking of, the Gaiety? Panto; Pablo, what a muddle. Time was I could answer the questions on *University Challenge* with well-oiled confidence.

Panto; Pablo – I like that. He would have too.

Wherever it was, whenever it was, it was. The *Quadro Flamenco*, still so vibrant. Picasso designed and painted the set and, for the full duration of the performance, that was all I saw. Around his work the cast danced and sang an homage to Andalusian folklore, but for me all of that was just so much background. I was lost in the colour, the wit, the clever reality of the stage set. Picasso had replicated a nineteenth-century theatre complete with close little boxes draped in velvet and filled with characters of the era. I didn't know enough of the world to recognise any of them, but that didn't matter; the joke was the use of portraiture, and I got that.

Before that night I had never stood still for long enough to appreciate my surroundings fully and aesthetically, which was, Picasso told me later, the first step towards appreciating art. But that night I sat stone still and stared. I saw the nuances of colours and the skilful arrangements of form and, more than that, I felt them. With just the use of my eyes I felt the textures of cloth and smelled the dust-filled folds. It was something like magic, a heightening of life experience.

After the show I told all this to the man who had accompanied me, a friend from the Quarter who was desperate to get back to the Dôme.

'Don't you feel it?' I asked. 'It's like life but more intense. Like a heightening of life experience.'

'Yeah, yeah,' he said. 'Yeah, whatever, come on.'

But I let him go. I wanted to be alone to savour this new-found knowledge. The theatre emptied around me and I stood watching, appreciating everything that I had taken for granted before: the tilt of some lady's hat set so perfectly on her hard, tight curls; the narrow free-flowing planes of some young man's tailcoat; the crispness of starched cotton and the deep blue folds that sculpt white satin.

I waited until they were all gone before I followed them out into the dark. I intended to walk down by the river for a while. I romantically imagined myself tracing the light of the moon on its soft surface, but then it began to rain. I stepped back to shelter under the narrow overhang of the theatre's roof and I stepped straight into a man who was already standing there. The impact unbalanced me and so he closed his arms around me to hold me steady. They stayed resting on my bare shoulders long after I had recovered my equilibrium.

I was wearing a primrose-yellow dress that evening. It fitted me perfectly, glancing off every curve, from bust to ankle, and all those slight, young curves were accentuated with trims of ivory lace. I was carrying a plain white shawl, finely knitted with a silver thread worked through it, and

I was wearing a pearl-studded skullcap. Beneath that, my thick, dark hair curled wild against my cheeks. Despite the sophistication of my clothes, I looked my age.

'Women never learn how to control their hair until they are old and bored and have nothing better to do,' the man said, trailing a finger through one of my curls, smiling. 'You are not yet twenty.'

I nodded immediately, although it took me a few moments to decipher his accent. But that didn't matter, it wasn't his words I was agreeing to.

'I heard what you just said to your friend,' he said, dropping my curl and reaching for my hand. 'It reminded me of why I have to paint. A heightening of life experience.'

He asked for my name then and I gave it to him. He didn't volunteer his and I didn't ask for it; I had recognised him immediately. I had often seen his picture in the papers and once he had been pointed out to me on the street. That time, something more than his fame had caused me to turn and watch him move away from me. There was something about his hair that stirred something maternal in me. Something about the way it fell forward and the way he continually ran his hand through it to drag it back. And there was something about the fleshy set of his lips that fascinated me; they seemed to be forever in motion, forever humming out the tune of his thoughts. But Picasso was so much more than the sum of all these parts.

It was Pablo's vibrancy, bouncing off his canvases, that elevated his work just as it elevated his speech, his humour, his walk. Everything about the man created the same emotion in me as his work did; everything about him heightened my life experience.

I will never regret loving him. Although we spent such a short time together, he shaped my horizon and distorted my perspective. He told me that the world was filled with beauty and he taught me where and how to look for it. And he taught me well. From that summer onwards I saw the beauty of life everywhere. I see it still in the turn of the rain when the wind catches it, in the limp curl of a sleeping dog's tail, in the hard, brave grit of a street girl's smile. And I saw it in your dying eyes, Mother, in the claw of your hands grasping and pulling on your bedclothes. It's a hard, natural beauty, but one that Picasso revelled in and one that he managed to capture on canvas.

Mother left then, kissed me and left. Maybe I shouldn't have mentioned her death. When trying to describe the potency of life maybe it was insensitive.

And Picasso's approach to living was potent. He loved life and all it had to offer; that's what comes across in his work, and that's what came across in his manner of living. He was never really unfaithful, but sometimes he just loved to love women. Just as he was never a drunkard, he just sometimes loved to drink. And he was never obsessive about his work; he just sometimes loved to paint to the exclusion of everything else.

When Picasso and I first met he was the father of a three-month-old. Something new was born in the man when his son, Paolo, was delivered to him, and that was why he could never love me with anything more than his body. Whatever we had together was never strong enough to threaten his commitment to his family and, from the very start, I was aware of that.

From that very first night I knew that all he saw in me was wit enough to render my brand of beauty attractive. But from that very first night I saw my world in his eyes. My breathing became laboured almost before he touched me; the anticipation of his hands was enough to choke me with emotion. Sometimes I even envied his canvases, his brushes, the tools of his trade that would stay with him, mean more to him.

I loved his laugh; it was Spanish. The man laughed in his native language and he snored in Spanish and he drank in Spanish. Picasso's involuntary noises belonged to the bullfights, and the olive groves, and the small, white churches with red, tiled roofs, and the big-set men with deep-set eyes and their tiny glasses of clear, fiery alcohol.

He gave me memories of Spain long before I visited the country to collect them for myself. He made his homeland vivid for me with words long before he illustrated his descriptions for me with charcoal sketches of young, proud men drawn high on to their toes looking disdainfully down at the animal charging for them, or bright little watercolours full of white light and dusty townscapes, or portraits of old men with tight, drawn expressions sunk into the deep crevices of weathered age.

But on that first night all knowledge of the man was still ahead of me. But still, on that first night, dressed in all my finery, with the rain dripping down my back and the hum of the sleeping city pressing down on us, I made myself as wantonly available as any street girl. It was me who kissed him, reaching out to him, my lips grazing the corner of his mouth. It was me who slipped my arms under his jacket, under his shirt. It was me who guided him and whispered encouragement and endearments into his ear and it worked. I charmed him sufficiently to hold him for a summer.

We never met much in Paris. Oh I was always welcome in his studio on the Rue de la Boétie but I was never comfortable there, I don't think he was either. I think the splendour of the space and the haughtiness of the address separated him from who he was. By 1921 he was growing into who he was to become but, at that time, I think his soul still belonged to poverty: to midnight dinners of sardines and cheap wine; to worn-out shoes and cold, wet winters; to all the ardour of conversation and youth; to Braque and the energy associated with the beginnings of cubism.

I think that that was why he had to negate his surroundings before he could work properly. His studio in the Rue de la Boétie had once been a spacious five-roomed apartment with all the trimmings suitable to such a central address, just off the Champs-Elysées. The fireplaces were marble, the mirrors above them gilted and ornate. The floor would have been a rich parquet if it had ever been as much as swept and the view framed the light and life of Paris, a postcard of the city complete with the Eiffel tower. But all of that was before, when I knew it it was nothing but Pablo's studio.

He had opened up the entire space. All the doors were either pushed back fully or removed from their hinges. Every room was filled with the debris of his work: the papers and magazines he never could part with; the endless sketches and scribbles that were later elevated to works in progress, or works on paper, but at the time were nothing more than doodles. And all the filth of his living: the cigarette butts and packages; the empty bottles and forgotten food; the newspapers over everything, soaking up the paint, draped over the canvases, worked into the floor. I loved the smell of the place. It smelled of excitement. The oils and the fumes of paint, the sweat and the smoke of the man combined with the height, seven floors up over a city, to produce an atmosphere where anything could happen.

Picasso set up his easel in one room, in the best-lit one, and, in there, he kept a few sticks of furniture and a violin hanging from the corner of a large blank canvas. I saw a picture of the place once, in a book, just as I remembered it. Just so exactly as I remembered it that I stared hard and long, trying to see around corners, shining my eyes into the shadows, looking for my young self. I saw the chair I used to sit on, empty, it chilled me. I used to sit there when I called. Sit half-on half-off a broken, filthy chair and Pablo would talk to me. He never worked in front of me there, but he would talk to me. I wonder if I knew then how happy I was. He told me, '*Dans les mains on voit les mains.*'

He told me, 'Always wear gloves when you lie. The face can be tamed, but a man's hands never lie.'

He used to sketch his hands frequently; that was his form of self-portraiture. He left his face for others to study. He told me that he hadn't done a self-portrait since the day Apollinaire, his friend the poet, had died. Later he did one for me: I hold that up as proof of his feelings for me. After all, I knew too well what it took for him to study his image in the mirror. He told me, 'If I never look in a mirror, I will never know my age.'

It was a philosophy that worked for him. He avoided mirrors and managed to keep his youth intact. I wonder at the tragedy of his death. I wonder if he died of old age while still retaining his passion for life. I hope not. I hope by then his passion was for death; he was always attracted by the unexplored.

He used to laugh at my hands, turning them around in his. He used to pinch them, pressing his thumb down deep and, for a moment, after he released the pressure, my young flesh would hold the imprint of his thumb.

My hands betrayed all my youth. So much so that later, when dealing with circumstances I felt were beyond my years, I wore gloves. I stopped when I realised they were no longer necessary. I was in Berlin then and my hands were thin, with long nails painted hard, emerald green. They were cut and scarred by work and misshapen by chilblains. They were street hands. Hands that told their own story, that were far more interesting than the soft little pads that Pablo had held and laughed at, but they were no longer capable of holding any impression.

During the first few weeks I knew Pablo I spent a great deal of time sitting in his studio, listening to him talk, watching him play with my hands, wallowing in the joy of his presence, but still that place was never ours. It was a place of conversation, of work. Pablo's brand of honesty could never be comfortable with sordid fumblings and, in his studio, any movement we made towards each other seemed to be echoed by a movement below us. Either by his wife Olga's, firm, neat step or worse by the cries of Paolo. So Picasso took his family and left Paris. He rented a villa in Fontainbleau for them, one large enough to incorporate a studio for himself, and he rented a cottage for me, one close enough to visit but remote enough for discretion.

I told Phil a story just one question away from the truth, but that question was never asked.

'I'm tired,' I said to Phil and he just nodded. We were all of us tired, all of the time.

'I think I need to get out of the city for a while.'

He agreed Paris was nowhere to be in the summer.

'A friend has asked me to stay in Fontainbleau.' I stopped and waited but the question never came, instead Phil laughed.

'You go,' he said. 'You go kick up a storm, babe. Think I'll wait around here for a bit and see what's going on. See what Bob's doing, I'll let you know.'

We were sitting opposite each other on the terrace of the Rotonde and I reached my hand over to his and let it rest there. He didn't say anything, and then, for all the world like two old, married people who have learned to read each other's minds, we both turned to look at the pedestrian traffic passing before us. That was the end of any pretence between us. Phil had found something new in Robert McAlmon, and now it was my turn.

CHAPTER 12

I left for Fontainbleau in June. I left all my city finery behind in the Rue de Fleurus and just packed a few simple dresses. I thought I was being frugal, a little milkmaid in the woods, but Phil had only taught me one way to shop and his way charged extra for simplicity. 'Tailoring is all in the tailoring, babe,' he told me. 'A guy's only ever as good as the cut of his jib.'

Phil paid for my summer wardrobe, and my travelling expenses, and he kept paying the allowance he had settled on me. I took it all. I felt no guilt then and even now I find it hard to associate anything as negative as guilt with that glorious time. I doubt Phil would expect me to. I think that, back then, he still needed me a little. I think he wasn't yet secure enough in the choices McAlmon had introduced him to to do away completely with the idea of a wife. However he was secure enough to realise that an absent wife would always be the more preferable option, and so we parted on the best of terms. He accompanied me to the train station and we kissed as politely as any parting spouses would. He even bought me flowers for the journey, a little posy of violets to cheer my carriage.

The rest of the journey I made alone. But my expensive simplicity made it that little bit easier for me. I was wearing a tight, straw hat and a plain, navy-blue dress, one that I thought terribly suitable for travelling in. I fancied myself the picture of pastoral innocence. But my dress lightly skirted my breasts and swung heavy and loose from my hips, stopping that fashionable six inches above the ankle. My short coat matched it perfectly, being cut from the same cloth. My stockings were silk and so were all my underclothes; you could tell that much from the smooth fall of my frock. My shoes were cut from a soft, rich leather and my trunk was so new it still smelled of wax. On the small, rural platform at Fontainbleau, people stared.

I put on my gloves and allowed a porter to take care of me. My groomed appearance demanded his full attention even before I had the opportunity to ask for it. Leaving all my fellow travellers to fend for themselves, he settled me and my trunk on the back of a cart and directed the driver to take me to the address I had written in the front of my notebook. At first my driver was respectful. He hazarded a few comments and I replied as best I could. Although by now my French had progressed far beyond my initial schoolgirl mutterings, the man's accent was thick and completely unfamiliar so I didn't encourage any full-blown conversation. Even so it was a pleasant journey until we reached my cottage.

It was tiny, three rooms and a primitive outhouse, totally screened from the narrow dirt road, almost lost in a deep wild green growth. A thin grassy path led the way from the gate to the door and my driver pulled my trunk up that far for me.

'*Combien?*' I asked and he sneered and held his hand out for an amount that I suspected was inordinate.

I wasn't aware of it then, but in retrospect I can see that the discrepancy between my appearance and my surroundings labelled me as definitely as leather, fishnets and stilettos would today. The man finally left but not before he had shown me exactly what he thought of me.

He told me that he figured that a girl staying alone in such a place was no longer above him, that I should be friendly, that he would kill his sister if she turned up with all my airs. He lunged for my breasts and pushed his tongue into my mouth. He pawed his way under my clothes and I pushed and screamed and kicked and bit and he finally left. After that I was happy to stay alone in my cottage. Aside from Pablo, the only human contact I had during that long, hot summer was with the housekeeper from the neighbouring château.

My cottage was on the grounds of an eighteenth-century château. The house was closed up while I was there. The family was in Switzerland with their two sons, both of whom were suffering from TB. But a Madame Germain, their housekeeper and my acting landlady, remained behind, living in the kitchen wing, working herself dry trying to maintain some semblance of normality. It was Madame Germain who told me about the two sons: she mentioned their suffering from TB as if it were a minor inconvenience. She worked with the certainty that the family as a whole were due home at any moment, although back then no one ever really suffered from consumption, they died from it.

As well as being responsible for the house, Madame Germain tended to the kitchen gardens. The larger farm work was delegated to a skeleton staff, an old man and three shell-shocked veterans. I had nothing to do with them and my only dealings with Madame Germain were limited to her providing me with food. We were never friendly. She never had the time; she was too devoted to her vocation as a Catholic retainer to a Catholic family.

The château had been built to house a large staff, but when I was there all there was was Madame Germain. It needed her, busied her and curtailed her, and she tended to it, loved it and allowed it shelter her. It was all she was. Her hands were thick and hard from rooting in the earth, from dragging vegetables out of the thick, black soil. Her back was stretched and supple from flowing with the movements of the seasons: bending over herb boarders, weaving through fruit bushes and reaching into apple trees. All of her, from her head with its tight coils of grey hair, to her short, thick body tucked firmly into tweeds, to her rounded, muscular arms, were just as much a part of the fabric of that great house as its walls. Picasso thought she was beautiful. He would make me find out where she would be and then he would follow her through the course of her day. Discreetly out of sight, he would sketch her hard round body as it stretched and bent and toiled.

Once, she showed me around the château. She unhooked a huge brass ring hung with keys of all sizes from the cold kitchen wall and walked me through that ghost of grandeur she had committed herself to maintaining. Once we passed the narrow tunnel connecting the kitchens to the main house she dropped her voice to a respectful level and then whispered me around room after room filled with the shrouds of a family. Dust-sheets covered everything; pictures had been removed from the walls, leaving patches of darker colours; carpets and rugs had been rolled up, leaving the floors bare and cold. The walls were covered with intricate papers and the ceilings were edged with gilt. The floors were scrubbed clean and the windows were still opened on a rota basis. Poor Madame Germain was fighting the family's disease on the home front and was failing; the house had all the atmosphere of a tomb.

The kitchens, though, were different. The kitchens and the chapel were both still alive. One was warm with the smell of cooking, the other with the smell of incense; one was still busy with the needs of the body, the other still busy with the needs of the soul. Madame Germain was responsible for feeding the working men and she took it upon herself to pray for us all, including me. Just like my driver, she thought I needed saving, and I liked the idea of being saved in such surroundings.

Three or four times a week I went over to the château to collect whatever food Madame Germain had for me, and she fed me well. She provided me with home-baked bread, warm and crusty with a centre that melted in the mouth, and eggs – large, brown, speckled double yolks because she thought I needed filling out – and pure, yellow cream, and golden soft butter, and firm squares of white cheeses flavoured with chives or thyme, and thick milk that clung viscous to the rim of my deep blue jug. There were also extras: drop scones made with shavings of mature cheeses, and pastries cupping clots of cream mixed with jam, and baskets of strawberries, and fat bunches of herbs bound together with twine and thick green bottles filled with warm rich wines.

It was easy to weigh myself down too heavily with these delights and often the mile-and-a-half walk back to my cottage took me twice as long as it should. Then one day Pablo produced a weathered boneshaker of a bicycle and

I would fill its basket fit to burst before bouncing my way home over the rough-cut tracks of the estate. It wasn't just Pablo that made that summer perfect.

Although I was still living off Phil's charity and Pablo's infidelity, I felt free. That cottage was the first home I had that I didn't have to share, and those long, golden days with, or without, Pablo, were the first that I experienced completely independently. Even my one-sided affair gained some degree of independence being, as it was, played out on my territory. Because almost immediately I claimed that cottage as my own.

As I have said it was tiny, three rooms and an outhouse set in a quarter acre of gardens and smothered by growth, but it was so much more than that.

My bedroom was dominated by a huge brass bed weighed down with a heavy, buttoned quilt in the lightest shade of blue. It had a tallboy painted white and a wicker chair painted yellow. There was rush matting on the floor, so recently laid it bounced like grass under my feet. The window wouldn't shut and, just under it, there was a flower-bed run wild with thick bunches of lavender. At night I was smothered by the release of their perfume and in the morning I was woken by the dull drone of bees.

My kitchen had a blackened stove in its centre and a pale pine table worn thin in the middle from generations of scrubbing. It had a cold stone floor and a chipped sink wedged under a pump. It had a dresser that was painted blue but was flaking to reveal layers of colour: yellow and red and dull dirty brown. And that dresser was crammed with chipped bits of crockery, curling postcards, yellow newspaper clippings, hanging cooking utensils, balls of twine, mousetraps and so much more, all the dirt of a discarded life. Ivy had pushed its way through the rotting window frame and had taken a firm hold all over one wall. It was creeping up to the ceiling and its leaves had mutated, growing broad enough to trap all the sparse light of that dark little room. Sometimes I would use those leaves as plates; they made my bread and cheese taste green.

My sitting-room had a rug covered in faded clumps of forget-me-nots, and a settee that smelled of nests and straw. It creaked when you sat on it, and sagged to the floor in the middle. My sitting-room also had a fireplace with a wrought-iron surround and a mottled, warped mirror above it that distorted my face beyond recognition. The first time Pablo saw that he laughed and said, 'What's this doing here? I invented this.'

My outhouse was a rotten old plank of wood laid over a hole, but on the ground, dug into the dirt, were two unsuitably ornate footrests, white porcelain with blue flowers. The door wouldn't shut, wouldn't even close over, and at night bats would sweep over my face while I, terrified, tried to relax my bladder.

My garden was rampant with life and filled with the vibrancy of the wild. I cleared the small stone yard and there, under the clutter of fruit trees, I sat night after night with my young heart's dream. We used to drink far too much and watch the purple evenings fade into silver starlight. I never remember those nights getting dark. But I do remember the smell of them, the thick smell of earth that clung like home remembered.

'It's the most natural thing in the world to die and be buried,' I said one evening, and Pablo answered, 'Of course. That is what drives us to live.'

During the days when he was working I used to dance. During that summer Pablo worked a lot and I danced a lot.

I danced in my garden and, because it was set three miles back from the tar road and shielded from the dirt road by a wealth of growth, I could dance naked. I danced in step with the life around me. Springing high from the grass I twirled and twisted in time with the drone of insects and the flutter of birds. I flung myself at the dance with too much enthusiasm and no control, but that didn't matter; there was never anyone there to see me.

I'll always remember those mornings, before the sun burned too brightly. When the grass was still wet with the cool of the night and when the warmth of the day touched my inner thighs, the arch of my back, the soft, white curves of flesh that usually lie hidden under the fall of a woman's breast. I turned cartwheels and felt myself open and close to the sun, round and round, opened and closed. My hair grew long and wild and my body hardened and turned nut brown.

I used to wash in the stream that just skirted my garden. It was cold – pure green cold – but the sunlight could always convince you otherwise. I would untie my hair and lie on the round worn stones that lined its bed and the water, in such a rush to pass, would part into ribbons at my head and fall in loud gasping sheets by my sides.

I wore fewer and fewer clothes. My Parisian silks stayed in my trunk under my bed and I dropped my dresses over my head and delighted in the feel of my naked body moving inside their light confines. I wore a plain blue cotton dress with a plain round neck and a sweet white trim and I wore a white lawn dress, short and sleeveless. I wore a shirt of Pablo's that he had left behind. It smelled of him and rustled like him and, when he wasn't with me, it felt like him.

I used to sleep through the heat of the afternoons and cycle in the evenings. Once I cycled over to the Picassos' villa and hid behind a tree. I saw Olga there sitting out front on the steps that led up to the hall door. Paolo was with her, wrapped in white, lying on a blanket at her feet. Olga was dark and graceful, and her body bent towards her child with all the devotion of the concerned Madonnas that dominated Picasso's work during the latter part of that summer. I stayed watching for a long time. I watched the sun dapple across the stuccoed front of the villa. I saw it dazzle and blind the windows. I saw it warm the wood of the shutters, and then, once I was sure of its effect, I left.

I didn't need reminding, but perhaps I needed proof. The villa still stood strong against its environs; my cottage was barely holding on to its structure, losing its battle against nature. Just as I would always lose if I was to pitch my strength against the solidity of Olga cradling her child. I cycled back to my world, so young but already defeated.

I remember Picasso as being delightfully happy that summer. He was boyish in his enthusiasms – for me, for Paolo, for Olga, for the drink in his hand as much as the canvas in his studio. He talked endlessly, filling me with his ideas, his hopes for his work, and he loved me. He loved me in my plain blue cotton frock. He told me that I was like a peasant girl in the field.

'And that is art,' he said. 'Art isn't to be found in the exclusiveness of aesthetic discussion; art should be brought down to the peasant girl in the field.' And then, laughing, his hair falling free over his face, he lowered himself onto me.

He told me about line and the importance of definition in form. He told me that the artist needed, above all, to be confident in his vision. That this confidence can be traced in the strength of his line, and then he told me about his vision, about how he wanted to portray his world.

'Since the renaissance we've been bound by the conventions of perspective,' he said.

It was night and we were lying under my apple tree. I was thinking, *Stars be gone, stars be bright*, as a branch, fat with growth, swung back and forth in the breeze, rhythmically blocking and revealing my view of the sky.

'We are told to read a canvas using only the language of perspective,' he said. 'Why? Why when there is so much more?'

'What do you mean by "more"?' I asked, lazily reaching my hand under his shirt. I was still just a child and only wanted to talk about love.

'What about time?' Picasso answered, and I just shrugged, so he continued. 'A woman running for example will always be a lie if we only freeze her in space. Isn't it more honest to say that she is coming towards us in time? Her forearm sooner that her shin and foot, her face distorted as it turns?'

'But time?' I was confused. 'Do you mean to paint things for the future?'

'No, no, no. That is nonsense.' And because of the harshness of his tone I sat forward and tried to concentrate on what he was saying. 'I'm talking about trying to capture a moving object as it reaches the retina,' he told me, 'as it is raw, as it is fully present, just in the moment before the brain deciphers the jumbled image and renders it familiar and dull. I want to show the world as it is, not as what our limited senses perceive it to be.'

'No you don't,' I whispered, remembering London, hearing the rustle of those ever-present whispers. Picasso didn't hear me though, I didn't intend him to, I had no way of warning him about the horror he was trying to explore.

'This is what the artist can do,' he was saying, and I just nodded. 'And isn't it right that now, in the twentieth century, in this, our renaissance, that we move our art forward into a new dimension?'

I nodded again.

But, along with all of Picasso's enthusiasms, there was a sadness. A sadness that he personified as a scrawny dog that every now and then shadowed his days and haunted his nights. He had lived too hard a life not to have been touched by some sorrows. He had seen friends and lovers die, he had known great poverty and he had watched the war as an outsider.

He told me, 'I took Braque and Derain to the station at Avignon; I never found them again.'

Their bodies survived the trenches but their youth couldn't and youth was something that Picasso always prized. He found himself in Harlequin, always young, always in love. He whispered that I could be his Pierrot. I laughed, sitting on his knee, swinging one leg over another, wearing only his unbuttoned shirt and drinking my wine straight from the bottle. The drops that ran down my chin ran into his mouth. He was laughing, his good, hearty Spanish laugh and I said, 'We could run away together to join the circus.' And, for a moment, I believed it.

'Yes, two little clowns making sweet music,' he said.

'And we know what tune we'll play,' I whispered, dropping my words right into his mouth. He swallowed them before answering.

'We'll whistle our way to damnation.'

'Oh no!' I gasped, pulling away. I was appalled. 'Our tune is a hymn. Love is religion. We can make our own rules, obey our own circus god.' Picasso laughed a little, then was silent for a moment and, when he answered me, it was in a different tone of voice, paternal, firm.

'Don't you know, little girl, Pierrot and Harlequin never meet their hearts' desire?'

The mood was broken. The evening was broken. Picasso set me gently on to my feet and got up to go.

'And, little girl,' he said, 'for you to whistle any hymn you would have to put on all your clothes and a dour face, then you would have to call in a priest to set the score. I have a wife and a son and no priest would write the hymn that would omit them. Some rules cannot be broken. No, little girl, we can never fool ourselves into believing that this is a hymn.'

I didn't see Picasso for a while after that but, when he came again, he brought some paper, some charcoal and some pastels with him. I was delighted. I had never seen him work before. He was a magician. He worked with line and light in such a way as to contain the world. A simple line combined with a few hatching strokes produced a tree, a piece of fruit, a parched flower, a matador ready for the kill, an olive grove wilting in the heat, an old man waiting, cap in hand, outside his church. A flick of his wrist and I, in all my bewilderment, had dropped from his chalk. I clapped and shrieked for all the world as if he had pulled a rabbit from a hat and he indulged me with his tricks for a full afternoon. Towards evening he got up to go and I knew by the way he bent his head before he pulled the door behind him that he was going for good.

'Don't,' I said, before I could stop myself.

'I will. It will only get harder after this,' he answered low and sad.

'It will only get harder for me and I am willing to take the risk,' I said thickly, emotion more than tears clogging my speech.

He came back to me then. I was kneeling, naked on my bed. The room was warm with an evening glow but I was warmed by something deeper.

'You think that it is only you who feels this?' he gestured around our room, and then brought his hand down to touch my breast, then his. 'It will get harder for me too.'

And there was all my joy and all my loss. I loved him enough to understand that he was a selfish man, selfish for himself and selfish for his art. There could be no arguing with the situation he presented to me and so I let him go.

I never cried. I watched him walk down my narrow, grassy path and step into the late afternoon of the world and all I felt was proud.

Later that evening I found a package under the apple tree, one of his soft-backed, spiral-ringed notebooks wrapped in brown paper. On the cover of the notebook he had written 'from me to you' and, in it, on the lower right-hand quadrant of the first page, was a rare self-portrait. I turned the page and there he was again, in the same place, only his chin was slightly different. On the next page his nose had shrunk, I flicked through the book and, magically, Pablo's face melted into mine.

We met again often. We met on the streets and in the bars. I used to track him down, which was easy; he had his haunts and his habits rarely changed. For a while he seemed pleased to see me but in a remote way; any possibility of intimacy was politely avoided and so being with him always hurt a little. But still I'd track him down. Sometimes I just needed to stand near him at those times when I couldn't much stand what was going on in my life, and he always allowed me that much.

I never told anyone about our affair. Sometimes I was tempted to brag, but as time passed I began to believe in it less and less. I was afraid that if I tried putting it into words it might evaporate. It would become just a story, a piece of gossip rather than the heartfelt emotion it was to me. Also, if I'm honest, I knew I would have run the risk of ridicule. After all, what could a man like Picasso see in a child like me? But I was seen with him often enough for people to notice it and for some to be impressed, though I'm sure all they thought was that I was a model at best, a star-struck lackey at worst. Still I seemed to be tolerated and that in itself was impressive. It raised me in McAlmon's opinion for one and, later on, I think it was why Hemingway and Fitzgerald took the time to look in my direction. I might have looked and acted like all us girls struggling on the fringe, but a connection to the great Picasso, no matter how tenuous, did set me apart.

I returned to Paris very soon after Picasso left me. I left my cottage to sink back into the earth. I doubt that it survived another round of death and growth. I wanted to leave before autumn set in, before I was claimed by the decay of the season and so, with my spirit, if not my heart, still intact, I readied myself for Paris. I dressed in my silk underwear and blue travelling suit. I tucked my wild hair up into my hat and I took the time to wash the dust of the summer out of my gloves. I fastened my stockings over my dark brown legs and I hid my freckles under a thin layer of powder. I dragged my trunk as far as my gate and waited for the lift I had arranged with Madame Germain. One of the shell-shocked young men was to drive me to the station in his pony and trap. He did so silently. His eyes fastened on the road ahead, his left arm and left leg shaking and twitching continually.

On the platform the porter ignored me and I had to call for his attention twice before he took charge of my trunk. Back in the Gare de Lyon, while I stood by my trunk scanning the crowds for a porter, the well-groomed people of Paris stopped to look.

A couple of days later our concierge in the Rue de la Fleurus stopped me on the stairs.

'You have changed, *ma petite*,' she said. 'You walk now from your hips but you keep your eyes cast down. I think perhaps you think that you are in love.' She was laughing so I answered defensively.

'No.'

'No, you are not in love, but yes, you think you are. You cannot be in love because you are not yet twenty. It takes a woman until old age, like me, to know what it is to be in love. And it takes men until old age to know that what they know as love is lust and so they look at their wives and pack their bags. But their wives, they watch them go and they laugh because once a woman is old enough to recognise love she is wise enough to know that it cannot be found in her husband.'

She laughed loudly at that and slyly touched her finger off her nose, but she was wrong. I was young but I had recognised real love in Picasso and he had recognised it in me. Our truth was that he loved everything and so his passion for me was part of his passion for life, whereas my passion for him was my life.

CHAPTER 13

The first thing I did in Paris was cut my hair. I thought of you while I did it, Mother. Remember how you pulled and tweezed it into ringlets, how you forced the comb through it, how you pinched it into tight, singed curls, how you prided yourself in it. You said it was your mother's hair and, like good teeth, was an undeniable proof of breeding. I thought of you as they hacked the weight off me, but mostly I thought of Picasso.

He had loved it long. He had slept on it, kissed it, plaited it and then he had left me so I cut my hair. I cut it well short, a close-fitting cap of curls, just like the girls in the magazines. And I wore black. Picasso had loved my white lawn dress and my sweet blue frock and then he had left me so I wore black. Two plain dresses that I bought cheap and hacked into two unadorned tubes that covered me from neck to shin. As I said, no one ever knew about my affair with Picasso. Phil had never asked for a name and I didn't think that anyone else deserved one, though Flossie tried her best to worm it out of me. She took to pointing to any passing man calling out, 'Look, your lover! Why do you treat him so mean?'

The more men the more she cried, the more outlandish-looking the man the louder she cried. She created quite a reputation for me in a very short time. But still I kept quiet about my summer, still wore my widow's weeds and never admitted to anyone the real reason why I was in mourning.

And I was in mourning. I was mourning the death of my hope. Picasso had given me back a little of what London had taken from me, but then he had left me and this time I had grown too far from Phil to expect him to rescue me. All I had when I returned to Paris was Paris itself and I was surprised to learn that that was enough. I felt that the city had stretched to suit my new needs. I was too young yet to understand that cities are built to house despair – no matter how low you fall, the gutter will always be there to catch you.

When people asked me about the severity of my clothes I answered, 'Shouldn't we all be in mourning for the war? If needs be I will be the lone memory of the dead.'

To others, to those who had actually lost their boys in the trenches, I said, 'Black is the blank canvas of couture. This is fashion cut to its basics. This is Gertrude Stein's prose and Duchamp's urinal.'

And everyone laughed and applauded and thought my stunt 'too, too real' and 'oh so daring'. But, as with all stunts, it died after its initial impact and I returned to my colours.

On my first night home Phil and Robert brought me out to dinner. They sat close together, thigh to thigh, arms around each other, and told me all about the summer I had missed; all the news and all the gossip. There wasn't much. Kiki had found a new lover, Nina and Flossie had created a few scenes, Laurance Vail had smashed up another bistro. I laughed and listened and let it all wash around me. It was nothing to me now, and I was nothing to it, it was all just a show and I showed them all I was a player.

Looking into Robert's eyes, I saw in them the same detachment I felt and I understood that he was searching for the same something that I had lost, the same something that London and love had stripped me of. Whatever it was, I couldn't name it, but I recognised it in Phil's eyes, and Robert did too. It was what attracted Robert to Phil, I could understand that, but I never understood what attracted Phil to Robert. It worried me; I felt very protective towards Phil's boundless optimism, couldn't bear to think of anyone stealing it away. In the very beginning, after that first night, I did try warning him about Robert.

'He's cold,' I said and then, noticing Phil's lack of enthusiasm for the subject, set about rephrasing myself. 'He's just so objective, he's just looking for an amusement.' I couldn't explain it any better than that. I didn't fully appreciate what I was talking about, and Phil couldn't understand a word of what I was saying.

'Ah, Bob's all right,' he said stiffly. 'He's a great guy, best friend I've made over this side of the pond.' And that was about as close as Phil ever came to reprimanding me for I don't know what, maybe for losing myself in London, maybe for misrepresenting myself from the beginning.

'Well, just don't go falling in love,' I said, laughing, trying to lighten the mood, and then I let it go, let Phil go off with Robert. Though that implies that I had some power over Phil and the situation, and I hadn't. Phil had embraced decadence with just as much enthusiasm as he had bohemia, and my brand of, by now jaded, innocence couldn't compete with that.

I stayed living in our flat. It had two bedrooms and I had nowhere else to go. Phil never said anything about it. I had a key so I continued to come and go and so did Phil. As the months wore on I saw less and less of him. First he limited his socialising to the strictly men-only clubs, then he began branching out a little. He started moving in circles that were too dark for me.

There's no one to blame, no good to come from blaming anyone, but McAlmon's bored cynicism always did scare me. During the summer, just for a lark, Robert had introduced Phil to the depths of Parisian society. To the warm cellars and broad beds strewn with vacant bodies. Beneath the happy, glitzy world of ex-patriots, France was still raw from its recent carnage and Paris, being the city it was, was largely responsible for containing the pain. It called out to the broken and the maimed, the bitter and the frightened and they travelled there in trains and coaches, on foot sometimes, and arrived only to find that they hadn't the strength left in them to fight against the dollar. They collapsed in doorways, in the seedier rooms that were always for rent around the left bank, and on the soft, velvet cushions of the opium dens. There was a price to be paid for that luxury, but afterwards there would be oblivion and that was what they were all aiming for.

This was Phil's Paris now and he soon settled deeply into it. He began to depend more on the opium dens than on Robert's company and he began to only move about at night. I took the situation to Robert, placed it square on his shoulders and I still remember his reaction, a defiant toss of his head combined with a contradictory shrug of his shoulders.

'Hell, how was I supposed to know he'd take to it so keenly? We all went once or twice, once or twice was enough for anyone. After all, kid, we're all just tourists really and those places are a sight to see.' But Robert's shrug tossed his eyes off balance, sent them scuttling over my shoes, settling on the ring he wore on his little finger. He twisted that ring as he spoke on.

'I did my best. We all did. Didn't you? He's a good man. I hate to see... Say, what's all this anyway?' And he smiled straight back up at me. 'So, the guy's got a bit of a taste for dope, so do lotsa people. Him and me we're planning a trip for Christmas. Nothing like a bit of skiing to clear the head.'

I nodded but I knew, just as Robert did, that a taste was never enough of anything for Phil. He tried explaining his all-consuming fascination for opium to me once. His face lit bright with the force of his innate enthusiasm.

'It's like the world; just, well, like it just softens, babe.'

'But why do you need to soften it?' I asked, and I really needed an answer. Phil's reality had always seemed so perfect I wondered why he could want to alter it.

'Hell, I don't need to, it's just like, well like a new thing to do. Like moving to a new city, or finding a new place to drink all full of new people.'

It sounded innocent. Sounded like just a new way of coping with boredom and I could understand that. I nodded and Phil smiled at what he interpreted as my acceptance, but neither of us knew then what we were condoning. A rich young man battling with boredom was one thing, but he took his fight to the wrong place. The only antagonist the opium dens presented was despair.

But the opium dens weren't the only places that housed despair. Sometimes you could stumble upon it in broad daylight, on the terraces of the cafés or cluttering up the avenues in the Luxembourg Gardens. Even back then, in 1921, Paris was seething with what was to come. Italian Jews were pouring in, fleeing a country that no longer welcomed them. The anti-Semitic laws weren't in place yet, but public opinion was paving the way for them. I avoided those people: their eyes saw through what we were; they were watching for what was to come and, through the rustle of their foreign language, I could always hear that hiss of truth, '*We've stretched the earth too tight over corpses.*'

So I avoided them, them and the Russians. The astounded, terrified, disenfranchised gentry that kept gathering around their chosen bars and restaurants. They sat hunched over tables, whispering their horrors to each other.

'We have lost everything,' they told each other over and over, waiting for some realisation to come from the chant, but the repetition only served to trivialise their situation. Their circumstances could not be contained by mere words, but still, words, so many words, kept bursting out of their silences, driving them together, driving them to look each other deep in the eye and say with so much meaning, 'We have lost everything.'

They still called each other by title, they still wore their fine clothes long after their bodies had shrunk with hunger, they still kept the jewels they had risked their lives to smuggle out of their homeland, but all of that was superficial and they knew it. Everything their grandeur was based on had been destroyed. But still they scanned every face they passed on the streets, searching for the young Romanovs, and every rumoured sighting held them rapt and hopeful.

It was a wonder that all this mad desperation did not spill into something more harmful than mysticism. If these broken people had looked for physical retribution, Europe would have erupted far earlier than it did. But, instead, these people searched for spiritual comfort and they found what was given to them.

There were the communes, the mystics, the sects and the gurus. And there were the others too, less well known but far more fun. There were the gypsies, the thieves, the con men and the showmen and they all told us girls the same things. They all told us we were beautiful, princesses, born from some great past life, intended to succeed. They told us that men had died in the war for us, that they were proud to do it, that they were by our sides now, their hands resting on our shoulders. Sometimes we were told that we would meet love, sometimes fame, sometimes wealth, but once we were told something that sounded like the truth and we never played that game again.

I met Ivan during a binge with McAlmon. We used to call these binges being 'out for the weekend' because they usually lasted a couple of days. After one such 'weekend', spent mainly with McAlmon and Vail, I remember waking up naked on a barge moored under the Pont Neuf. It was a Sunday afternoon and above me a Pierrot was juggling to a crowd of children. My clothes were all with me, folded neatly on top of the cabin, but I had to wait a full hour freezing under some smelly tarpaulin before I could make a break for it and grab them.

During this 'weekend' however I remained safely indoors. Myself and Robert were both drinking gin and had been since noon; it was now long past midnight. It had been one of those marathon nights during which we all separated, and met, and named new friends and collected new stories. In the Capitol a quartet played thick, clanging jazz and myself and Robert stayed to dance while others drifted around us coming and going. Later we were in some small bistro somewhere around St Germain when we were joined by Ivan.

Robert, Kiki, Flossie and I,
All slumped at a table, too blue to be high,
Robert, Kiki, Flossie and I.

Ivan gave us no second name and he smirked when he said Ivan, he didn't need us to know anything more about him. All in good faith we gave him the money he asked for and waited for the usual flow of compliments. He stood when he spoke, he sat to think but his proclamations were made standing and, as he was over six foot tall, his prophecies literally came from on high.

Later we laughed at them but what he told me has always stayed with me. I can still hear his voice, so low and heavy, drawing out every vowel, fumbling over every consonant. And I can still see him, looming so dark over our silly, drunken confusion. His eyes sloped inwards, stopping close together just over the bridge of his narrow nose. His eyebrows were grey and his hair black. His mouth was thin and his chin was long and bald, a hairless beard. He smelled strongly of something foreign and decadent, something clawing.

He told me, 'Your spirit identifies too much with the now.' And then he stopped. He seemed confused and it took him a moment to phrase his thoughts. He stared down into me and I dropped my eyes, opened my mouth on too loud a laugh and tried pulling my hand away.

'So forget the future, what's going to happen now?' I demanded, but Ivan wasn't listening. Holding tight to my hand, gazing somewhere over my head, he was proclaiming my future.

'These are your days,' he said. 'You will live and die with this age but it will take your flesh a long time to wither. You will see others go before you and you will envy them. You will work hard in your life and you will learn much. In the end you will know what you know now.'

It was an epitaph. He had denied me any hope for a future, leaving me with just the promise of time enough to stagnate. I have worked all my life to prove him wrong and, in the end, all I learned was that he was right. I had always, until relatively recently, presumed that life was about the accumulation of knowledge. I know now that that's merely an assumption of youth.

I forget what exactly he told Robert, but I remember him laughing at Robert's attempts at life; that was what he called them. He was referring to Robert's sporadic flashes of heterosexuality, his sporadic bouts of work, of drinking, of bitching, of abstinence. He told him that he would kill himself in his effort to live.

And then he took Flossie's hand and muttered endearments that were almost more terrifying than any truths. It was as if what he saw in her ran past words and into pity, but pity is soft and Flossie shrugged when he was gone and said that she was happy enough to grow old with pity.

'I'll be pitiful then right enough. Grey, balding breasts and hair sagging to my knees.' Ivan's reaction to Kiki was similar, but for her he found words and she listened to them with tears streaming down her cheeks and one eyebrow shaved into a coquettish arch.

'Don't trust in your youth,' he said. 'It will leave you in time. Don't trust in this city; it will isolate you. Don't trust in your friends; they will leave you. Don't trust in fame; it will forget you. Don't trust in money; it will bankrupt you. There will be a time when you will walk through this world of yours as no one.'

In ethos perhaps Ivan was right, but some of his details were wrong. Kiki was never forgotten, and her friends never left her: it was she who left them. She left when the Nazis came. Her spirit was so linked to the quarter, it couldn't survive its annihilation. Outside of Montparnasse, she saw herself as a no one.

As soon as Ivan left us we went home, quietly and separately, and I didn't see anyone again for a long time. I got sick. I caught a cold, later a cough and then my throat dried up. I took to my room and wrapped myself up in my gold coverlet. I was sick for weeks with the grippe. Outside, Paris was suffering an epidemic. The *Tribune* ran a series of articles plotting the course of the disease and warning Americans of its symptoms; hospitals were teeming and hundreds were dying.

In the beginning, our put-upon daily Thérèse cooked light meals for me twice a day, but the grippe was infectious and her mandate did not include nursing. During one of my more lucid spells I found her neatly worded resignation propped up against the copper kettle in the kitchen.

Phil came and went sporadically. Arriving early in the morning, leaving for nights on end, sleeping deeply through the days, he never thought to check my room. Occasionally he ate the light meals that I couldn't face, occasionally, while she was still there to ask them, he answered Thérèse's questions about my health with enthusiastic gusto.

'Oh yes,' he boomed, 'Just swell the last time I saw her.' And he never realised how long it had been since he had seen me. He left a note saying that he was going away with Robert for Christmas. He was gone for five long days and I thought I would die.

The fever burnt my reason, sent me shrieking into the night, nights that lasted days. My room was sometimes clogged with heat, sometimes hollow with cold. My hair clung icy and sweaty to my face. My cheeks caved, my stomach hollowed, my skin mottled and my lips cracked. I howled through a delirium of heightened colour and illogical fears. I was Harlequin, my lozenged suit swirled around me and the world turned its back on me. I was stiff in the comfort of my parents' house and the oppression weighed on my head so heavy, fit to burst. I stretched out for the gate in my father's garden wall, clawing the air over my head. I was in London, sitting quiet at a table in a bar, watching a man, watching him move closer, and his eyes watching me, his face split open on a scar, his skull grinning obscenely and I cried out for the warmth of Pablo and summer.

I woke all those days later still crying but lucid. Now I was crying for such abandonment. So many friends, so much cocky young wisdom, notice from the greatest painter of the age and the patronage of Phil Anderson Junior, all of this and still I had been left alone, all curled up in my grand, gold coverlet. There was no one to blame. No one had promised me anything different. I figured it was my fault for not taking proper control of my life. Since leaving my father's house I had been in hiding: in hotel rooms, in Phil's arms, in Picasso's cottage, in noisy bars, in Flossie's boisterous laugh. Curled up in my bed, folded up in pain, I promised myself a new life. One where I made choices rather than merely adapted to what I was presented with.

Phil found me one morning collapsed on the bathroom floor, exhausted by the effort it had taken me to leave my bed, but I was almost better then and, as he carried me back to my room, I told him that. I told him how long I had been sick for, how feverish I had been, how close to the horrors of death I had come, and all the while I was looking deep into his eyes, searching for that generous glow of empathy that used to light his world for him. It was gone. The words Phil used to comfort me were only words, but still I listened to them gratefully, they were all I had.

As soon as I had fully recovered, I left Phil. I left all the security he offered me. I took to the streets, trusting to my wits to get me by.

Initially Phil was appalled by my decision. I suppose he still saw me as his responsibility, still related to the package that had once housed such an innocent young girl. For the first time in a long time, and for the last time, he held me close and whispered endearments.

'Marry me,' he said. And the proposal was so at odds with my thought processes at the time I laughed. Laughed the romance right out of the man. He moved away slightly, shifted the tone of his voice in to a conversational mode and continued, 'You know me, babe, so it won't be, well…it won't be a down home, apple-pie, picket-fence type of affair, but maybe we could do well together. You and me, we still get along just fine, don't we?'

Is it just now, after all these years, that I can remember a whine of neediness? Did I hear it then and just ignore it? Was I right in thinking my refusal came as a relief to him?

'You don't have to marry me,' I said, still smiling broadly. And never for a moment did I think that maybe I had to marry him. I wonder how things would have changed for him and me if I had accepted. I wonder at my stupidity, my selfishness and my dubious notion of a moral code. I thought that whoring my way around Europe was a more honest option than settling for family, security and sweet soft luxury. And how close does honesty ever come to kindness? I never gave as much as one kind thought to Phil's needs. But I thought of mine all right. I refused Phil's offer of a settlement, but I did allow him to come nest-shopping with me.

The result was a delightful clash between my new room and my new possessions.

As a child I had always loved the story of the Little Princess stranded in her garret in London waiting for rescue. It was that romantic image of poverty that decided me on my fifth-floor walk-up in one of the oldest parts of the left bank, on the Rue des Boulangers, close to the Place de la Contrescarpe. My decision may have been swayed by romance, but it was weighted by finances. My room was cheap, after living off the dollar for so long it seemed very cheap. But once I started really living off my wits I discovered that it was a sum to be earned and I respected it as such. Soon I learned to respect every centime.

My street was a lively street. Lively and loud with dance, and drink, and sailors and sex. It scared me, but when you're eighteen it's easy to confuse fear with excitement. It took a lot for Phil to leave me there, but finally I persuaded him to and then there I was, one cold evening in late February, proudly surveying my independence.

I had one room.

One cold, grey room perched high over the city roofs. It had no paper on the walls, just a bare layer of thin paint. Flesh-coloured plaster crumbled into dust with every movement, every breath of wind. The lino-covered floor was stained with wear and worse; a kitchen of sorts was hidden behind a thin wooden divide and consisted of a two-ringed gas burner, a sink and a cupboard. There was an open fire that would spit out dirt from its congested chimney-stack, but still I used it, blinking through the belches of smoke that frequently deadened the damp little spark I had managed to create. My mattress stank. It sagged from the weight of all its former occupants, and it crawled with bugs, nasty ones that bit.

There was a toilet on the ground floor that had to be shared. It very much reminded me of the outhouse in Fontainbleau but without the access to fresh air and without the ornate footrests. Every night it was pumped clean but still every day the smell would kill you. I took to using the toilets in the bars. I washed at my sink, foot by foot, shin by shin and up and up. I don't think I was ever very clean.

And on top of all this filth I unpacked. After first dousing my bed with a thick layer of powder, and wrapping it well in a protective blanket and then, to be sure, a protective sheet, I covered it with my gold coverlet. I hung all the glory of the Parisian fashion houses up in my worm-holed wardrobe and, on the back of my flimsy door, I hung my winter coat, my spring coat and my fur-lined dressing-gown. I unrolled my new kiln rug, fresh from the loom and still vibrantly red, in the middle of the room and on it, alongside my bed, I lined up all my dainty, prettily embroidered shoes. I arranged my sparklingly new china tea set in my cupboard: light, thin, white with sweet little blue birds climbing all over it. I left the cupboard door open; I thought the tea set was too fine to be stored away out of sight. Over my grimy, rotten window I slung an orange velvet throw. The tiny, rickety table, big enough to sit one, was swamped in white linen and the two armchairs, worn, bristling and sparse, were lavishly covered with plump eider cushions rich in colour and texture.

For my first night Phil had given me a hamper of what he called essentials and so, my first meal in my new home was of caviar and champagne, sushi and *foie gras*. I laid out the food and the picture was complete. I had created the Little Princess's magic garret on the morning after the Indian gentleman had made her dreams come true.

CHAPTER 14

Ruth was startled by her mother's grip. She had been lying peacefully, drooling her dreams – Paris, McAlmon, Picasso – and then she reached out, clawing at Ruth's arm in distress.

'My throat,' she croaked, rolling a little in the bed; 'I'm so hot.'

Ruth checked her forehead; she was hot and clammy, so she rang for a nurse. Nurse Kerr was there immediately. Extraordinarily composed for such a young girl, Ruth thought, but then nursing is a vocation, not something you grow into.

'Now then,' Nurse Kerr crooned, 'nothing to get upset about.' And it wasn't. Old Mrs Egan loosened her hold, swallowed the liquid that was held to her thin, parched lips and allowed herself be settled back down on to her pillows.

'I always knew you were different, Claudette, love,' she sighed and then, as Ruth laughingly told Deirdre later, she started on about Hodgson Burnett's *The Little Princess*.

'See, I told you,' Deirdre said. 'She's just rambling on about her reading. Remember how she was always on at us to read more.'

'It's our duty to past generations, and to our own, to honour what went before.' Ruth answered in an approximation of their mother's delicate voice. Deirdre laughed a little.

'Good way to go, though,' she said. 'I must remember to cut out horror and concentrate on romances. What do you think? A rake of Mills and Boon should see me out happily.'

' "He took her in his thick, manly arms…" Hmmm, not a bad way to go.' They were sitting in a cheap Italian restaurant, over the remains of a pizza and the dregs of a bottle of wine. Ruth felt relaxed, first time in ages. Christmas was only a week gone and it had been a strain. Her daughters' presence had only added to the tension. She said as much to Deirdre, who laughed again, this time in a more heartfelt way.

'See, that's what people don't tell you about all that empty-nest nonsense; nine times out of ten it's a relief to see them go.'

'Nonsense, you can't tell me you don't miss James?'

'Course I do. I miss toddler James and football-practice James and even sometimes spotty, teenage James, but I don't want married James with family loading more washing on me, or expecting a babysitter whenever. They grow up, they go away, that's how it is.' She sounded less definite though, and her light-hearted tone faltered slightly.

'It's sad, though.'

'It's life, though; that's how it is.'

'We didn't grow up and go away,' Ruth said.

'Mam wouldn't have it,' Deirdre answered. Ruth was going to argue but then she stopped. Deirdre was right. The weight of their mother's expectant love had always kept them close. Her approval had always been paramount.

'Remember when I wanted to move to Holland? "Really, Holland, dear?"' Deirdre's impersonation of their mother was much better than Ruth's. Sharper, an edge to it. 'Don't you think it might be dreadfully boring? Tulips – and those accents! She ridiculed it right out of me. But you know I think she was disappointed I didn't go. She talked about it a lot later. I think she expected us to rebel a bit.'

'But sure there was nothing to rebel against, she let us do everything we wanted.' This time Deirdre's laugh was loud, raucous even, very out of character. It was loud enough to draw attention and when she got it she ordered another bottle of wine.

'God poor you!' she finally splurted out. 'Don't you know she allowed us to do nothing... or Dad.' Ruth made to disagree, but Deirdre talked over her. 'Think about it, every decision you made, didn't she put her oar in? Didn't you always end up doing exactly as she said? And remember that "I-love-you-anyway" face whenever we dared step out of line? And we, all three of us, went along with it. You're still doing it. Fretting every time she turns in the bed. She's completely out to lunch now and still you want her approval.'

Ruth was shocked, shocked speechless. Noting her reaction, Deirdre laughed again.

'Don't they say no one has the same family? I'd a younger sister, you'd an older one. I'd younger parents for a while, god knows.' She was trying to soothe the harshness out of what she had said but it didn't work.

'She may have offered her opinion,' Ruth said firmly. 'You could call that interfering, but she did always want the best for us. She was devoted to all of us, Dad too.'

'She wanted you to be a teacher, me to be a solicitor and Dad to wear a sports jacket. That's why I never said a word to James about what he should do, or wear, or study, or where he should live or anything.'

She was sounding smug now and Ruth registered what she was saying as a dig at her parenting skills. Deirdre was finally entering the Best Mum Competition.

'And you think I interfere too much?'

'I didn't say that.'

'You didn't have to.' Strangely though, Ruth wasn't annoyed; in fact she felt relieved. If Deirdre was right, her big sister who knew better, then these feelings of displacement and guilt were normal urges. She could relax a little. Say no to overnight babysitting, let Brian fend for himself sometimes, stop probing Ellen for details, leave Isabel to get lung cancer.

She said nothing about any of that though – not yet, it was too new a concept. Instead she brought the conversation back to their mam.

'But you think she wanted you to go to Holland?'

'Yeah, I think she would have liked someone to stand up to her. It's just somehow, even though we did everything right, somehow she wanted more.'

'You think we disappointed her?' Ruth asked.

'See, you're doing it again,' Deirdre said, exasperated. 'I tell you she wanted an argument and you want to go running to her with it saying, "Is this argument good enough?"' She said it kindly though, so Ruth laughed at the conceit.

'How's Paris these days anyway?' Deirdre asked. 'Any more heroin?'

'I think they've moved into opium dens now,' Ruth answered, matching her sister's cynicism. It was easier that way. There was a question hovering in her head, but she felt too afraid, too exposed, to ask it.

If you think I reared my children the same as Mam did… If you think I treated my husband the same as Mam did… Why don't my family respect me? Adore me? Love me?

Because it was true of them all. Deirdre could be as revisionist as she wanted, but she did love, adore and respect her mam. She had become a solicitor, had married Mark, hadn't lived in Holland and had gotten rid of that dreadful perm. She had done it all for the love of her mam. Any argument around that issue was mere semantics and both sisters knew it.

But she said none of that, kept her question to herself and, instead, she said, 'Seems they were mad for opium back then and the place was full of Russians. Or maybe just the opium dens were; I lost track.'

'Maybe it's the morphine they're giving her now that's triggering some kind of wishful memory.'

'Or some kind of repressed one.' Ruth couldn't help it, believing in it a bit; for some reason she wanted to. The minute she said it, though, she knew it was a mistake. Her mother's snatches of fragmented memories were far too fragile to withstand Deirdre's scorn. And, with a bottle of wine in her, Deirdre was not prepared to let such a comment go. One eyebrow shot up immediately.

'Really? Are you serious?' she sneered.

'Only a little, she seems so definite and I was thinking, she never really spoke that much about her time in France, did she?'

'I suppose there wasn't that much to tell, really. It must have been very quiet and monotonous, year after year, the same nuns, the same things to teach. She seemed to like it, though, remember her telling us about the convent and how it used to be a grand house? And the gardens, she seemed awful impressed with the work the nuns did in them.'

'Yeah, nothing she ever grew matched their stuff. They even made their own cheeses, didn't they? They must have had a small farm; I never asked her about that. You're right, though, she did seem to like it. But isn't it funny how the religion never stuck? Remember how she was always talking about how restful and spiritual their chapel was, but she never went to mass or anything here. You'd think she'd want to find that comfort again.'

'I suppose she had to go when she was with the nuns. Maybe she overdosed on it back then. See, she did talk about it quite a bit. And what was that girl's name? The pupil she was so fond of?'

'Claudette?'

'Ah yes, Claudette. Remember when we were bold she'd always tell us how sweet Claudette was?'

'Well, Claudette obviously left some impression; she's still going on about her. I think she thinks she's one of the nurses.'

'See, it's all just messed up in her head. Fact and fiction, Mills and Boon for me. Cheers.'

The sisters talked on, talked through their second bottle of wine, talked nonsense until the meal was over and they were walking towards the bus stops that would separate them and then, driven by Deirdre, the conversation took a formal tone.

'I've said I'll give the keys to the estate agent by the end of the week. Is that all right?' Ruth nodded; that was all that was expected of her. 'So the place will have to be clear. It could do with painting, but I don't really think that's necessary. The auctioneers say they can come during the week and collect the dining table and those other bits. Will you arrange that with them? I'm sorry, but I've taken way too much time off work as it is. There's nothing else I want from the place. I was there at the weekend, so anything you want now is fine. And the stuff for Kerry, we can just hire a storage space and get some delivery company to take it away for the time being. Is that OK?'

'I was thinking that I might drop it down myself,' Ruth answered, although the thought had just now popped out of her mouth. Now that she had said it, though, she was warming to the idea; a few days alone in Kerry would be something to look forward to.

'If you want,' Deirdre answered. 'But I'd say the place is almost falling down now, sure no one's been there in a couple of years, have they?'

'Suppose not. Not since Mam's fall really. Remember how worried we were about her being down there alone after Dad died?',

'Yeah, twenty-odd years ago and we thought she was so old then,' Deirdre said laughingly, and then Ruth told her about Brian's misjudged comment about the 'tough old bird'. In this context it seemed very funny, and both sisters laughed.

Half an hour later Ruth closed her hall door behind her.

'Only me,' she called out. Brian didn't answer. Probably didn't hear her over the drone of the television.

She joined him. Sat straight down beside him on the coach without first checking the state of the kitchen, or asking if him if he needed anything. She tucked herself under his arm, took a drink out of his glass of wine, and said, 'God but that was a hard day.' She didn't ask about his day and she didn't stay long enough for a conversation to develop. A couple of minutes later she yawned and declared herself fit for nothing but bed. She left the way she had come in, avoiding the kitchen. If Brian was surprised, if he even noticed, she couldn't tell; he said nothing aside from his usual, 'Night, love.'

CHAPTER 15

Claudette comes in a lot now, drifts in and out; quiet as ever but much more mature, maternal even. I guess that means that I was right about her, that she lived long enough to grow into her potential. Or maybe she died young enough to avoid bitterness. Back then, in the life, a girl would have to die mighty young to avoid that though.

And for me the life started in the Gypsy Bar. I started to work properly there, and proper work meant I was expected to do more than dance. The patron knew me as one of a crowd and I think he assumed that if he employed me he would be assured of the crowd's custom. Unfortunately for him, though, the crowd had scruples. Phil was still so well regarded that, by association, it was hard for anyone to see me as anything other than respectable, though that definition was used quite loosely back then. But still, for a while, McAlmon and his companions stayed away and I was relieved. I would have hated to have to face them during my first few weeks.

During those weeks I took my cue from the other girls. I pranced and pouted and shrieked with delight whenever

I was approached. It wasn't what I wanted to do though. I had imagined myself dancing for my living, sometimes singing, but I soon learned that girls like me, girls whose youth made up for their inexperience, were two a centime. Diaghilev's Russian Ballet was sweeping Europe and, as a result, all the young girls yearned to dance. I was just one of the masses, but still, as a proper employee, I was expected to work. So I worked like all the other girls worked, and I found the job hard; hard and mean and grubby and debasing.

In the beginning I barely dragged myself through the nights. My mind led, pulling my body behind. Night after night, I talked myself into position. I told myself that it couldn't be that bad, so many of us were doing it. I told myself that it was all old hat to me, hadn't I done it all and worse during those days in London? If I was honest, wasn't it the same job I had done for Phil before he had lost interest?

It might have been but still it was hard. It was a job, a way of life, that bruised the senses and the girls I worked with were no comfort. They were all as hard as the life they were in; bright-eyed with fangs bared and claws sharpened, they spat instead of spoke. They approached everything with harsh good humour, laughed at it all, cursed everyone. For the first time I saw something other than hilarity in Flossie's brash approach to life and I winced at my ignorance. No wonder I had been left with my illness. What kind of friend was I?

I took my cue from Flossie though, Flossie and the gaggle of girls around me. I thought that if I adopted their attitude it would have to help, but it didn't. The work still debased me. It clawed under my skin when I was sober and so I drank. It loosened my tears when I was drunk and so

I took to popping uppers, but then it just burned into my over-active conscious. It's still there, branded sharp and lurid. Just a few short weeks later and I was going under, and then I met Peggy Hopkins. She was a Ziegfield girl fresh over from New York.

'I've come to see,' she said. 'Come to see and come to spend.' And she laughed, winked and patted her outrageously large handbag.

She was still very young but she had already gone through numerous husbands, five I think, and had gained substantial amounts of money from every match.

'You just call me Peggy,' she said. 'I picked Hopkins out of a telephone book and every other name I've had I picked out of the society columns. They all don't mean nothing, so Peggy'll do between us girls. What's your name?' she asked, and I said, 'Jane.'

'So what is it you do, Jane?'

It was two in the morning in the Gypsy and I was wearing a slip and stockings rolled down to my knee. I gestured at my uniform and shrugged.

'God, girl don't you know the first thing?' Peggy gasped. 'You can't do this job and be a Jane.' She patted the chair beside her and I sat down.

'You call yourself JoJo,' she said to me. 'Like this.' And she wrote it on a napkin with two capital Js. 'And with your colouring, Fox would go well; sounds good, like Foxy, don't you think? So you call yourself JoJo Fox but don't go giving out your surname to just anyone. A surname is like a kiss on the mouth. Nothing but a wedding ring should buy them that kind of intimacy.'

And that was just the start. She went on to tell me all sorts such as, 'You go look in a mirror, JoJo, and you tell yourself how pretty you are and then you go look at those men with your pretty-girl eyes. Take it from me if you do that they'll pay just as much for the privilege of a dance as anything else. And you roll your stockings up high and you wear a dress that comes down well over your knees. Men are such fools that even when they're paying for it they like to think they're the first. Trust me, you play this game right and those dead-beats will think they've seen it all when you've let them catch a sight of thigh.'

And she showed me how you could do this. How you could cross your legs innocently, showing as much as you saw fit, while still keeping your expression Sunday-school sweet, then she said, 'You can talk as dirty as you like; talking never did any harm, but the harm does come. You get ready for it, girl, and stay ready. And when you do get yourself into trouble you take the trouble to get out of it cleanly.'

She paused there, waiting for me to say something that showed I understood what she meant. But I didn't say anything. Oh, I understood what she meant by 'trouble' all right, I just didn't know that there was any 'clean' way to get out of that kind of bother.

'Cleanly?' I asked eventually, and so she explained.

'There are some things you don't trust to the management and you don't trust to the man. You take it from me, JoJo, when you fall pregnant you don't go where a man sends you, you go where a girlfriend sends you and you go there with more money than you've ever dreamed of owning. There's no one going to risk their reputation if anything goes wrong. No one's going to send you to hospital if they mess up, they're going to send you to the bottom of the canal. So you go to someone who won't mess up.'

I nodded in agreement but still, when the time came, I did it wrong. Kiki knew the name of a man but Flossie knew the name of another. I went with Flossie's, he was cheaper. He prayed with me before and after and I joined in with the after one. I think my getting out of that place in one piece had a lot more to do with divine than medical intervention.

'Take it from one who knows,' Peggy said, slipping me a wink. 'Take it from one who's played the game to win.' And she reached for her oversized handbag and hugged it tight. She told me that it was filled with jewellery, gold, diamonds, rubies and pearls, all presents from men and mementoes from marriages, told me but didn't show me.

She told me that she kept it with her at all times, that she didn't trust banks, safes, locks or honest faces. When she went back to New York she told the same story to one of Hearst's reporters. She stupidly told him that she carried that bag everywhere with her; wonder how long it was before it got snatched? That wouldn't have mattered, though; for girls like Peggy there was plenty more out there for the taking. Hearst's reporter went away impressed. He coined the phrase 'gold-digger' especially for Peggy.

I only met Peggy the once. It was said that Paris depressed her, that she couldn't find anyone rich enough to marry and so she went home to the money markets of New York. But still, one meeting was enough for me. I immediately assimilated all she told me and it worked. Life at the Gypsy became a little easier, and I became a lot harder. I soon mastered the art of being friendly while still giving the impression that the men baying for my attention, the men flinging their money at me, were below my contempt but maybe deserving of my pity. And there's nothing puts a man off his performance more than the feeling that his partner, rigid with manners, is bravely, pityingly enduring the brunt of his sorry efforts. Of course some didn't mind, but soon I had work enough that I could choose to stay away from that type. Soon I was seen as a sort of trophy. The men queued to dance with me and then later, all fired up by my slow, curved writhing, or my loose-hipped jerking, they went in search of the cheaper girls – girls who pranced and pouted and shrieked with delight. Girls who later could be relied on to whisper endearments and moan in ecstasy.

After a few weeks of doing this it was noticed by the house band that I could dance some life into their music. They were looking for a singer so the patron checked me out and decided that I could hold a tune. He was right, I could – just about – but then that was all that was needed. And so I was put on stage, right up front singing. There was never much room for a chorus line in the Gypsy, just a few girls scattered about, writhing away, but still I outranked them and that was something.

Of course this didn't make me very popular with the other girls. A few tried imitating me and a few tried threatening, me but mostly they were all too lost in apathy to do much more than curse me, and I was way past bothering about a few curses. I just ignored them and then the girls got to ignoring me. I didn't mind, not one bit; those girls had only heart enough to keep their blood flowing – their company was always just that. Just the noise of chatter, it never ran to friendship. But then Claudette joined us. Bright little Claudette who really couldn't have been that much younger than me, but was so hung about with country freshness that she still glowed with childlike innocence. I took to her straight away, tucked her right under my wing.

I remember her standing by the bar on her first night. Little Claudette with her round, brown eyes and flowing chestnut hair. A man held her by the waist, whispering in her ear. Her face turned red, pounded darker and darker with the beat of her pulse and then it dropped and the toes of her dainty red slippers were splashed black with tears.

'Babe, you want to dance?' I was in front of them; my hands flung high and my back arched on a yawn. 'Man, I could do with a man tonight and you look like man enough for me; you mind, honey?' I asked Claudette, but she was already gone, slipped from his grasp, racing towards the toilets. I minded her as best I could that night and after we closed up I took her back to my flat with me, sat her down and gave her all I got.

'Hell girl!' I said to her, 'Hell don't you know the first thing? You can't do this job and be a Claudette – you call yourself Detta and you go look in a mirror and tell yourself how pretty you are…' She listened all right, and what I told her must have helped her a bit, but still the life was too hard for her.

We had all come to the city searching for god knows what – fame maybe, fortune, bright lights, freedom – but Claudette had come looking for love.

'There are no young men in my town,' she told me. 'All old farming men with no teeth, and my mother she said I would have to have one of them. My father had already picked one.' And she shuddered, a child's shudder that ended with a giggle. 'No hair, no teeth, and so big!' Her arms spread wide over an imaginary belly. 'And so I ran away and have come here to where men will kiss your hand, and where they will waltz with you until dawn, and where they will give you gold goblets filled with sparkling wine to drink, and where they will buy you presents that come in tiny boxes wrapped in bows. And why is it that they click their heels before they leave a room?'

129

She was hugging her knees and rocking backward and forward and I pitied her position regarding the toothless farmer, I cursed the movie, or magazine, or penny romance that had brought her to this. This squalid room, this sordid life.

'The city is full of young, handsome men.' she said, willing me to agree, and so I nodded. 'So I just must keep myself until I meet one.'

It sounded simple when she said it, but the actuality of that statement proved impossible to achieve. She had started off trying to get work as a milliner, then as a shop girl, then as a waitress, then as a maid, then as a bar hand, but no one would take her on and city streets are expensive.

'They say it'll take too long to train me,' she told me, but looking at her I knew the truth. She looked too frail to carry the weight of a fifteen-hour day; she never had a hope. She was soon left without choices, left searching for love in some trick's eyes. And often, out of desperation, she was tricked into seeing it there.

'He was nice,' she would say. 'He smiled so sweetly.'

The other girls laughed at her. It got so that even her regulars would laugh at her. They'd roll her over and tell her they loved her and then, later, she'd sit curled up on my kiln rug talking up a dream for herself.

'He says he loves me. He says when we're married he'll bring me to the ballet every night and serve me breakfast in bed every morning. He says we will have a boy and a girl and a big oak tree in the garden.'

In the beginning I'd try stopping her, but that was before I saw that she was just doing what we were all doing – coating her reality with sugar, except she was using words instead of drugs. Once I realised this I started helping her, filling in details for her.

'You'll have a stone yard,' I'd tell her, 'squeezed under the clutter of apple trees. And you won't need a big house – three rooms will be enough. You'll have a bedroom with rush matting so recently laid it'll bounce like grass under your feet…'

'Yes, and my kitchen?'

'It'll have a pale pine table worn thin in the middle from years of scrubbing and a big dresser painted blue.'

'And my sitting-room?'

'Will have a rug all covered over in faded clumps of forget-me-nots.'

'And my bed will be brass and will have a buttoned heavy quilt.'

'And your window will look out on a bed of lavender.'

It was a game that heartened us both.

So life went on and it was OK for a while. I had my flat, some friends and a platform to perform on. And I liked performing. I liked breathing in heavy, blue smoke and breathing out deep, dirty tunes. Every song was the same. Starting with the whisper of sex, they'd work themselves up to a climax, ending with me standing feet spread wide, head thrown back, hands flung high in the air, twinkling to the notes, my body twitching wild. Those songs always had more to do with movement than tune and that was how I got my reputation as a singer. The word spread that that was what I was mainly doing, some grand singing, and so my friends turned up to see, bringing their friends with them.

And that was how I reached the attention of the Duchess de La Salle, one of the great militant lesbians of the age. By then, by the early Twenties, she had outlived her fashion and was seen by most as rather tedious, but I hadn't been around in the good old days when Paris was heaving with homoerotic tensions; when Colette's husband Willy published the *Claudine* books and every good Parisian husband sought out a lesbian for his wife. I hadn't known of any of the great dames of those days, I hadn't even met Gertrude Stein and her Alice, Sylvia Beach and her Adrienne and so I was impressed by the Duchess in her tails.

She sought me out in the Gypsy, leaving les Deux Magots, which was her haunt at the time, to sit oh so close to the stage. She lit the cigarette at the end of her long holder, gold and black and scarlet at the tip, and she turned to her companion.

'I love to be within licking distance,' she said, and all through my set I was aware of her tongue, moistening her lips, pouting out for the scarlet kiss of her cigarette. As I reached my climax I shook my hips in her direction, I arched my back for her and, to a chorus of approval, I swung my breasts free of my sweat stained blouse. I blushed a little as I tucked them back out of sight, but I smiled for her as I did this and she smiled back.

After my set, without waiting for an invitation, I joined her at her table and I stayed there for the evening. I was intrigued by her and by the slim man by her side who was wearing a perfectly cut suit and some very feminine accessories: rings, a bracelet, a long string of pearls and earrings. His cheeks were rouged and his lips reddened. His long coat had a vibrant blue trim and his hat was that same colour. He was introduced as Prince Yusupov. And that's who he was, and he was every bit as glamorous as the books and films describe him.

During the course of the evening I heard the whispers that circulated around him. They said that he was one of the men who had killed Rasputin, and most of us laughed at the thought. But those who knew nodded emphatically and finally I was persuaded to ask.

'The girls,' I gestured behind me, 'they've told me a strange story about you.' He turned to me then and in his eyes I read the truth, but still I asked the question.

'Are you the man…?'

'The very one,' he lisped and then ducked his head giving the impression that he was reluctant to say anything more, but that was just an act. Rasputin was still hounding him and all the drink and all the glitter of decadence couldn't hide that.

'Are you?' I gasped. 'So what was he really like?' I asked and that was all the prompting poor Prince Yusupov needed to start his story. He started it low, seemed to shrink a little into his fragile self and his accent became more pronounced.

'Large as a bear, he was,' he muttered, and I had to lean in close to catch the words. 'Large as a bear with sharpened teeth and thick, coarse hair that sprouted out of his face and neck and hands. Physically he was an animal, but animals can be tamed, they can be nurtured. But him! His breed was not of this world, he was answering to a lower order. And do you know how you could tell?'

I shook my head.

'His eyes.'

And that, just that much, that was enough. I didn't want to hear any more. I knew the rest; I had seen those eyes in London. For a week I had seen the world through them. In the cold, lonely dead of night I still saw my nightmares through them.

We have stretched the earth too tight over corpses.

'No!' I cried and got up to go, but the prince held tight to my arm and pulled me down, right in close to his smeared clown's mouth.

'Yes,' he spat at me. 'His eyes. They were cold with intelligence. Do you understand that? He wasn't wild or mad,

133

he was intelligent and merciless. Can you understand the horror of that? Someone who controls you, who hates you and has no mercy for your humanity. Do you understand?'

'Yes.' I said, pulling away as hard as I could. 'Yes, please let me go.' But he wouldn't. He kept his hold on me and kept on talking, shoving his words into my face.

'We had to do it, but it was almost beyond us. No one will ever believe us, but we saw it. That man-monster died many times. He was poisoned and he died, then he was shot and he died. Over and over again he died and every time his spirit reared up. We could see the power in his eyes moving his body, lumbering his dead flesh towards us, and dying, and rising, and coming towards us, and dying again, and rising again.'

He let me go then and reached for a drink. In a moment he was himself, his smile bright under his make-up, his empty glass raised for a refill. I never asked him about Rasputin again.

Just for fun, I slipped under the patronage of the Duchess and the Prince and, for a while, we became good friends. I remember nights of hilarity when we three, the two cross-dressers and the whore in full costume, would parade through the Latin Quarter looking for a party, following any trickle of laughter that fell out of the night. Us three feeling just fine from the gin fizzes bubbling through our veins and the crumbled pellets of hash quietly soothing our minds. On those nights we would stop just to laugh at the world; arms around each other, holding on to each other, holding each other up and, sometimes, on special nights, the world would stop just to laugh back.

CHAPTER 16

I haven't laughed in a long time. A good proper laugh, one that chokes, and cleanses and corrupts. The kind that leaves you as spent as lovemaking. There's been no room in my life for that kind of laughter, not for years. William wasn't the sort of man to bring that kind of emotion out in a girl. Strange, but up until now that's never seemed very important.

But laughter is important, back then especially. Laughter was very important during those inter-war years. The horror of the First World War was fading and the horror of the Second was still far enough away to ignore. We all sensed its approach but that just made us laugh all the harder. Later, when I was in Berlin where the steel cold breath of war was chilling the streets, then I didn't laugh. But during those long lamp-lit Parisian nights, during my young years, when my world was filled with artists who had lived hard enough to learn that their life was their work, then I laughed. The men and women I knew then knew that the wilder they lived the wilder they worked and so there was always something to laugh at, there was always some party to be found.

All kinds – the intellectual, the political, the lavish and the beautiful. The most spectacular of these must have been the ball thrown by the Comte and Comtesse Pecci-Blunt. Everyone went dressed in white, as requested, and everyone followed the music outside, as instructed, to flit delicately over the lawns. White suits and white gloves guided white dresses and bare backs over the dark green of the grass and under the deep blue of the night. And onto those bare backs, onto those white studded fronts, caught and carried on the generous sweep of those dresses, Man Ray and Lee Miller projected a hand-coloured film by Méliès. Man Ray laughed.

'Larvae to moths,' he said proudly. 'I have coloured the night.'

But the best parties of all were the grand celebrations of debauchery that were open to everyone. Laurance Vail was very good at hosting these. Before his marriage to Peggy Guggenheim, he would roam the quarter stopping people and giving out his address and, after he was married, he more or less continued doing the same thing, only now he called his parties an 'at home' and Peggy insisted that they only take place on Sunday afternoons. I suppose she was hoping to civilise the event, but of course that never happened. There was no civilising the blousy, boozy belt of youth that would descend on her home every week. Once we had gone, poor Peggy would disinfect the whole place. She thought we oozed dirt and sin, and maybe she was right.

The Vails' parties were good but I think the most famous parties of this type were the ones given by the American painter and entertainer Hilaire Hiler. Hiler knew what a party was all about and he served his straight up. I remember one held in a hall – a big hollow place that was furnished with just the bare essentials – as Hilaire said, 'Fancy trimmings are just excuses for a bad guest list.' Instead of tables, there was a large bench full of tubs of beer on ice and jugs of punch and instead of elaborate entertainments a small orchestra battled their music over the noise, and we did the rest. Hilaire always invited everyone, and so he had included the older generation of burlesque performers, and we saw this as a challenge and we set our hearts into the night, determined to outperform them, and we did. Kiki sang and myself and Claudette danced.

Oh, I remember that night well. I remember how Claudette danced, how people watched, rapt, and how one young man stared. It wasn't her moves they were looking at, it was her glow. That girl – she could catch the light, wear it draped over her skin like a shawl and then, when she danced, it would ripple and flicker and flare like fire. Later on, much later on, after the night had settled itself into noisy drunkenness, Claudette came looking for me and it was only then that I realised I hadn't seen her in hours. She was looking a little dim, a little smudged. Her lipstick was smeared, her kohl had run and the straps of her dress were torn, but her eyes shone bright. Bright with tears or wild with happiness, I was in no condition to say which.

'You OK?' I asked. She nodded, dreamlike.

'Some man…' she said, allowing the statement to trail into the inevitable, and I laughed.

'Does he love you?' I asked.

'Oh no, no, no.' She shook her head violently. 'Not him, look he tore my dress.' And she flapped her broken straps at me light-heartedly, in direct contradiction to her words. 'The brute! A few francs and he thinks he has the right to…' And her words trailed off, lapsing into a memory neither of us felt the need to dress in language. I put an arm about her shoulder and she turned and smiled directly into my face.

'But I am in love,' she whispered. 'He rescued me,' and she pointed to the young man who had been staring at her, a man I'd seen around a few times. 'He beat that brute off me. I've been, you know, with him a few times now and he says he wants me just for him. Well, he will when we can afford it. He says he loves me, we just need to save hard and in spring, when the bluebells are out, we should have enough. He says he'll take me away with him then. I told him we wouldn't need much, just three rooms with a big kitchen dresser painted blue and packed with all the clutter of past lives, and a small bedroom with a big brass bed. . .'

'Yeah, yeah,' I said. But I'd stopped listening; I'd heard it all so many times before. I was watching McAlmon fling himself about the floor. He was shouting, 'As high as Nijinsky!' And we all laughed knowing that he was high on something other than the love of ballet.

But we did all love the ballet. The Comte de Beaumont set about hosting evenings that out-Diaghileved Diaghilev and some say he succeeded. We all went to see the sets by Picasso, Miró, Max Ernst and De Chirico and we all stayed to listen to the scores written by Satie and Stravinsky and we all silently cheered the Dadaists who shouted from the hall that the fringe had sold out to the establishment.

And then, of course, there were all the usual parties. The weekend gatherings that, for weeks on end, could fall in on each other and carry us all spinning through months of idleness and regret, and drunkenness and laughter. But what was the harm? We were all young and we were all game. Those of us who could worked, those of us who couldn't encouraged and, sometimes, the best encouragement you can give an artist is to ensure they lose themselves in living for a while. Or, anyway, that was what we told each other.

No one ever wanted to admit to the amount of time wasted, the lives and the talents squandered.

For a while I let myself go along with everyone else. When I wasn't working I was posing, draped around the Duchess, or outsmarting Flossie with filth of my own invention. Laughing, dancing, drinking, one eye always on the lookout for Picasso, one ear always cocked for the boom of Phil's enthusiastic greeting and, as a result, every night out was a disappointment. But the next night might prove better. The party I missed was always the best one. The headache I woke with would dissolve in the next shot of whiskey and so the days spilled on and the nights gathered momentum and I lost track of when I last spent any time with Claudette.

The Duchess was taking up a lot of my time, something Flossie couldn't understand.

'That old tart, wizened old fart!' she'd chant, and though I laughed in agreement I still followed the Duchess whenever she called to me. She flattered me, physically and intellectually; bought me presents, dressed me, fed me and spoke to me about the academic side of Parisian society, Gertrude Stein, Shakespeare and Company, Natalie Barney's salon, movements ongoing and past. I listened and nodded and paid her in kind with ducked head and pouted lips. But such posturing couldn't last forever; in time dues would have to be paid.

We were returning one evening from a late supper, the two of us in a taxi, driving aimlessly, as yet no specific address had been given. I was relaxed rather than drunk, and I was tired. I allowed the Duchess trail her hand lower than my shoulder. Softened by the warmth and the thick soft leather I didn't stop her when she trailed it lower still. I was thinking of the comfort of her rooms, the security of her wealth, the ease of passivity. I was thinking too hard. She pulled back, sat up, lit a cigarette and, looking away from me, staring out on to the grey streets, asked, 'Where will I drop you?' I was confused by the sudden change of mood and muttered something about not minding. She laughed.

'And that's the trouble, dearest,' she said. 'I think you should at least pretend to mind. I'm old enough to know that I must at times pay for passion, but I have no intention of shelling out for indifference.'

She was right. So I asked her to drop me at the Dôme and that was the last I saw of her. And that was the beginning and end of my formal introduction to the academic movements of the time. I don't think I ever even visited Shakespeare and Company. Maybe if the Duchess had met me earlier I would have been more interested in following her into the depths of her physical or intellectual life, but that hadn't happened. By the time we met I was a whore and that state has a lot more to do with the spirit than the flesh. I was all right with it, comfortable with myself, but I was honest and knew what price I had to pay for that comfort.

Purity of thought made me nervous; vulnerability, sentimentality, compassion, empathy, integrity – all these traits and so many more made me nervous. So I couldn't respond to the Duchess's advances, nor could I respond to the passion that drove the great movements of art that surrounded me.

And nor could I respond to the innocent trust Claudette placed in her friends.

This is my excuse for abandoning her.

CHAPTER 17

It was coming into spring time, cherry blossoms budding, twilight lengthening the days and bluebells skirting the trees in the Luxembourg Gardens. I hadn't seen Claudette in weeks and then she came calling all lit up – wide-eyed and flushed.

'The bluebells are out,' she said, nodding at me, expecting a response, but I had none to give her. I'd forgotten.

'Don't you remember? My man? Didn't I tell you?' And she had but I, being the type of friend I was, had to be told again.

'Remember the young man at Hiler's party? Remember he said he loved me and would take me away when the bluebells came out?'

'When you had saved enough money for him.' It was a cruel statement but I was used to speaking like that to Claudette, injecting a grain of reality every now and again.

'For us, yes. For him to take me away.'

'And have you enough now?' She looked momentarily confused, but only momentarily.

'We should have, yes; yes, we should have. He's taking care of all that side of things.' And she physically shrugged off her doubts. She drew herself upright, scaled her joy as high as her sparkling eyes and no logic could reach her up there.

'He promised. This is our time. We're going to go to Provence and we'll rent a little cottage. He's a carpenter by trade and there'll be plenty of work for him. I'm going to have a herb garden and a vegetable patch. We won't need much space, just three rooms will do. We'll have a pine table in the kitchen worn thin in the middle from generations of scrubbing and a chipped sink wedged under a pump…'

And I let her talk on. I didn't take anything she said seriously enough to be worried by it. She left early that evening, kissed me goodbye and swore she'd write. I never saw her again and she never wrote. Afterwards I occasionally saw someone who looked like her young man around the quarter, but I never approached him. I was afraid that it might really be him, that he might confirm what the girls in the Gypsy had told me.

They said that Claudette had been working the streets for her man, that she couldn't take it any more and that her body had been taken from the Seine. But no one had any real proof, no one actually saw a body. So I laughed at the girls when they told me this. I sneered at them, told them that they could slap tragedy onto everything they heard if that's what they wanted to do, but it only labelled them as pathetic and jealous.

I chose not to believe their story. I still do. If Claudette wants to be remembered in her cottage in Provence, then that's how I'm going to remember her.

So here, for posterity, is the fact of it.

Claudette proved us all wrong. She met a young man in the city. A tall, handsome man who had the power to flush up her cheeks and sparkle up her eyes. He was a carpenter by trade, a country man who longed to get back to where he was comfortable. So he worked as hard as he could for a while, saving as much as he could and, with the utmost compassion, stood by while Claudette did the same. As soon as they had enough money they left the city together and started their new life in a tiny three-roomed cottage. His first job was to make it homey, while Claudette's was to tend to their small garden, just enough room for a vegetable patch surrounded by herb bushes. Claudette never wrote to the friends she left behind because her life in the city was something she wanted to erase. She would never have grown into the confident young mother she became if we were still there reminding her of what she had once been.

She just did what I did when I left the life. I slipped straight into the construct Mother had built around my absence. Straight into the willing arms of my waiting, wooing William. Straight into the binds of duty and motherhood. It's like learning a language; you try that hard at being someone else and then, over the years, you start thinking in their thoughts, dreaming in their dreams. Of course that's all smashed to pieces now. Where's Miss Piss of the parish when I need her?

So I told myself, and anyone who bothered to ask, my version of Claudette's disappearance. Told myself and them that there never was such a happy ending, but no matter how often I said it, I still hurt for Claudette. I told myself it was because I missed her. I took to drinking more than usual, took to drinking and taking chances – always a bad combination – I got pregnant.

I started working in The Jockey Club. I left the Gypsy after my abortion. I had to do something to re-establish some pretence of control over my life. I hadn't the money to move and I had already cut my hair, so I changed my job.

It was a bad time. It was a wet season and a bad time. My
body was sore; it hurt when I walked and my heart was heavy
with the decision I had been forced to take. I suddenly saw
children everywhere and every time I did I had to remind
myself that the children from my quarter never smiled so
broad, ran so fast, grew so tall. That the children from my
quarter, born to women like me, had rickets and sullen little
faces. They flinched when you reached out for them and
they spoke the language of the streets they were born for.
I had done nothing wrong. I told myself this.

And so I changed jobs and started singing in the Jockey. All
bright smiles and some too many drinks. All lewd innuendo
and shrieks of forced delight. Me and Kiki up on the stage,
both of us painted with tight bow lips and high jade eye-
shadow. Her in a dress and me in tails and a lot of thigh
slapping thrown in; everyone said that we were a riot, and
everyone went to the Jockey. It was the new place in town.

It was run by Hilaire Hiler. He had decorated it and
he directed the cabaret. He was an earthy man, ugly and
enthusiastic, and he translated those two traits into his art
and into his cabaret. He painted grand, big, lusty scenes of
life and then twisted his grand, big, lusty face into a comedy
of itself and roared out some tremendously dirty ditties.
He was a good man to work for, always honest and never
judgmental. It was he who made the Jockey, turned it into a
good place to spend a night. A good place to come and drink,
and laugh, and love, and sometimes fight, but sometimes it's
good to fight.

The Jockey was on the Rue Campagne-Première, close
to Rosalie's café and I loved Rosalie's. It was run by an
Italian who boasted great pre-war associations. He spoke
of his friends Whistler and Modigliani and of nights in the

Chat Noir with Somerset Maugham and George Moore. He prided himself on his family-friendly menu and that was just what I needed after my ordeal, some small taste of security. The floor in Rosalie's was tiled and the chairs were wooden; there was something clean about that. And I needed to be around clean things.

I remember the summer of that year. The warm breeze blustering and blowing and the nights falling with a hint of soft light lingering about their edges. I remember the clean sweep of showers that washed over the city. They brightened up the gravelled walks of the Luxembourg Gardens. There was something clean about them and I needed to be around clean things.

Details became important to me. Like the detail of a wooden chair being pulled across the tiled floor in Rosalie's. Or the detail of a waiter standing in front of you, early in the morning, in any one of a number of cafés, with his long, starched apron shining clean and white and behind him the wind hurling past the clearly polished windows, and the warm, home smell of coffee, and the sweet, dark taste of chocolate, and the slightly oily feeling of croissants, and the way your coat dripped from its peg by the door, and the way the papers were hung on poles, and the awkwardness of an iron table leg being settled on to a warped, wooden floor.

It was these details that cured me of my abortion. These details and so many more that dragged me back to life. By the end of May I felt the sun hot on the back of my neck and I thought that I was cured.

One night in the Jockey I told Robert all about it. I said that it was over, that I had been cured by the details, but he just laughed and asked, 'Then how come you're talking like a crazy lady?'

And it only took that much to destroy me. There and then, dressed in my tails with a show still to do and all around me the noise of the young world screaming and laughing, there and then I started to cry. Robert stayed quiet for a while just holding on to my hand.

'You need to be away from all this,' he said finally. 'You need to be quiet for a bit.' And I nodded and tried to stop myself imagining my cottage in Fontainbleau.

'I'm waiting on a friend,' he told me, 'and we're going to make ourselves some plans to get away from all this; drop by, you never know what you might hear.'

Robert's friend was Hemingway. For a while those two were close, but their friendship never really rang true. Even back then, when he was still so young, Hemingway was very publicly proud of his heterosexuality. Robert McAlmon should have been the type of man he would make a show of avoiding. Later, of course, he did deny the association, but that night he seemed happy with it and the two settled down to drink together as back-slapping, guffawing, good old pals.

In fact their friendship didn't survive long enough to catch up with its appearance. They had just met, at Rapallo where Ezra Pound was living, and they had both decided that they expected the same things out of literature and that, on that basis, they deserved each other's company. For a while they did, and when they parted each said that they deserved better. But all of that was months ahead; that night in the Jockey they were friends busy making plans for each other.

McAlmon had set up Contact Press by then and had promised to publish a collection of Hemingway's stories and poems. So, that night in the Jockey, they had plenty to talk about – Hemingway's potential, Hemingway's talent, Hemingway's book, Hemingway's passions and Spain.

Hemingway wanted to go to Spain; McAlmon was pitching for Berlin but he was doing more listening than talking. Didn't have much choice, Ernest was talking up a storm, he was desperate to see a bullfight. I was sitting close enough to their table to hear a lot of what was being said and I heard him tell McAlmon all about the fights.

'It's a thing that every man should experience,' he said. 'But for a writer it is essential. We are here to record life and how can we do that if we don't witness it in its extremes?'

He talked on and on, using grander and grander words, but still it took him a long while to infuse Robert with any kind of enthusiasm. By then, by the summer of 1923, Robert was already an old man; already too cynical to achieve anything substantial, already jaded with the lifestyle his wife's money had presented him with. Very few things excited him any more but, eventually, the lure of the bullfights and the blunt force of Hemingway's language stirred him sufficiently to announce.

'Very well then, Spain it is; away with us to Spain.' And he raised his glass ready to toast his decision, but Hemingway shook his head.

'My wife is pregnant and I am not a rich man,' he said.

'Well my wife's a lesbian and she's rich enough for all of us!' Robert shouted.

That was one of Robert's nicer traits. He was unbelievably generous but, by distancing himself from his money, he could give without seeming at all patronising. Sadly, though, this was a virtue that a lot took advantage of. Because Robert always mentioned his wife when he mentioned his money, those who leached off him were reminded that they had an excuse to despise him. After all they were just taking from a friend; McAlmon had gone that step further, he had prostituted his name for his fortune.

'Well in that case…' Hemingway agreed, raising his glass as high as Robert's.

'In that case let us toast my goodly rich father-in-law, Sir John, and remember to send him a post card. JoJo!'

I came when I was called, it was part of the job, and I slipped my hand into Robert's when he held his out for it.

'This is my friend Ernest,' Robert said proudly and I smiled at his enthusiasm.

'Pleased to meet you,' I said sweetly.

'And this is my friend JoJo.' Ernest barely looked up. 'Singer extraordinaire, sufferer of fools and confidante to no less than the great Pablo himself.' Ernest took my hand.

'Ernest has an interest in all things Spanish,' McAlmon continued. 'The women, the flamenco, the olive groves, the women and the bullfights and the women.' Ernest looked slightly uncomfortable, muttered something about marriage, and myself and Robert both ignored him. Robert pulled me down onto the seat beside him.

'So, Sir John Ellerman, my goodly rich father-in-law, is sending us all to Spain,' he continued. 'We three are to go on a fact-finding expedition. We are to explore and document these bullfights the natives speak so enthusiastically about. We are to dance with the women, eat as many olives as they offer us and avoid the flu. We are to sample every drink that we can find. We are to stay in hotels that expect us to indulge in unruly behaviour and if, on our return, we actually remember any facts, we will have failed our brief and Sir John and all the angels in heaven will weep.'

I laughed and got up to go. My set was coming up and my head ached with the noise and the smoke. I laughed because Robert's proposal sounded like a joke. But he was serious. He held on to my hand as I stood before him and, looking straight into my eyes, whispered an intimate plea so at odds with our surroundings that it resonated with pure sincerity.

'Please say you'll come, JoJo. Please let me make it up to you.'

'Make what up?' I asked but, before he could answer, my question trailed into understanding. 'You don't owe me anything,' I said softly. 'It was over between me and Phil anyway.'

'May have been,' Bob said shrugging, trying to sound flippant, 'but if it wasn't for me Phil would still be around keeping an eye on you, wouldn't he?'

'Would he? I doubt it. Phil's problem was his enthusiasm just burned up his world; he'd have got bored with everything eventually, even me. He'd have moved on, he was always one to try whatever was going.'

'Maybe, but maybe he couldn't have tried what he never knew about.' I couldn't argue with that, so I didn't.

'You need to make your peace with Phil, not with me,' I whispered and then, to dispel the weight of gathering guilt, listed the reasons why I couldn't go in an affected upper-class accent.

'But what about my job? My room? My public? My commitments? My career?' McAlmon jumped on the joke with obvious relief.

'Staff, darling, staff. What do you pay them for anyway? I'm only talking about a quick trip. A week, maybe two. Your palatial quarters will be maintained; your valuables can be secured; your secretary can cancel your engagements; and your ever-loving public will, I'm sure, be happy to forgive you.'

I laughed then, just to silence him, and he took that as a 'yes'. But I had no intention of going with him. It took me a while to understand why I was so set against the idea, but finally I realised that it was a matter of control.

My life may have been a mess, but it was mine. I had an aversion to slipping back into the comfort of charitable security. I had no wish to trail behind Robert, drinking his drink, laughing at his jokes, suffering his moods and realising that I couldn't repay him with anything more tangible than my gratitude. That was reason enough, but perhaps it wasn't the whole truth. Maybe I didn't want to give McAlmon the opportunity of relieving his sense of responsibility for Phil. Maybe I needed someone to feel worse than I did, someone to blame.

'So that's settled then,' Robert said. He was so well used to getting his way he didn't need my verbal agreement. He slapped my bottom and turned back to his drink and his friend, who was looking rather sulky at this addition to his trip. I stayed put though, stayed standing right by him until he looked up at me again.

'Where is Phil?' I asked.

'We went to Berlin a few weeks ago and he wanted to stay on. So I guess he's in Berlin,' Robert said and, although that was an innocent enough answer, he muttered his words into his drink, avoided my eye and flushed up with guilt.

I noted his reaction but didn't know how to question it, so I didn't. Years later, in Berlin, I got my answers.

CHAPTER 18

Brigit Egan was weakening by the day now. Slow breaths – in, pause, out, pause. Ruth sat still, automatically matching her breathing with her mother's. She wondered at the action of death. Her father crumpled forward over the lawn-mower, and now, twenty-five years later, her mother dissolving into the air that barely sustained her.

She dipped her head low, hearing words floating on the exhale. The name Claudette came and went.

'Here, for posterity, is the fact of it,' Brigit breathed out. Ruth silently collected all that was given and it all sounded so real. What biographer would bother with such details about one more street girl? Were these heartfelt mutterings just chanting the bones of a novel?

And even if they were, her sweet mam, hounded to death by these memories! Where was her father? Where were herself and Deirdre and all those Christmas Eves? All those bedtime stories? All those summers in Kerry? Those annual trips to the circus? She did try; Deirdre told her she was stupid and she agreed. She did try, but she still couldn't stop herself from taking it personally.

'Miss Piss of the parish, where is she now?' Brigit spat and, despite herself, Ruth laughed.

'I never did go to Spain.' Brigit said. Sounding lucid now, sounding firm.

'You did. Remember, with me and Deirdre?' But, as usual, there was no recognition of the names or associated memories, just a rasping breath, a disconnected rambling.

I didn't go to Spain but I went to wave Robert and Ernest off. Hadley, Hemingway's first wife, came as well. He kissed and cuddled her, nuzzled her and groped her and I walked away revolted by the spectacle. I remember thinking at the time that a man who needs to show so much affection in public has something private to prove. I think in Hemingway's case he was trying to prove to the world that he loved his 'Feather-kitty' and that his 'Feather-kitty' loved her 'Beery-poppa'. He was trying to prove that he hadn't noticed their age difference, that he didn't mind in the least being kept by her money.

And, aside from trying to convince the world of all that, he was also trying to prove himself a man. He was drinking already. A bottle of whiskey sticking out of his battered tweed jacket and the stench of it heavy on his breath. His case, tied with string at his feet and his weary-looking wife tucked under his arm. The sight of that clichéd pose of masculinity annoyed me and obviously had the same effect on Robert, who began prancing. Prancing and preening, rolling his eyes and hitting on the porters. It had the desired effect. Hemingway broke his pose and all but stamped his foot.

'Would you stop it, you fucking fairy!'

Robert smiled oh so sweetly, slipped a sleek, silver hip-flask out of the inside pocket of his impeccably tailored suit and answered.

'Fucking? No dear, only when I get lucky. At the moment I'm a drinking fairy.'

I left them to their fights and their drinks and I was happy to. I promised Robert that I would keep his favourite seats in his favourite bars warm for him, gave him a big kiss, turned and extended my hand to Ernest. He didn't take it; instead he cupped my elbow and walked me a little distance from our small group.

'Hadley's alone,' he stated and, from over his shoulder I could see that he was right. She was standing by the open door of the carriage just waiting for Ernest's final farewell. 'Will you look out for her a bit, what with the baby and all?' I nodded for form's sake but Ernest wanted something more than that.

'You will, won't you?' he persisted, allowing me sense a rare glimpse of true sincerity. 'Please do. Promise you will. She's lonely and pregnant and so far from home I know that I'm not half of what she needs and she'll like you. She needs a girlfriend.'

'She doesn't need me,' I said and I meant it in the nicest possible way. I couldn't imagine that frumpy, pregnant middle-class lady perched by me in any of my haunts. 'She needs some pillar of the parish to take her to knitting parties.' I wonder if he hoped I would introduce her to Picasso in his absence, have the friendship all up and running for him by the time he came back. But maybe I'm doing him a disservice.

'She needs a little help with the day-to-day business of life, especially now with the baby on its way, but most of all she needs company,' he answered as firmly as all his machismo could muster. I couldn't argue with that. Then he slipped me a comfortable wad of notes and I had no intention of arguing with that, and so I did what he asked. I promised to call on his wife. And I'm so glad that I did.

I visited Hadley Hemingway very soon after. To be honest, I was bored. At that time my social life had completely merged with my working life. A night in the Jockey sitting at a table drinking was not much different to a night in the Jockey standing on the stage singing. A night perched on some young man's knee flirting was not much different to a night perched on some old man's knee simpering. One night laughing, cursing and bitching with the girls was just like the one before, the one to come. I was bored and so I went calling on someone new.

Hadley Hemingway was a good woman. A kind, open, happy woman; proud of her husband and blooming in her pregnancy. She welcomed me as a friend of Ernest's but kept me as one of her own, even though I had introduced myself as something of a 'daily'. I offered to do some cleaning, half-heartedly asked would she like me to cook her something, if she needed any messages. But she just laughed me out of that role.

'What a way you expect me to treat a visitor?' she said and I shamefacedly told her about Ernest's money.

'So he thinks he has to buy me some friends?' she asked, but she was smiling and seemed flattered that he had thought to look after her in his absence.

'I've spent most of it already,' I explained. 'But I've got enough left to get us both a good lunch.' And that's just what we did.

We liked each other immediately. She had the sort of face that I hadn't been around in a while. It was pale, slightly chunky with rich red hair and an unfashionable collection of freckles. When she was feeling good with the world her hair and skin glowed, when she wasn't they faded. She was that transparent.

When I met her first she was glowing and I was attracted. I thought that if I sat close enough, listened well enough, I could catch a little of what she was. I thought that all I needed was the company of women like her and I could be guided home; women who liked hill-walking, who loved their husbands and who took to pregnancy. Women who spoke about alcohol in terms of flavour rather than quantity, who played the piano and kept a basketful of needlework on the go; women who could turn a slum flat into something resembling a home; women who still had confidence enough in people to greet a stranger with a broad smile and a firm handshake.

I don't know what she ever saw in me, but that first afternoon we spent together, sitting on her bed in that tiny flat on the Rue du Cardinal Lemoine, started with us sipping tea and ended with us talking deeply and honestly.

We firmed up our friendship over that summer. By the time Hadley and Ernest left for Canada in August, we were close friends, all three of us, though both Hemingway and I forced our relationship a little for Hadley's sake. It only took a little forcing, after all I was good-looking and he was good company. We did have good times.

It was an almost unbearable summer, so hot and still and tense. Everyone with sense left the city, but then I knew so few sensible people I hardly noticed. The papers were reporting deaths from the heatwave and we were all hooked on reminding each other of the details of winter.

'Do you remember how we couldn't sleep because our faces over the blankets would be freezing?'

'Do you remember feeling the cold through the hole in your glove?'

'Do you remember how we would love to drink soup in the middle of the day?'

We were all ready to burst by Bastille Day and burst we did. We burst out of the bars and danced through the streets. The Select set up a table outside, on the road, and we ate off it and later danced on it. Laurance Vail led some coup against the patron of the Rotonde, and a lot of Americans ended up in court and even more ended up in the papers. By this time America was desperate to read proofs of debauched behaviour abroad and, during those Bastille Day celebrations, we did enough to keep them happy. There was even a photograph of me reproduced in a Chicago paper under the heading, 'YES MOMA I CAN CAN CAN.'

It showed me high-kicking my way down the table outside the Select. For a while I was worried that my parents would trace me through it but, as Robert pointed out, there was no way they could unless they were used to recognising me by my underwear.

It was a fun time to be young and through it all the Hemingways came and went, toing and froing from Spain. Ernest's trip with Robert had cemented his passion for the country. He loved the sport of the bullfights and when he couldn't get to them he chased the race meets and boxing fights in and around Paris. Hemingway went everywhere with his notebook and Hadley followed with her lumbering belly.

She told me that once in Pamplona, after sitting for hours under a belting sun looking down on bull after bull being hacked to death, she fainted. She slumped against Ernest who must have merely shifted her weight off his shoulder, because she woke on the ground. She thought it was funny.

'When I came to and sat back up,' she told me, laughing, 'he was saying that it was too hot for that kind of thing. I was totally confused and asked him what was it too hot for, and he said "snuggling". As if! It was hot like an oven and there I was rising like some huge, solid soufflé in it and he's thinking that I was wanting snuggling! Men!'

I laughed because she had stopped to give me time to.

'You know?' she asked me then, still smiling, 'You know what I did at the bullfights?' I shook my head. 'I knitted baby clothes. I kept my head down and knitted and I counted all the stitches all the time in my head to block out the noises. It helped, but nothing could stop the smell.'

She laughed again then, so I laughed too but, for a while after that, I restricted my visits to times when I could be sure that Ernest would be off somewhere writing his angular prose. And that was quite an easy thing to do. He always had someplace to go, some invitation to honour; he was very successfully inventing himself as the next genius. Gertrude Stein had him tucked under her intellectual wing, and that was introduction enough. All of Paris was open to this new, talented, handsome, charismatic young man. But between Ernest and Hadley plans had been already made and they didn't fall in with this new definition of self. I could read the signs of stress. Ernest was often absent and Hadley was fading.

The Hemingways had planned to leave Paris that August. They were going to go to Toronto where Hadley would have their baby and where Ernest would earn their keep as an ace reporter on the *Daily Star*. We, our gang, used to joke about it quite a lot. We used to sit around the bars, describing pictures of suburban bliss to each other.

The Hemingways, we said, would take a house comfortably set back from the road, behind the safety of a cherry tree and a well-tended lawn. Hadley would wake every morning early. She would put on the coffee and cook Ernest a breakfast and, every morning, he would groan a little, saying he didn't much feel like it, but she'd insist he eat it and then she'd kiss him goodbye. The rest of her morning would be spent walking baby up and down the broad avenues that circled their home. Occasionally she would stop to chat with the neighbouring matrons. She would bake for the afternoon and then, in the evenings, she would bath baby and doll herself up something fine for her returning husband. She would always be ready to greet him at exactly six thirty three with a smile, a well-mixed cocktail and a good steak dinner.

Ernest would leave their leafy home every morning at eight fifteen and head in to his office in the city. Once there he would roll up his sleeves and apply himself to the job at hand. All his colleagues would respect him. They'd tell each other that he was first-class reporter, an all-round type of guy, and he would think that they were all right too. He would eat his lunch every day with some of them at a diner where the waitress, who used to be a bit of a doll, would flirt with him and always pour him extra coffee. All the boys from the paper would go for a drink after work in a rough kind of bar, but Ernest never would. He'd tell Hadley that, 'The boys only do it because they've no one as fine as you to come home to.'

Ernest would always arrive home at six thirty three and then Mr and Mrs and baby too would spend their every evening together. Sometimes Mrs would sit on her Mr's knee and they'd stay close like that, saying nothing much. Sometimes they'd listen to their wireless and maybe do a bit of dancing, and sometimes Ernest would sit himself down at the dining-room table and write himself a mighty good little story.

It was a joke, all of it. It had so little to do with our perception of living that we felt comfortable laughing at it. But the closer the Hemingways came to sailing, the less funny it sounded; it began to seem real. We weren't telling fairy stories any more; we were describing how things were going to be. Ernest grew grimmer and grimmer and Hadley tried harder and harder to keep the joy flowing. I think she felt responsible, as if her pregnancy was tying him down, and I think he was happy to let her think that. I don't think he ever reminded her that it was her money that had freed him up in the first place.

They were due to sail away sometime towards the middle of August, I think, I know it was still very hot. I saw a lot of them during the days leading up to their departure. I helped them pack. Ernest wasn't good at anything domestic and the long heat of the summer, the trips down to Spain, the stress of the move and the anticipation of the sea crossing were showing on Hadley. She was frequently sick and always exhausted. And they were both very busy with people. Hemingway had claimed a lot of friends during his stay in Paris, and Hadley had made a few deep connections. They had a lot of goodbyes to say and they took the time to say them all thoroughly, even a little dramatically. So they were busy and I was happy to help.

I spent a week of afternoons with Hadley packing, lifting, cleaning and chatting away cheerfully, trying desperately to paint a fascinatingly cosmopolitan scene of domestic harmony in Toronto. I talked about sweeping scenery and award-winning stories, new friends and the all-encompassing fulfilment of motherhood. It was hard work but I liked Hadley and I was going to miss her; I enjoyed lavishing my time on her. We'd sit on boxes, drinking coffee out of chipped mugs and talking hard about the positive side of everything.

'And of course we'll be back,' she said over and over. And over and over I said, 'Unless you love it over there.'

I was, unselfishly, hoping that they'd stay. I was hoping that Hadley and her baby could be given the time to relax in the comfort of mediocrity for a while. She seemed so worn out by bohemia.

The Hemingways were to set sail on the 17th of August. They did their last goodbye tour on the 16th. Their flat was empty and ready for its next tenant, their crates were dispatched and their sailing was postponed. For every other passenger due to sail on the *Andania* it was an inconvenience, but for Ernest it was a calamity. The move had sucked their finances dry; a hotel was out of the question. Or so he said, but it was always hard to know with Ernest. Maybe he thought that the fact of his staying in a hotel would ruin his carefully crafted persona of starving artist. Maybe he didn't want to stay with any of his more affluent or important friends because he knew that too long and close a proximity could tarnish his reputation of good-humoured raconteur. Or maybe he just saw and jumped at the chance of creating a mystery. But anyway, for whatever reason, on the night of the 16th of August, himself and Hadley arrived at my door.

The sailing was delayed for nine long days. For ten long, hot nights they slept in my room. Ernest begged me not to tell anyone of their whereabouts and so I didn't, although everyone was asking. After a couple of days I was sucked into his smug pleasure at the intrigue and no longer had to work at keeping my mouth shut. I was enjoying myself.

Everyone had a theory, but only I had the truth. Even when the Hemingways finally left I kept my silence and their disappearance during that time has remained a mystery. I never dreamed Ernest would end up so famous; his moves, moods and writing scrutinised with such intensity. Many of his more obsessive biographers have taken the time to document his absence during this time and I love reading their various speculations. All those versions of the one truth; it makes me feel documented. It places me between the lines of history, a place where most of us settle.

Aside from our cramped conditions and Ernest's refusal to let either him or Hadley move outdoors; aside from the sleepless nights, the foul stench of flesh and the claustrophobia; aside from our frayed nerves and my growing indignation at being treated with such little respect; aside from it all, we had the most marvellous time.

To pacify Ernest's lingering sense of paranoia, I told the world that I was sick and I cut all my engagements down to a minimum. I left myself more or less free to be at their disposal and, to be fair, they paid me handsomely for my trouble. When they were gone I found a twenty-dollar bill on my mantelpiece and back then, in Paris, twenty dollars meant something.

We spent most of the time talking, singing and playing. Hadley would sit at my table and run her fingers up and down its edge pretending it was a piano. She would start by singing scales and go on to more and more complicated pieces. She entertained us with masterful performances of mime and music.

But Ernest outshone her. In that closed environment, with no one to impress, he relaxed into the man he could have become. He was a big man and in my small room he loomed huge. He made a great burlesque play on this, dancing around imaginary fighters, taunting imaginary bulls and then, when he had exhausted himself leaping and shouting, he would relax us all by telling us stories. They were good stories; they sounded real, as if they were painfully sharpened by experience. He told us all about himself as a boy and he made it all seem funny, and once he told us all about himself as a writer. He said, 'I want to strip language bare. I want to cut out everything except the truth. I want every line of my writing to say one true thing.'

'But truth is never that easy,' I argued. 'Truth is always subjective. Memory, recall is never collective and so can never be absolute.'

'It should be collective. A thing happens. A thing is recorded. That is absolute – anything more or less is lies.'

'But what about viewpoint? What about someone else's opinion?'

'I have my own knowledge of events and as a writer I have to have absolute confidence in it.'

'Will you give no quarter to another's interpretation?'

It was Hadley who asked this. It was my question and I wish she had left it for me. Her having to ask this of her husband rendered her too vulnerable. Ernest looked at her before he answered and when he finally replied, his voice was sad.

'I cannot afford to,' he said and that was his truth. He remembered, or he invented, his realities, and he allowed for no discrepancies. Invariably those around him pointed out his omissions, his exaggerations, and invariably he discarded their versions – eventually he discarded them. But that was all to come.

That night I remember Hemingway told us a story about a young boy fishing with his father on the banks of a river late into the night. The boy was happy because he could handle his rod well and because his eighth birthday was just a week away. The boy caught a fish much larger than any his father had landed, but he didn't say a word because, just as he was about to call out, he noticed the tired slump of his father's shoulders and he saw the moon bounce off his father's grey hair. His father, however, heard the heavy noise of the fish leaving the water and he walked over to his son to congratulate him on his catch. The boy, wanting to be kind, denied any responsibility.

'It leapt out at me, Daddy,' he said. 'Must be because it's mad at us or something. Leapt clean out of the water it did.'

The father hit the boy for being a liar.

The Hemingways came back to Paris the following January with their new son. Their sweet suburban dream barely lasted six months.

CHAPTER 19

Ruth stood in the dust of her childhood home. Outside it was getting dark, inside it was cold, hollow and bare. Childishly she had left the lights and heating off; she knew that she was purposefully romanticising this goodbye, she just didn't know why. Did she really need such theatrics to instil emotion?

She was upstairs, staring into the emptiness of bedrooms and bathrooms. Everything was gone now except for the colossal wardrobe in the master bedroom that must have been built in situ, there was no way it could fit through the door, let alone the down the stairs. And they had left the finely finished shaker unit in the bathroom. It had been custom sized to the alcove and it seemed a shame to remove it. Downstairs, still shrouded, the enormous sitting-room couch and sideboard were all that remained. Slabs of some long-dead Victorian grandeur, fitted for homes built to a different scale, probably worth something in their day, obsolete now. Time passes.

Ruth had talked herself out onto the front porch where the last five bags of rubbish waited for her, last bin day, and still it didn't impinge. Not the cold, not the gloom, not the passage of time could impinge. She could feel the shape of the garden surround her. Half an acre almost, enormous by suburban standards and always so well maintained. All the neighbours said it, all the time.

'How do you find the time, Brigit?' they cooed.

And she did do it, even though it demanded so much, and more and more as age crept on. From her bedroom window Ruth would watch her mother bend and weed and prune and plant her way through the seasons. She only ever watched; there was something very private, almost religious, about Brigit's connection with the garden and the produce she brought from it into the kitchen. Soft fruit heaped on the table, jars waiting to be sterilised. Parcels for neighbours, wrapped apples, pungent onions, the deep green of lettuce and cabbage, swollen tumours bulging ugly. And through it all her mother's hands, firm and deft. And still it didn't impinge.

Ruth picked up the first two black sacks; they were very light, mainly filled with old papers. On the top of one she caught sight of the empty, battered sleeve of *Highway 61*, and there it was, suddenly, emotion enough to punch her square in the stomach. She was twenty what? Twenty-two or three and this had meant the world to her. A far away, beaten up, mouthy, young world. She had got married to those tunes blaring in her head. She had stood by her solid dependable husband in church and at home, she had had Catherine. She remembered hoovering to the squall of *Blood on The Tracks* played far too loud for suburbia.

Behind her she saw the sweep of headlights before she heard the crunch of gravel. She turned to face Deirdre reversing her car to a halt but she didn't realise she was crying until Deirdre caught her up in a light-hearted hug.

'You eejit, I knew this would be what you'd be doing.'
It's not what you think, Ruth thought, but still she was so
thankful of her sister's presence. She allowed herself the
luxury of crying properly, just for a moment though, before
she forced a laugh behind the tears.

'You're right, I'm a big sentimental eejit. Come on, we'll
put these out.' And she gestured at the remaining bags while
pushing Bob Dylan's battered face out of sight.

Deirdre had brought a bottle of wine.

'One last drink in the old place,' she said, and so they sat
themselves either end of the enormous sitting-room couch,
wrapped in coats, drinking from the paper cups Deirdre had
remembered to bring, staring into the empty grate, the faux
Art Nouveau tile surround.

'Miss Piss of the parish? God but that's wonderful!'

'I know,' Ruth agreed. 'Where did she get it and who was
she talking about?'

Deirdre answered straight away. It was meant as nothing,
a throwaway comment, 'Sure it could be any one of us.' A
moment passed.

Ruth felt the words settle like a judgement and then she
asked, lowly, scared, 'What'll we do without her, do you
think?'

'We're without her now and we're doing fine. Maybe it'll
be the making of us.'

'Maybe,' Ruth agreed and it was the first time she had
agreed to anything so negative. Deirdre didn't say a word,
she just waited, and then it came. 'But we all loved her and
respected her so much and I don't understand... I don't
understand where I went wrong.'

There was a long silence. Deirdre stayed waiting, quiet,
and Ruth drank.

'You didn't go wrong.' Deirdre finally said but, not knowing the context, her tone lacked conviction.

'You see I thought all I needed to do was love them, unconditionally, like mam did us. But they think I'm a fool; I can see it in them. The jokes stop when I'm around, it's like chasing ghosts. It was horrible at Christmas. I'd hear them, even Brian, and then I'd follow the laughter and it'd stop.'

'You're their mother, they depend on you for all sorts; let them have their jokes.'

'But we never felt like that about Mam, did we? I don't remember ever wanting to exclude her.'

'That's 'cos even the jokes were hers.'

It was dark outside now. Deirdre got up and switched on the bare overhead bulb. It helped. Ruth felt suddenly stupid. She smiled a little and stood up.

'Way past clearing-up time,' she said in the parody of a barman. Deirdre didn't laugh.

'A lot depends on your definition of unconditional love,' she said as she re-corked the remains of the wine. 'You say potato, I say control.'

For the last time they closed and locked the porch behind them and one after the other drove down the short avenue. And, despite the poignant sound of gravel crunching, crows settling, rain pattering, Ruth forgot to look back.

CHAPTER 20

Time seems to have slowed now. There was a tree when I came and the evenings are still long and dark. I suppose I must be here a few weeks, maybe months – it seems longer. The bed feels hard, hard under bones, and the blankets seem heavy, a weight to lift with every breath. So many years passed so fast and now a moment lasts a dream-long eternity. They're right though, all those old heads that tell you; youth speeds by fast, screams right by you. Maybe the same can be said of a century, the early decades race through, the later ones limp on home.

There was certainly something fast about the Twenties. Something that flung gin in girls and girls in short skirts. Something that chased motor cars out of cities and sped them down country lanes. We called it everything but the truth. We laughed. One afternoon, sitting high up in some boy's convertible, I waved my scarf and shouted about youth and freedom. We told each other that it was all just fun.

Just for jolly!

Why not when we've got the lolly…

And then we'd run on to the next fun riot and another weekend would disappear. We were always moving; there was always so much to do, everything was ahead of us. We would seek each other out and then, once we were safely cosseted in groups, we would dance and sing and squeal with laughter.

Everything was too, too funny.

Every girl a darling, every boy a honey.

We stopped talking, there was suddenly too much to scream about and so we all screamed together, and if no one listened it never mattered; you soon came to realise that you had nothing much to say.

Oh, we made so much noise, as much as we could, but it was never enough to drown out the truth. That truth that still haunted my nights: *we have stretched the earth too tight over corpses*. The whisper was louder now; most people could hear it if they listened and so we made so much noise, as much noise as we could.

And we ran, tripping over ourselves, squealing with what we called the energy of youth but we all knew the real reason we were moving so fast. We all knew what we were trying to run away from. We knew that the war had left world politics in frayed disorder; we knew that the Germans wouldn't stay starving forever. We saw boatloads of Americans flooding Montparnasse where easy luxury could be bought for just a few dollars. We saw trainloads of them journey on to Berlin where easy sin was offered for less. We had recently learnt that wars were dictated by economics and so we knew that we were being pulled down towards the inevitable. We went down dancing though, and don't time just fly by when you're all dressed up and your dancing shoes don't pinch?

For a while I was at the heart of it all. I wore a fringed dress that stopped mid-thigh and my trick was to send all those tassels flying while holding on to the penultimate note of whatever song I was singing. I went down a storm and managed to earn myself a modest enough living. Aside from the Jockey, where sometimes Picasso would come to see me, I used to do some nights in the Jungle and later on in Bricktop's. Afternoons, if I needed money, could be spent in the Boeuf sur le Toit, where, although I was never officially on the books, I was welcome to work on the lonely-looking men who drank there. I was welcome to make them feel right at home.

Hiler was involved with the Jungle, I think; it certainly had much the same feel as the Jockey: the same people, the same songs. It was a good place to go and a lot of people went there. One night a very handsome young man came in. He made a bit of an entrance, blocked the door while he flicked his coat off his shoulders with a flourish, and took his time about sitting down. He had the look of fame about him; he was torn between the bore of being recognised and the indignity of being ignored. Happily though he didn't have to suffer any indignity at the Jungle. It only took a moment before the whispers started circling the room.

'It's Valentino. It's him. It's Rudy. It is.'

The young man heard and relaxed. He emptied his glass and raised his hand for another. The patron himself was there to pour it for him. There was a brief exchange between them and then the band was ordered to lower the music. Of course, ever since he had come in, everyone was covertly staring at Valentino, but we gave up all pretence of doing anything else when the patron stepped into the silence that the band had cleared and up on to a table.

'Ladies and gentleman,' he called out. 'Tonight we have the pleasure of Mr Rudolph Valentino's patronage.' The very young, very handsome man bowed and we all clapped. 'And he has very kindly agreed to tango for us. He will pick, as his partner, whoever amongst you pleases him the most.'

There must have been some applause, but us girls had no time to contribute to it; we were busy. For a brief, blinking moment every desperate one of us forgot our public persona. For a brief, blinking moment we were all mentally back before our bedroom mirrors and all our private, preening quirks were exposed.

We licked our palms to smooth and glisten our curls; we scraped at our teeth with our nails and then polished them with our fingers. Breasts were plumped up into shape, stockings were smoothed all the way up to the thigh, jewellery was straightened, shoulders squared, stomachs sucked in and lipsticks randomly applied. Cheeks were pinched, fingernails checked, perfumes sprayed and our best smiles rehearsed. It only took a moment before we were fixed and set, but obviously a moment was too long. By the time we were ready to look up and dazzle the great Valentino with our all, he was gone.

He had made his decision and was moving towards the dance floor with his arm draped lovingly around some young man's shoulder. They started to dance and the band followed. We all watched and knew that his decision had been perfect; my, but they danced. They moved so close together. Body to body, face to face, their eyes fixed on one another and their lips barely separated by that sweet sigh that breathes all the promise of sex and so is the essence of eroticism. They moved with the slow, tight, erotic tension that is integral to the spirit of the tango and, strangely, their parade of homosexuality just worked to heighten their masculinity. Their strength was in their every movement, from the sharp workings of

---

their shoulders down to the firm stamp of their feet. When they were finished us girls all sighed before we roared our applause.

That was the Jungle, just one of the clubs, just one of those nights. There were always others, other places, other people. Cocteau had a hand in the starting of the Boeuf sur le Toit. He used to go there quite a bit with his young love Raymond Radiguet. We all watched poor Radiguet fade away and we all watched Cocteau die a little with him. There was a genuine feeling between them. They had their jealousies, Raymond had his affairs but, in the end, he chose to die with Cocteau and that has to mean something.

And then there was Bricktop's. Bricktop got her name from her bright red hair and she got a lot of her popularity from the fact that Josephine Baker, one of her protégées, had rendered black dancers fashionable. Before Josephine a place like Bricktop's would maybe have had a cult status, but would mainly have been left to cater to its own. But now Bricktop's was not only the place to be seen in but Bricktop herself was given a front-door invite to all the best houses in town. Cole Porter was a good friend of hers. It was said, certainly by her, that she was one of the few singers he liked to hear sing his songs. She was probably right though because it was said by everyone that he wrote 'Miss Otis Regrets' specifically for her to sing. He used to invite her over quite often to sing or teach his guests the new steps and she'd march straight through the front door of his home; no slinking tradesmen's entrance for her.

'My "master" days are over,' she'd say. 'God's my only master now and the Bible tells me he'll be waiting for me by his front door. If I'm good enough to knock on them pearly gates, I'm good enough to knock on any door in town.'

She took it all for what it was worth and for her it was always worth laughing at. I loved working for her. She was an American who claimed to have an Irish mother, though I never believed her. In my book black people never came out of Ireland no matter how many generations separated them.

Bricktop never minded my scepticism though, she just saw it as another of life's jokes.

'All it takes is a taste of chocolate mixed with the cream,' she'd say. From the moment we met she took an immediate liking to me. I asked her one night if she needed anyone for her cabaret and she employed me on the spot without even the pretence of an audition.

'I know that accent, girl,' she said. 'I've heard your voice before. That was the voice I heard when I had the mumps and was sick for nights. And that voice sang to me; it sang me out of all kinds of nightmares. Still does, that voice is in my head and it does me good to see such a pretty face behind it. You stay by me, girl, and I'll tell you what to do and you'll tell me when to get lost and we'll get along just fine.'

I worked some nights and I missed some weeks and I never appreciated that she was offering me a real place in her life. Things might have been a lot different if I had stayed by her. We lost touch after I left Paris but, over the years, her name has cropped up. I heard that she opened a club in Rome after the war and there's a rumour that she retired to a convent in California. It wouldn't surprise me if she did, there was always something spiritual about her; something graceful in her understanding and tolerance of people.

She was a big woman moulded out of hard flesh and lots of it, but she had slim ankles and fast feet. She could out-Charleston us all and that was what she was best at, although she was a good singer. Mostly though she was busy running the place, and she left the entertaining to us. She would sit up in her cashier's booth and direct the night. I never saw her lose control of any situation and I saw a lot of situations that needed controlling. The secret of her authority lay in the way she talked to the drunks; she never seemed patronising or judgmental. If a man had to fight she just asked him to do it outside; if a man had to vomit she asked him to do the same. And they always did as she asked; her tone of voice could reason the fight out of the most belligerent of drinkers.

And that was just another of the clubs. Another place to fill your night with noise, another chance to earn a few dollars. We were all getting tired though, I could read my humour in the faces of my friends. Everything becomes mundane in time and we were bored with our continual pretence of present hilarity and our refusal to acknowledge the reality of the future. Wars and calamities aside, I still had a lot to fear and very little to hope for. I remember one night Flossie pushed her blotched, blurred face in mine and whispered, 'I was prettier than you.'

I figured I had four, maybe five, years left.

By 1925 this mood was almost universal. The Paris I had known began to fragment. The bars all changed to suit the influx of American clientele. The cafés followed, then the shops, then the theatres. The air itself was changing; more cars on the streets, more hot dogs under grills, more jazz tunes on the radio. Many of the old gang were gone. A few had gone home; a few had moved on naturally, pairing off, having children; a few had moved on aimlessly, wandering Europe, losing their bearings; and a few had died.

The Dôme and the Rotonde had been renovated to suit the times and the times were suited to nothing more than easy luxury. Hemingway used to complain about the rich leaching off the talented. They may have done but, in my experience, it seemed that the talented were easily courted. The cafés were filled with them, the geniuses holding forth – a restaurant devoted to Joyce, a café devoted to Picasso and, as yet, just a stretch of the bar devoted to Hemingway. The tourists came to sit and watch; the rich came to buy.

They filled the bars, then filled themselves with legal alcohol. They toured the studios and bought paintings by the yard. They slunk into Shakespeare and Company and bought up all the banned books they had heard so much about, and then they hunted down the artists themselves and tried, and very often succeeded, in buying them.

They were laughable really, all those severe young men and flat-chested young women earnestly searching for their identities. In the beginning we used to make fun of them. I remember once, when I was strolling down the Champs-Elysées with Picasso, we were approached by a grim-looking boy of maybe twenty. He stepped straight into Picasso's path and proudly introduced himself as an artist. He obviously expected an enthused response and became quite unnerved when Picasso merely stopped and stared silently back at him.

'It is you, isn't it?' The boy finally asked and Pablo sadly shook his head and answered, 'Unfortunately no.'

'But aren't you?'

'No, I'm not.'

'But you look exactly like…'

'Not quite. If you look closely you will see that my nose is too small.'

'Well yes, now that you mention it. I'm so sorry to have bothered you.'

'Quite all right.' And we walked on and waited until the boy was out of earshot before we laughed.

There were lots of similar stories, a lot of them exaggerated, and I'm sure a lot of them fictional, but another one that I saw for myself involved a very beautiful American girl, very rich and very well connected, a friend of Peggy Guggenheim's from back home. She had come to Paris to be photographed by Man Ray and, although he turned her away from his studio, although he took the time to explain to her how busy he was, although he recommended a host of other photographers, she would not leave him alone. She sent him presents, followed him around his social engagements and courted Kiki and anyone else she fancied might have some influence over him. Of course we all made up stories of how close we were to the man and for a month or so we all dined out on that poor girl's desperation. Eventually though Man Ray faced her with an absolute refusal and she came running back to the Dôme, flushed with success, to tell us all about it.

'I am to go home,' she announced and then she sat back and waited for us to ask why. Eventually I did. I felt that I owed her that much after all the drinks she had bought me.

'So you got your portrait taken then,' I said.

'Oh no,' she answered shaking her head, 'but now I understand why Mister Ray won't do it.' She paused there for a moment to look coyly down at the tips of her smart little shoes and, when she raised her head to continue with her explanation, she was blushing. 'He says that I am too beautiful. He says that my face is angelic and that his portraiture only works because it plays on the humanity of his subject. He says that he has not got the expertise to capture perfection. That if he photographed me he would only succeed in doing me a disservice and that that would not be fair to either of our reputations.'

As I have said, in the beginning we laughed at these stories but, in the beginning, we thought that we were invincible. By the time Hemingway had left Hadley for flat-chested Pauline Pfeiffer with her ample income and her sleek-bobbed beauty, I already knew that we had lost, that we had sold out.

And I've been selling out ever since, Mother. I sold my children down that same road, but god knows that took little or no effort. An easy life breeds nothing but complacency, and what greatness is born from that? I should have thrown them out onto the streets and watched to see if they'd bounce back. Or was there anything left to bounce off of at that time? Did the war make failures of us all?

It's this sense of failure with which I associate the Fitzgeralds, Scott and Zelda. I met them first in 1925 after *The Great Gatsby* had been published and had failed to live up to its commercial expectations. And after Zelda had failed their marriage by having an affair and had failed the youth-fuelled spirit of the age by trying to commit suicide.

For me the Fitzgeralds *were* the Twenties. At first they were the success of those early years when everyone was young and everything was new. They were clean, hard work, they were the Charleston, the beautiful young things. They were fast cars ripping up those tired old country roads; they were loud music and sweaty, fine dancers jumping jungle-free all over the boards of staid old theatres. They were cocktails at seven; the flash of magazine photographers; the skimpiness of this year's bathing suits; the biggest movie theatres and the tallest yachts. They were neon lights.

But when I knew them they had already aged with the decade. By then they were in the frenzy of those middle years when too much energy generated too much activity and no one took the time to stop and plot a course. By then they had become cocktails for breakfast and time-wasting bickering. They were speeding cars racing towards something new, always something brighter. They were faded old friends disproving potential; they were bored sexuality bordering on decadence; they were mind-numbing drugs and meaningless stories. They were lost.

They crashed in 1929. By then Scott had identified himself too deeply with his times to distance himself from the Depression; it lodged in his heart and then he was no help to Zelda at all.

I happened to be with Hemingway when he first met Scott. It's true, I was, even though I know that if everyone who claimed to have been there really was, the place would have burst. All those memoirs, all those nobodies riding on the coat-tails of celebrity! But I was there.

It was in the Dingo. But, to be perfectly honest, saying 'I was with Hemingway' is a bit of an exaggeration. I was just in the Dingo at the time, sitting within earshot of the two. Scott was very drunk and very handsome. He was also very impressed with what he had read of Hemingway's work and he was very vocal in his praise. Later Hemingway said that such fawning repulsed him, but at the time he sat up and glowed red with pride. 'Do you really think so?' he asked, and, 'What makes you say so?' and, 'Do others agree?'

He kept the conversation centred on himself and his work for as long as he could, ignorantly ignoring his companion's genius, and Scott let him. It was that meeting that set the tone for their friendship: Hemingway was to be courted and Scott was to be charming. It was a relationship that suited them both. Scott was always attracted to men of the world and Hemingway was more than willing to play that part in return for the professional favours that Scott, as the established voice of the generation, was in a position to provide.

That first afternoon Scott had arrived in the Dingo already very drunk, and then he drank some more. He was soon out of control and so, inevitably, his conversation slipped away from literature and on to sex.

'Did you sleep with your wife before you married her?' he asked, an innocent attempt to shock, and it worked. Hemingway, the big hard-drinking man, bristled like a Middle American school marm.

'I refuse to answer that,' he snapped, and behind him I mimicked, 'I'll thank you to mind your own beeswax, young man. I don't think I've ever been more insulted in my entire life.'

There was a lot of laughter at this, but Hemingway didn't join in with it; he just squared his shoulders under his worn tweed jacket and muttered something into his drink. I didn't catch what it was, but Scott must have because he immediately decided that it was time to leave. He slid off his bar stool and, in so doing, pitched himself right into my arms and so I left with him. I had no choice but to, the man couldn't stand up by himself. I walked him outside and managed to keep him propped up while I tried hailing a taxi. It was hard work though, he was a heavy dead weight and he kept twitching and giggling. Finally he pulled my face around to his and, trying desperately to look serious, slurred, 'Let me tell you something. D'you know something?'

'What?' I asked.

'Clothes maketh the man... spend too much money on his wife.' He spluttered and then he collapsed onto the path, with the force of his laughter dragging me down with him.

Very soon after that, after their first meeting, Hemingway and Scott went off on a trip to collect Scott's car from Lyons or somewhere around there. The car was just an excuse, though; the trip was really about male-bonding and drinking and, on that level, it was a roaring success. For a long while after it, the two newly bonded friends were often seen together raging through the nights and drinking through the days.

Zelda was rarely with them; she was the kind of woman who terrified Hemingway. She was not attracted to him and so she had no time for him. She yawned through his descriptions of bullfights, she talked over him and, with very little effort, she absorbed all of Scott's attention. Hemingway wasn't used to fighting for female attention and so, with Zelda, he never even tried. My, but he missed out.

Zelda was, she just *was*, and there can be great power in that. Most people thought her beautiful but she wasn't; she was just expressive, always burned up with something. She was passionate-looking and most people assume that the starting point of passion is beauty. It doesn't always have to be, though; sometimes passion can be self-fuelling. She was the only woman I've ever met who was actually schooled in charm. She had a way of talking that enlivened language; from the moment she greeted you you knew she was special. When she held out her hand to say 'how do you do' she didn't hold it palm down like the affected girls of her class did, she stretched it full out. And she didn't drop her eyes, she held them steady. And she didn't emphasise the 'you' in her question; instead she faintly emphasised the first 'do'. It worked a charm, and that was just the beginning.

She had no time for small talk. Hemingway claims that, from very early on, he knew she was mad because once, out of the blue, she asked him if he agreed that Al Jolson was better than Jesus. A viable question, I would have thought, dependant totally on your definition of 'better'; a worthy topic for discussion.

I met her first in the toilets of Bricktop's where I was putting the final touches to my face before my set started. I've often read that Fitzgerald was frequently quoted as saying that his biggest claim to fame was discovering Bricktop before Cole Porter – I'm not too sure about that, though. I was called out then but, from the stage I kept an eye on Zelda and, from behind the flutter of activity that always surrounded her, she watched me. When I finally stepped down – hot, wet and half-naked – she ran up to me and took my hand.

'You dance like the wind,' she said, 'like the soft winds of Ireland. I don't know how to do that. I never knew such winds; our winds blew hot and dry and that would be an old woman's dance. Will you teach me how to dance like you?'

Of course I said that I would and so, for a while after that night, I would go to the Fitzgerald's apartment on the Rue de Tilsitt every Tuesday evening at four to teach Zelda some steps. The first day I went I repeated Bricktop's words to myself.

'My master days are over,' I told myself. 'If I'm good enough to knock on them pearly gates.' They let me in the front door all right, but that was as far as any real friendship went. I was staff and even for these young, decadent bohemians, staff was staff. I didn't mind, the work was light and the money was good.

As it turned out though we did very little dancing. Zelda's heart was too full of distractions to allow for dedication, or else too dedicated to distractions to allow for progress. Either way she was very skilled at distracting everyone around her, and that included Scott, whose wasted talent was already beginning to haunt him. One of the main benefits of being regarded as 'staff' was that you were ignored, or, worse, seen as inconsequential. To ignore someone you have to first think of them; the Fitzgeralds didn't even see me as worth that much trouble. As long as I stayed in my place, facilitating them, my company was tolerated. I liked it like that, it enabled me to see them just as they were.

They drank a lot.

'Just the one cocktail before dinner,' Scott would say and drain a tumbler filled mostly with gin.

And they talked a lot, well mainly Zelda talked. Scott used to try to make the most of my visits. He would usually disappear off at some stage to spend time with his writing. He was never let stay away for too long, though. As soon as Zelda noticed his absence she would lure him back. She would shout questions at him through his closed door – jokes, offers of drinks, offers of amusement. Poor Scott, he was never strong enough to hold out for any length and, every time he came running back, he sank a little further in his wife's estimation. He did manage to write a bit though. Sometimes he would make me recite things to him, or read passages of his own work back to him. When Zelda ridiculed this as narcissism, he took the time to explain to her that it was because of my accent. He said that the 'melody' of my accent gave life to his words. She continued laughing, but I bowed my head. I was flushed with pride and ashamed of being found taking such public gratification in something that was just a chance of birth. I was proud though. Ever since London I had felt hampered by my voice. I thought it labelled me as parochial and that knowledge had often silenced me. I cleared my throat then, in preparation of saying something 'melodious'. But Zelda just went on, talking right over me. I lowered my head again. Melodic accent or not, this was obviously my place: head lowered, waiting for the time when I would be called into use again.

For the first time since I had left home the social norms I thought I had left behind were beginning to catch up with me. Money mattered again. Oh, I know Phil had had money, but he was a child and I was his toy. And Robert had money but he hadn't earned it, had no respect for it. The Fitzgeralds had money and it mattered to them. No matter how bohemian they claimed to be they were still just a couple of middle-class kids with money. I saw it the first day Scott asked Ernest his 'shocking' question; I saw it in the way he squared his shoulders for a fight whenever confronted with proof of his conservatism; and I saw it in the way Zelda indulged herself by 'talking' to me every now and again. She may have thought she was crossing social barriers, but all she was really doing was practising her anecdotes on me. It was my place to ooh, aah and laugh at the right parts; it was hers to perfect the rhythm of the tale. Don't get me wrong, though. I had no problem with my role; it came easy to me. I loved Zelda's stories and was always flattered by her company.

She told me all about the soldiers who came to camp in her town.

'We used to have such fun,' she said; 'such dances. My mother made me wonderful dresses, a new one for every occasion, and they were all beautiful; orange and red, pure white and deep blue. They fell as soft as petals and so, to compliment them, I always wore fresh flowers. I used to make sure that my corsages were kept damp all night so that I always smelled flower-fresh. That's one memory I know was worth creating, so many young men wrote to me from the front telling me how they remembered my perfume. Now, isn't that sweet? Isn't that something? That when a man is nose deep in the stench of war he can still remember the smell of a pretty girl he once held in his arms. I did a good thing for them, the dear boys, didn't I? Even the church ladies would have to agree on that.' I would nod solemnly at this point.

'Oh, but the poor boys. It was all a game, nothing but a dear, sweet game. I pretended I loved them and they pretended they were going to see twenty. I used to twirl for them, order a moonlit sky for them, delay the dawn for them by keeping them awake all night. I used to keep my eyes open all the time and I saw their wonder, I'd hear the whisper of their thoughts. They'd tell themselves, 'This must be a prelude to death, because life could never stay so sweet.'

And they were right, life has never been so sweet since.

'The aviators used to fly in formation over my father's house, did I tell you that? Two pilots died in a field close by, they dipped too low over my porch. They flew so low I could see the crinkle of their smiles, and so I bowed to them and then they tumbled black and red out of the sky. Wasn't that horrible?' she asked, but she was smiling.

'Horrible,' I'd agree, but my face would be flamed with jealousy.

'I could waltz better than any girl in Montgomery,' she boasted. 'I could swim better, dive better, kiss better and rollerskate better. Perhaps I should have stayed there. Here, in the real world, no one salutes the skies for me.'

And I would sigh for her.

But such moments of doubt were rare for Zelda; she was usually filled with admiration for the creature she was. She was proud of herself and she expected to be proud of her husband. That was why she was continually pushing him forward, goading him, taunting him, challenging him. Hemingway, and a lot of others, thought her treatment of Scott was destructive, but

I think that they just didn't understand it. Zelda never wanted to destroy Scott; she just wanted him to live up to the potential she saw in him. She expected him to be brave, charming, intelligent and suave. She expected the world from him. She had fallen in love with him because she had truly believed him capable of delivering the world to her, but she had overestimated her man. Poor Scott, he loved Zelda enough to try to live up to her expectations, but she wasn't interested in mere attempts and she had no pity for failure, she had no pity for Scott.

I remember one night in particular. We were out, the three of us. We had gone dancing and Zelda had insisted I accompany her to monitor her progress. We had gone to the Jockey, the Jungle and to Bricktop's, but Zelda wasn't happy with any of them. The music was too slow, the crowd too dense, the atmosphere just too, too dreary. We had been out for hours and we were drunk. We were in the Select drinking beer because it was hot and because Zelda was undecided about where to try next. We were having a good time, well I was. I was sitting silently, clamping my mouth shut on the melody of my accent, and I was listening. Scott was berating two passing Americans, describing them as 'average fools'. 'Average' was his new insult and he thought it dreadfully funny; so did Zelda. She was laughing along until suddenly she tilted her head back, drained her glass and slammed it hard back on the table.

'We never swim!' she wailed out. 'I haven't swum in months. At home I used to swim all the time.' She looked straight at Scott when she said that and her eyes were filled with a challenge I didn't understand. I wasn't to know that she expected Scott to fill every hole her absent home had burned into her heart. She turned to me then.

'At home I would swim every night,' she said wistfully. 'I would dive deep into the black water, barely rippling the circle of the moon. I would lie flat on my back and float and above me, the sky, filled with stars, would stretch and bend to the horizon. I would lie there on the echo of the moon and, all around me, the reflected stars would wink straight back up at themselves, and I was one of them, an image looking for my soul in the sky. Now I never swim.'

No one answered her; there was nothing to say.

'But tonight I will,' she shouted, jumping to her feet, knocking over her chair. 'Tonight we'll swim in the city. Come on, Scott, we've never done that before. Oh, it will be perfect. We'll swim in the reflection of limelight.' And she was gone.

We followed close behind her, ran screaming down the street after her, laughing, thinking that it was all a joke. She was headed straight for the river, running right down the middle of the road. Passers-by stepped out of her way, traffic swerved, drinkers and late-night diners paused conversations, craning their necks to follow her progress. When she reached the Seine we stopped laughing. She kicked off her shoes, slowly pulled her dress over her head and stepped up to the water's edge. Dark, black, murky, dirty depths rushing past, slapping off the walls – and she was poised to jump. A straggling crowd gasped and Scott cried out, 'For god's sake, Zelda, don't!'

She turned around, pretended to teeter backwards and laughed right in Scott's face, 'Will you jump after me? Will you swim with me or save me?'

'For god's sake,' was the only answer he could give, and it was nothing. No match for her drama, no climax to her scene. Even I could see she had no choice, she turned and bent her knees on a jump, Scott was just in time, he grabbed her by the waist.

'For god's sake, let's go home,' he said, and so they did.

CHAPTER 21

For the most part I dealt exclusively with Zelda. I was her dance coach and so was in her employ. Not that I didn't have anything to do with Scott. As I have said I would read to him every now and again. Sometimes I would run errands for him and once I did him one great service that severed my connection with both of them for good. I witnessed a scene so humiliating that it rendered even my inconsequential presence embarrassingly painful.

Scott wanted to visit the celebrated Edith Wharton. All the biographers write about this, the great, grand meeting of minds, and over the years I've read many versions. Some come close, but none are mine. I should have written all this down, Mother. Shouldn't I have? It would have blasted your story about the nuns clear into the sordid truth, but what would have been gained? One more badly written memoir. Bill's dull, dependable love was worth way more than that.

Anyway, Scott and Wharton, the two greats. Scott, Wharton and little ol' me. It happened like this.

Scott and Wharton had met once before and, although Scott told the story as if it was an anecdote he was proud of, something about his way of telling it never sat easy. He and Wharton both shared a publisher, the great Charles Scribner, and they had met in his office.

Scott had burst in on Wharton and Scribner while they were having a meeting and had flung himself at Edith's feet, howling about her genius, about how he was not worthy to stand in the presence of the author of *Ethan Frome*. That was the story that Scott told and that much of it sounded fine, a little unfinished, but fine. I heard him tell it a few times and every time some one would ask, 'What did she say? What did Scribner say?'

Scott never answered. I got the impression that that great lady of letters and manners may have merely reached for his hand and asked him how he did. That Mr Scribner may have, very politely, shown him to the door. Of course I could have been wrong. Maybe Edith Wharton had flushed red with the charm of the compliment. Can't you just see her patting her hairdo and simpering with the joy of it? Maybe she even said something along the lines of, 'Oh you flatterer, you!'

Maybe Scribner had interjected with a hearty, 'Boys will be boys, eh? What ho?'

But I doubt it because Scott seemed desperate to meet with Edith Wharton again. He obviously felt that she owed him some ground. At the time she was living outside Paris and so Scott made it his business to make contact. He sent her a copy of *The Great Gatsby* and it worked. She wrote him a letter detailing her admiration of the work and inviting him to visit her to discuss it further. Zelda had no interest in going.

'All those hats and all that conversation, wouldn't you rather just die?' she asked and Scott shrugged.

'Guess you would,' he said.

And so Scott was to go alone to meet the great Wharton. She had invited him to her château for lunch and Scott was nervous. He set about drinking the night before and kept at it. Then, just as soon as the day was bright enough to call it that, he packed himself neatly into his Renault and fell fast asleep. Zelda was with him and it was she who decided I should drive him. I was due to teach her that afternoon, but she had long since been bored by my lessons.

She pulled the car up on to the path outside my flat and Scott leaned his elbow on the horn. Eventually I woke up, and looked out, and then, still in my night clothes with my hair and senses still blurred by sleep, I ran down to them.

'We're off to visit the wonderful Wharton for lunch,' Scott called out as soon as I appeared within shouting distance. 'But if the natives prove friendly we may settle down for the night.'

'We'll pay you extra,' Zelda said. She climbed out of the car and tossed me the keys. And then, without any further instruction, she walked away. Scott blew her a kiss and settled straight back down to sleep.

'I can't drive,' I called out to no one.

And that was just the start of the day.

It took a while. I made Scott some coffee, brought it down to him in the car. I fumbled through his pockets and took enough money for a baguette and some cheese, which he ate slowly. I eventually persuaded him to freshen up in the toilets of a nearby café and finally he woke into the moment, but only so far as to instruct me.

'I can't turn up looking like crap,' he said. 'You drive and I'll sleep, I'll be ready for them then.'

'But I can't drive,' I said again, and once again this trifle was ignored. It's a way the rich have of dealing with the world – they disregard the details that stand in their way. Scott didn't answer, just curled himself up in the passenger seat and settled down for a sleep.

I had no choice but to prove my incompetence, so I got into the driving seat, fiddled with the controls and, drawing on the little I'd learned from Phil on the two occasions he had allowed me take the wheel, I bumped us down on to the street and through the city.

I expected Scott to be jolted awake and into action, but he just continued in his stubborn refusal to acknowledge my incompetence while I, white-knuckled, sweat-drenched and terrified, lurched us from one near miss to the next.

'Turn here,' he would murmur occasionally. 'Head south,' he sighed before settling into rhythmic snoring. And so we drove south and the countryside, rich and green and deep, dark yellow, waved over and around Scott's jerking car. It was easier out of the city, far easier. The empty road, the clear warm air, the long-forgotten rustle of foliage and flutter of birds were calming. I was almost beginning to enjoy myself when Scott roused himself.

'Fancy a drink?' he asked. It was barely ten.

'Don't you think it's too early?' I answered, trying to sound light.

'Either too early or too late, depends on which direction you approach it from,' he said, and there was no arguing with that.

He leaned across me then, grabbed the wheel and swerved so sharply that I bruised my shoulder against the car door. We stopped in front of a small, dusty café. It was the first of too many stops. I drank water and Scott drank whisky, his eye fixed on the bottle behind the counter as he drained his glass. That was the code of the cafés; it meant that once he set his empty glass down on the bar it would be refilled. In the third place I rested my hand on his arm, but he just lifted my hand with his drink.

'We'll be late,' I said.

'Then ring them and warn them,' he growled, slapping a crumpled piece of paper with a number on it on the bar, and so I did. The man who took my message was perfectly polite about it all and I suddenly knew that Scott was making a horrible mistake. The telephone was at the end of the bar and, while I was on it, I could see Scott reach across to the barman and ask him for a kiss.

'Come, on garçon,' he was saying. 'Look at me! All puckered up and nowhere to go.'

Scott was asking for a fight. He was brimful of anger and frustration, desperate to prove himself somehow, but the barman was a big man who didn't feel the need to pitch himself against another man's insecurities and so he just laughed, and the fight had to stay in Scott. By the time we arrived at Edith Wharton's château, the Château de Saint-Brice, the fight filled him and there was nothing anyone could do about it, least of all Scott.

We were far too late for lunch. Wharton had invited two other couples and the party had had time to settle together. They had eaten together and, when we burst in on them, they were sitting in a tidy little group, arched around a pretty fireplace at the sunnier end of a delicate drawing room, happily digesting together. The room we were shown into was dense with social niceties with everyone knowing their role, and everyone enjoying the play. We stood by the door – me dressed as a daytime whore, the only way I knew how to dress, and Scott with the fight in his stance and the dirt of the drive on his clothes. He called for a whisky.

'A drink after that journey would go down grand,' he said, but the man who had opened the door to us ignored him.

'Mr Fitzgerald,' Edith Wharton stood up and positively glided over to us. She was perfect in manners and dress. 'Let me introduce you,' she said.

I immediately forgot the names; they weren't familiar to me although I think they should have been. The other guests certainly acted as if their names alone were used to commanding respect.

'And your friend?' Edith asked after she had done her part. But Scott just ignored her question, leaving me to introduce myself and so I did. I just gave my name, I attached no relationship to it; no one asked for one, but there was a short pause after I spoke, a little rustle of understanding before Edith gently linked us both and walked us to our seats. I was a nobody and have been recorded as such. How many times have I read about Scott and his 'female companion' making fools of themselves before the great Wharton?

'Your book, Mr Fitzgerald, has caused quite a stir amongst us,' she said, and her guests murmured enthusiastically. 'We were discussing it over lunch; such a pity you were delayed. Perhaps you would care for something to eat now?'

It was a lovely little dig at our manners, but Scott was in no mood for nuances.

'I'd kill a highball,' was all he said, and that killed all pretence of small talk. He got his drink, tossed it back, and refused to sit down. Instead he stood in front of the empty fireplace facing the ring of guests with his legs spread, his shoulders squared and his chin thrust forward.

'So, Mr Fitzgerald, are you working on anything now?' one of the well-dressed ladies asked, and Scott sneered out his answer.

'The writer is always working. All experience is writing. Facing you now I am writing. When I put this scene on to paper that's just the final step.'

'How interesting. So should we expect to be in your next novel?' another asked lightly.

'Doubtful, I write about real life. The realities of life.'

'And is this not a reality?' This time it was Wharton asking the question and Scott should have been warned by the sweetness of her tone, but he wasn't.

'Living here? Eating lunch and talking literature? No. This is escapism and that's the coward's way out,' he said loudly, too loudly.

'I see,' was all Wharton said, almost whispered.

'What can you learn here?' Scott continued, balling his words up into his fight, sweeping his empty glass over the room. 'How to arrange flowers? How to sew? How to dabble in watercolours? How to doctor the cruelties of life? There is no blood here, no sweat, and the artist needs both to produce anything of worth.'

'Or maybe all that bleeding and all that sweating merely dilutes the artist's energies. Maybe if his physical needs are served his mental faculties are freed.' Wharton answered, keeping her voice ominously low and sweet, but still Scott wasn't going to be warned; he just shouted on.

'No, an artist thrives on energy. Energy creates energy. Energy expended – why that's just a way to make room for more energy. All life uses energy, it's just that you've forgotten that 'cos this isn't living. Stuck out here you don't get to see anything, you don't get to know what's going on, what the new movements are or…or anything like that.'

I tried to stop him there. It was a pathetic effort, but I did try.

'That's a lovely brooch you have, Mrs Wharton,' I said, and she smiled at me.

'Thank you,' she said, but both her answer and her smile just served to silence me completely. 'Mr Fitzgerald,' she continued. 'You may have a point, but I think you are just accusing me of ageing. It is right that I am not now so much in the world and it is right that I should not be. Now is your time; it is my time to step away.'

'Age is no excuse,' Scott slurred back. 'You can be in the world and be poor, or old, or sick, or anything, but still be in the world. All you gotta do is continue to make the effort. You should come back up to the city with us, come see what's new to write about, find yourself some stories.'

'And do you think that stories only happen in the cities?' Wharton asked. 'Is human nature not made up out of the urban and the rustic, the social and the reclusive? Aren't we as much about beauty as we are about blood? But maybe you are right, maybe I am falling asleep a little here.'

She was a good hostess. She was pulling her argument in on purpose; she could see that Scott was no match for her and so to destroy him in her parlour would be dreadfully impolite. It would almost be as bad-mannered as arriving drunk, three hours late for lunch, with a whore dangling on your arm.

'Yeah, yeah you are.' Scott said triumphantly. He was drunk enough to think that he had won. 'Stories happen in the country, all right, but they're always the same old stories. They never shock, or teach anything like stories, really *good* stories, should.'

'Is it important to shock?' One of Wharton's guests took up the challenge.

'Yeah, 'course it is if it makes people think or see things different. People should never get complacent – they should always be made to question things. For example… Well, I could tell you all a story that would shock you, make you all think a little but…well… It's just it's a little racy. Don't know if I should, mixed company an' all.'

'Oh, please, Mr Fitzgerald. Please feel free to tell us your story. I will take full responsibility for any offence incurred,' Edith said and her tone had firmed up by now. It was hard with angry contempt, but Scott was way past noticing.

'OK then,' he said, shuffling his stance a little, squaring up to the climax of this drawing-room brawl. And then out it came, one more neat example of his middle-class mores.

'OK then here goes, you've been warned, can't say I didn' warn you. So, thing is, I gotta friend and he came to Paris with his wife. They didn't know the city, had nowhere to stay an' were kinda a bit on the skids, money-wise you know. So, anyway, they check into this cheap hotel, cheapest they could find an'…' He stopped there to try and drink from his empty glass. Wharton signalled for it to be filled for him and the room waited until it was. No one said a word, and I could tell that Scott saw this as a good thing. He thought that he had them all in the palm of his hand.

'Well, anyway,' he continued, as soon as he had taken a real drink, 'the two love birds stayed quite happy in their lil' nest for a while, but then they got to thinking that something was a bit not on the up an' up. Seemed to them that the place was a lil' bit too quiet during the day, but hell was it busy all night long! Busy with a lotta check-ins – lotsa guests with no luggage, if you catch my drift. An' then they gotta noticing that all the ladies they saw hangin' about all looked kinda familiar, but the men were always different. But hell these kids were jus' up from the sticks somewhere, they didn' know what was what an' so it didn' worry them none. It wasn't 'til they met some folks out around the bars an' they asked them about their hotel that they found out that they were… in fact…stayin' in a brothel.'

He took a dramatic gulp of his drink and then just stood, waiting for a reaction. But nothing came. Instead there was an expectant silence. Very soon it became obvious, even to Scott, that the gathering was waiting for him to finish his story, to come to the punchline.

'They were living in a brothel,' he repeated lamely, and Edith Wharton nodded before asking politely, as if she was trying to prompt Scott on with his anecdote, 'And did they not like it?'

'How much did it cost? Was it much cheaper than an ordinary hotel?' One of the other ladies asked and her friend answered for Scott.

'I think his point was that his friends didn't approve. They must have been religious. Were they?' Scott slumped backwards into a chair before muttering, 'Not really.'

'Then were the girls very noisy at night?' One of the gentlemen asked and the other said, 'Well at least those places are usually clean.'

It went on and on like that and the worst was that Scott knew that they were all just trying to be nice. They were just trying to make some sense out of his shocking story. We left very soon after that. Wharton walked us to our car and, as Scott got in, she held her hand out to him.

'Don't feel too bad,' she said. 'Just remember that the reason we are old is because we have lived longer than you. We have already witnessed our stories and suffered our shocks.'

Scott drove away without answering. He knew that her words of comfort weren't said to make him feel any better, they were said to prove what a perfect hostess she was. He didn't speak for a long time and when he did it was only to say, 'They beat me, JoJo, they beat me.'

He dropped me as soon as we hit the city. Drove away without saying anything. I turned up at their flat the following Tuesday for my lesson with Zelda but was told that the couple were out. I tried again the following week and was told the same. I never did get paid for my day out with Scott.

CHAPTER 22

Ruth didn't drive to the airport to collect Ellen. Ellen had rung the previous week saying that she would like to come home to see Grandma again. Ruth had explained that it was quite pointless at this stage and that maybe it would be expensive, or difficult for work if Ellen was planning on coming home for the funeral as well.

'Should be OK,' Ellen answered. 'I might stay on for a bit this time.' There was a break in her voice that Ruth didn't probe. Instead she explained why Ellen couldn't be collected from the airport. The flight was due in late on Friday afternoon, Brian would still be at work and Ruth said that she would be just too busy.

'But Friday rush-hour traffic,' Ellen whinged. That was the word, Ruth thought to herself, 'whinging', and then she said it, 'Stop whinging.' And she said it as she felt it, firm and exasperated. The rest of her explanation was placatory, but the damage had been done. 'I just don't have the time, love,' she said. 'I'll be in with your grandma all morning and then Catherine and her lot and Isabel are coming for dinner, and maybe Deirdre too. I can't do it all, and sure there are loads of buses.'

'I'll have to get two buses,' Ellen moaned and Ruth chose not to respond. But she had been right. By the time Friday evening came she was badly pushed for time. She had spent the morning with her mother, listening, consoling, muttering those coos of comfort that the old woman seemed to respond to. Deirdre had arrived just as she was leaving,

'Any change?' she had asked, settling herself at a distance from the bed, magazine open on her lap.

'No,' Ruth stroked her fingers one more time through her mother's balding hair. 'She's on about Scott Fitzgerald now. You were right, her favourites have won through.'

'So is she Daisy from *The Great Gatsby* or what's-her-name from *Tender is the Night*?' Deirdre laughed, 'God but she's got some opinion of herself, it was always there though beneath all that false modesty.' Ruth let it lie, there would be too many arguments if she picked Deirdre up on everything.

'You and Mark still coming to dinner?' she asked instead, unnecessarily.

'Of course. Is that OK?'

And it was. Family dinners always ran a little smoother with Deirdre there. Everyone stayed a little longer at the table, made a little more of an effort at general conversation and, afterwards, Ruth could be guaranteed of some company in the kitchen. It did mean she was cooking for eight adults, though, and so she felt severely under pressure. It was after four by the time she got in and, from upstairs, she could hear the drone of Isabel on the phone; she was always on the phone.

'I'm back,' she called up the stairs. 'When you're ready come down and give me a hand.' It took twenty minutes, but Isabel did finally arrive and between them things got done – roasting meat, steaming potatoes, cheeses unpacked, wine chilled, table set. It was enjoyable and, without even noticing it, Ruth had started to hum, some old Dylan song, 'Idiot Wind' it was.

'Mum!' Isabel laughed and Ruth laughed back.

'God, you know, love, that hospital really takes it out of you. Do you know what I fancy before they all arrive? A cigarette and a swift bottle of beer.'

'Mum!' And this time Isabel really laughed.

They sat out in the cold of the garden together giggling. It was fun. It made up for how sick that first cigarette in thirty-odd years made Ruth feel.

Catherine, Simon, children and paraphernalia were the first to arrive. Ruth let Isabel greet and arrange them; she was whipping cream and didn't stop when they all jumbled into the kitchen together. Catherine looked tired. The baby was wriggling in her arms, arching his back, resenting the change from the comfort of the car.

'Swap you,' Ruth said and handed the beaters to Catherine while she took the baby. She was good with babies, had him soothed and calm in a few moments. But she stayed on sitting at the table, holding him close, rocking gently and directing the ongoing preparations for the dinner. Even Simon stayed in the kitchen, away from the television, propped up against the fridge, beer in hand, awkwardly in the way. Leah leaned by her Grandmother's knee, silently staring, sucking her thumb, and Ruth was warmed by how proud she felt.

Ellen was the last to arrive. Still a little sullen from the trip, but easily bribed with the comfort of food and family. Dinner went well. Ruth watched Brian carve the slab of meat she had roasted, an old familiar sight now. Her father had done the same. When herself and Deirdre had been young, they had watched as the girls did now, and although the trite, related jokes were slightly different, the flavour of the scene was generations old.

'Taken the spring right out of this poor sheep's step we have,' Brian said, as he always did when faced with a leg of lamb, and this time Ruth joined in with the girls' laughter.

Conversation rattled away – even Mark made more of an effort than usual – and Simon was either actually interested in those boring anecdotes or too good an actor for it to matter.

Afterwards, in the kitchen with Deirdre, Ruth heard the girls laughing from outside in the hall. Deirdre looked at her a little ruefully and Ruth shrugged, 'I was just being silly,' she said. 'Sure they'd laugh at anything.'

'We're off now, Mum,' Catherine called and Ruth went out to say her goodbyes. She kissed them all.

'Take care now,' she said as she handed baby Jack back. 'Trust me, love, I've done this a few times and I can tell he's hardy enough by now to let his Mum get a full night's sleep. You'll be no use to anyone if you let yourself get sick.'

Catherine just nodded, looked to Simon to see if he'd heard, and almost seemed relieved.

Isabel was staying over for the night. The house felt full, rooms lit upstairs, voices and steps clattering up and down the stairs. Later, as the night closed in, while the others sat in watching television, Ruth stayed at the kitchen table, drinking that one glass of wine too many, flicking through a magazine, the dishwasher droning a mantra in her head.

'This isn't enough,' she thought to herself, and for the first time the admission didn't hurt or harm her. Instead it filled her with something close to hope.

CHAPTER 23

Time always moves on, it's just when you're young, for a while you move with it so you don't notice, but it moves for the young too, taking people, places and potential with it. And it took those with potential away from me. It got so that I didn't see much of the Hemingways any more. Funny, I never really read Hemingway. Of course I read all about him but when you don't like the man it's hard to like the work. And I didn't really like the man, but I suppose I didn't really know him well. No need to look so surprised, not in that way, Mother dear! Though I don't suppose he'd have turned me down.

He was going places and once he got there that was no place for the likes of me. And where he went Hadley went too. They were away a lot and when they were about they brought the mood down. People were beginning to take notice of Ernest's writing and he was all puffed up and unbearable. I found him hard to be around, especially when Hadley and Bumby, his son, were with him. Hemingway suited the casual dowdiness of his clothes. He looked good in the shabby costumes he insisted that he and his family should wear; they added that realistic touch of grit to his persona. But Hadley? She just looked old and Bumby looked sick. I hated seeing them looking like that, especially knowing what I knew, what Flossie Martin had told us all, about Ernest and Pauline Pfeiffer.

It was getting so that I didn't much like Paris any more. The decade, the city, had moved away from me. In the beginning we had all been nothing together – just so much potential – but the years had separated us. Those who had made it moved on socially and financially and the rest of us just aged. The Paris winters, the fear of the flu, the bad food and the long nights were all gathering about my eyes. I was still young, only in my early twenties, but I was finding it harder and harder to trade on my looks and, in my profession, that was a big disadvantage.

Over the years my steady clients began to fall away. For a while I was doing it all wrong; I was still working the way Peggy Hopkins had advised me to, but she had advised a much younger girl. I was still practising my modest act, smiling at the world with my pretty-girl smile, looking at my clients through my pretty-girl eyes, but no one was falling for it any more. It took me a long time to realise that to come across as credible I would have to drag my act down a little deeper, that I would have to match my lines to the wrinkles that had gathered around my eyes. I was in Berlin when I finally discovered this but, for a long while before then, I was poor, cold during the winter, very often hungry and very rarely sober. I found that it was easier and cheaper to get warm and rested with alcohol rather than go to all the expense and bother of making a meal and lighting a fire.

I seemed to have fewer and fewer friends. There were the girls of the quarter, but they were no joy – every bit as broke as me and every bit as bitter. The bright young things who cheered up our evenings with their generosity and who glittered up our lives with their glamour weren't around so much. They just stopped by every now and again on their way to the mountains, or to the festivals in Spain, or to the beaches of the Riviera and, in between visits, us forgotten ones sat pretty dismal in our own company.

I never saw Picasso any more. I still took the time to track him down, but he didn't have any time for me, and I very rarely saw McAlmon – and whenever I did it hurt. Although we had never really been very close, we had always managed to drag some fun out of the times we spent together, but not any more. I remember nights trailing after him from bar to bar, nightclub to nightclub and all the time he'd be searching for someone, someone bigger and brighter than every passing face. Sometimes he'd have a name for this person and he'd start a hunt for Kay Boyle or Laurance Vail or Djuna Barnes. Other times he'd just admit that he was looking for someone else, but he was always looking.

I suppose we were all looking for something. The trouble with me, and Robert, and all the others like us, was that we didn't know what we were looking for. People like Hemingway knew, though. He knew that he could never be a better writer than McAlmon, but he also knew that he was looking to be the best of his generation and so he didn't waste his time looking for fun, or oblivion, or any kind of meaning in it all.

And during all this time I was still working in Bricktop's, and the Jockey and the Jungle. I still turned up most nights. I still wore my short, fringed dress and I could still send those tassels flying. But my heart wasn't in it any more. There had been too many nights, too many men, too much fun, and now every flicker of interest, every well-mixed cocktail, just served to remind me of all those fine old times, when the nights were brighter and I was younger. When sweet Claudette stood laughing by my side, or when honest Phil Anderson Junior stood strong behind me. I had had just about enough of it all. I began day-dreaming of Fountainbleau and night-maring about my parents' house. I needed to get out of Paris for a while and I was open to any alternative. It was Hilaire Hiler's father who provided me with one.

We all called him Papa Hiler; he had that look and he had that way about him. He was a grand old man of entertainment, with friends and contacts in every seedy show on the road, in every battered small-town theatre. He could tell you urban tales that matched Damon Runyon's for wit and charm, and he was an expert on the history of vaudeville. He told it like a family tree, linking acts down generations – and he knew the circus. He came drinking in the Jungle one night with Hans Kaufman.

'JoJo!' he called to me after my act. 'Come meet my friend. My friend wants to talk to you.'

'He doesn't have to talk much,' I answered, all low and lazy. 'All he's gotta say is please.'

'No, no, he really wants to talk,' Hiler said, shaking his head reprovingly at me. It was an embarrassing start, but pretty soon we were getting along fine, me and Hans Kaufman.

'My name's Hans,' he said, smothering my hand in his giant paw. 'So, call me Hans, OK, baby doll face? Yes sir, we got no bananas.'

Hans Kaufman loved all things American. He was a big man, maybe sixty years old, but it was hard to tell. His hair was white, but his face never stayed still long enough for anyone to count his wrinkles and he had the sort of body that you just knew wouldn't lie down to die. He was always moving, working us all by his example. And by us all I mean his circus troupe, the one that I joined.

'You dance real fine, doll face,' Hans said to me that first night. 'You come dance with me, give all the guys a foxy cute lady to look at, OK?' His accent was so thick I had to look to Papa Hiler for a translation but, even after I got that, I still had to ask for further clarification.

'He runs a circus, a good circus,' Papa Hiler explained, 'and he's looking for a dancer. A bit of light relief between acts.' Hans nodded enthusiastically.

'Yeah, yeah, doll face,' he said. 'Some real foxy dancing, maybe sometimes with fire? Sometimes with knives?'

'Maybe not,' I said as firmly as I could, but still his face brightened into a smile, just as if we had struck a bargain.

'Yeah, maybe not,' he agreed, then he spat into his hand and held it out. It seemed the right thing to do so I took it.

I went to follow up on this deal the following day. Hans had directed me to some wasteground south of Montparnasse cemetery and there they were; a rag-and-bone collection of post-war Europeans. Eight caravans and twelve horses, the charred remains of maybe four fires, a few dirty children and some crumpled adults. A girl about my age was scratching her back against a tree, her loose dress riding higher with every downward movement, and an old man was urinating onto the wheel of a rusting van.

I had arrived in a taxi and my driver took one look at the group and offered to wait for me. I thanked him and then, screwing all my street smarts into a twist of bravery, I got out of the car and started to cross the field, carefully avoiding the filth of the horses. It only took me a few steps before

I realised that I was making a mistake and I was just about to turn and head back to my cab when a small piece of circus magic unfolded around me.

From out of nowhere it seemed a man appeared. He walked like an old man with his head lowered and his body lumbering heavily along. He was a clown, dressed in tatters and coloured handkerchiefs with his face painted monstrously sad. His skin was pure white, his blackened eyes seemed hollowed out by the pain of his art, and his mouth was blood red and drooping. An elephant was plodding along behind him, shadowing his movements, head lowered and body heavy. The elephant's trunk was lying across the clown's shoulders and I got the impression that it was the elephant that was leading the man. They walked straight towards me. I called out to them once they were within earshot, but I was ignored. They just walked on, coming closer and closer. I started back-stepping, stumbling backwards towards the road.

'No,' I said. 'Stop. No!' I shouted out, but they still ignored me. I tried moving out of their path, swerving left and right, but every way I turned they turned, bearing down on me. I heard my taxi driver call out, but then the elephant roared and I could hear the thud of a car door slamming and then the squealing spurt of an engine as he drove off without me. I stopped then; I had nowhere to go. So I stpped and stood facing them; the clown, the elephant and, behind them, the wild-eyed stares of that ragged snatch of humanity that had begun to cluster together. They were moving now, following the action, heading straight for me.

'What? What do you want?' I shouted as bravely as I could. 'Hans Kaufman asked me to come. I'm here to see him.'

But still no one answered me; they just kept moving forward in waves, the clown, the elephant and, behind them, all the rest.

They all shuffled, surged, towards me and, as if hypnotised, I surrendered. I stopped shouting or questioning and just stayed still, watching and waiting. The clown finally stopped when the toes of his busted out boots touched the tips of my battered pumps and then, behind him, the elephant stopped, and then, behind it, all movement, muttered conversations and rustling activity stopped. There was a moment when I swear even the air stopped and, for that moment, I faced thirty, quiet people facing in me in naked silence. I was past expecting anything when the clown finally raised his bent head.

'How do, foxy doll face!' he said, and I laughed, a good big honest laugh, and so did everyone else.

I was invited to that evening's entertainment and that was the first time I had ever been to a circus. I had seen snatches of it in Picasso's work, but that night I realised that to see a real circus was to see Picasso's canvases stretched over your head and to watch as their contents spilled out into the ring. For me the circus was every cliché of wonder come true. A truly spectacular world filled with gaudy, glittering tinsel, discordant, terrifying music, earthy, mucky smells and outlandish sights that tricked your reason and reached for your long-forgotten naïveté. It was that that charmed me – a chance to believe in magic again. Girls could fly, balls could disappear, animals could dance and I could one day, maybe, wake up by a man who expected nothing more from me than his morning coffee, his goodnight kiss. After the show, still breathless with wonder, I went looking for Hans.

'Hey, doll face!' he shouted out to me as soon as he saw me. 'You like, you come. Say no, you go.'

'I like, I come.' I answered and he hugged me. He offered to show me around then, to introduce me to the others, but I said that I had to leave. I was afraid that if I stayed the wonder would fall away. I already sensed that it was crumbling. I had already seen that the lights that sparkled that wasteground alive had not fallen from the night sky but instead were all, rather messily, feeding off a dirty, belching generator.

I didn't see Hans again until I left Paris with him four days later. I left Paris that quickly. It was coming into the start of another summer, and I was delighted for an excuse to escape all those dreary, empty months. That's all I thought I was doing – getting out for a bit – and so I didn't bother too much with goodbyes.

I spent my last night in Paris in the Dôme with Kiki and Flossie and we drank to it all. Glasses raised and heads held high, we sang and cheered, refused to reminisce, refused to talk about tomorrow, and so said nothing of any real worth but created one perfectly independent memory. Whenever I think of Flossie I like to think of her on that night, so big and blowsy, one arm around Kiki and one flung out to the world.

I stayed up all that night and spent the early morning hours packing. It didn't take me long; I didn't have that much. The clothes that Phil had bought for me were long gone. I still had my gold coverlet, though, and I took that with me. I left my kiln rug, my linen, my cushions, my throws and my tea set behind. I trusted them to Yvonne, a friend who agreed to move into my room and mind it while I was away. I wonder how long she stayed there. The last time I saw her I was in a cinema in Ireland and she appeared as a chorus girl, high-kicking her way out on a tentacle in one of Busby Berkeley's spectaculars. At least I think it was her.

It was very early when I pulled the door shut behind me and, for the last time, dragged myself down that dirty stairwell, and so I walked away from it all, a battered suitcase weighing one arm low and a rolled up coverlet tucked awkwardly under the other.

CHAPTER 24

The circus as an adventure is one thing; the circus as a way of life is quite another. It was never a way of life for me. To me it was always magical, a breath of charm in the grim, grey reality of life. But for true circus people reality is made up out of charm, and magic, and all the shadows that lie in their folds. They told me that I would never understand this because I was not born to the circus and they found this out on my very first day.

On that day, my first one, I rode with Mama. She was a large, elderly lady with great, strong arms and hard, grey hair. She had quite a heavy moustache and one very hairy mole. I never saw her perform but still she was an integral part of the group. She did some sewing, some cooking; she drank a great deal and knew a lot about birth control. Her caravan was one of the brighter ones; it was painted red, yellow, and green and was hung with silk roses that were blackened from the dust of the roads. When I arrived at the wasteland south of Montparnasse Cemetery, she was already sitting up behind her horse, a set of reins loose in her hand and an unlit pipe hanging from the corner of her mouth. Everyone else was running way behind Hans's orders, gestures and curses. None of them had time for me and so I crossed over to Mama.

'I'm JoJo,' I said, hoping she would understand. She didn't look at me and she didn't remove her pipe.

'Step up,' she said, and so I did. 'You will ride with me today and you will sleep in my caravan tonight.'

Her English was fluent, but she spoke with a heavy, sluggish accent. I thanked her but she didn't respond. I commented on the day, on the performance I had seen, on the journey ahead, but still she never answered. And so I tried sitting still and quiet for a while, but I was too nervous to keep that up for long.

'Your English is very good,' I said, after only a short pause, she didn't reply. 'Where are you from?' I asked. And then she slowly turned to face me and, keeping her pipe perfectly still between her lips, said, 'You are not of the circus. You are not born to it.'

'I can learn,' I answered defensively.

'No, you cannot.' she said firmly. 'No one can learn the circus. You ask me where I am from? I am from the circus. If you were of the circus you would have no need or words for such a question – you would just sit quiet by Mama and know that you have come home.'

She wasn't trying to be hurtful, her tone was almost friendly; she was just telling me how it was. Then she lowered her reins and carefully removed her pipe. She put both on her broad lap and asked for my hand. I held it out to her and she turned it so the palm was facing upwards.

Out of the corner of my eye I could see a few people gather around us, their arms filled with bundles and their faces still set on their chores. They were just lingering by, curious to witness the outcome of what they knew was coming. Mama cleared her throat and coughed up some phlegm right into my palm. I tried pulling my hand away, but she held it firm; she was staring straight into the mess she had spit up.

'No!' she said loudly and the few who had gathered moved on without commenting on what they had seen.

'What did you do that for?' I barked at her. 'That's disgusting. I'll have to wash my hand.' I felt prissy, and angry and ridiculed. With my one clean hand I was rummaging through my bag trying to find a handkerchief. Finally Mama handed me a rag.

'I was just checking if I was wrong but I wasn't, you are not of the circus.'

Later I was told that if Mama spat some dust onto your palm it meant that you had the grit it took for the life; if she didn't you hadn't. It was a test that no one questioned and maybe they were right not to. They were certainly right about me. The circus was never more than an adventure to me.

I remember it in extremes: very busy, very tired, very hot and very cold. I remember the roar and clatter of movement; the sharp spit of stones split under heavily weighted wheels, the grumble of our one ancient engine pulling more than its capacity, the rhythm of horses' hooves, the thump of leather against flank, the howl, and whinny, and restless pawing of caged animals, the strange snatches of songs and curses, the high good humour and the earthenware jug of whisky weaving its way through it all.

I remember how the necessities of life suddenly loomed impossible. Water was always an issue, water and heat. Every day we would have to work to fill our water containers and gather enough firewood for warmth, and cooking, and washing.

And I remember the weather: cool and bright during those early mornings in summer, before the dust and the heat would clog the air. And I remember crisp autumn days when your skin would tingle with a taste of winter even though the sun was still shining, but then the nights were so cold, and winter was so hard. Winter blistered your feet and hands with chilblains; it kept you awake at night huddled close to a stove, half your body roasting and half freezing, and it exhausted your days. So much effort was spent trying to get warm or keep warm there was very little time for anything else. I remember my shoulders froze into a tense huddle, I don't know if my posture ever recovered; my dancing certainly didn't.

The weather matters when you are in it all day and all night. When it rains it rains on you and when the sun shines it shines on you, it all becomes personal. It comes down to you and the elements, and there's no one but your god to curse. So curses matter then too. I learned a rake of them during my time with the troupe, a curse for all seasons.

But still, no matter what the weather, every evening on the road was a party. We would light a triangle of fires and pick the hottest one to cook on. Food always tasted good, god knows why; black burnt scraps of meat floating in a stew of greens and vegetables. Maybe it was the greens that did it. Mama always produced them. During the day's journey she would collect an assortment of leaves and bright little flowers to add to whatever grey mess was in our dinner pot.

Then, after dinner, on the stretch of ground bounded by our fires, we would dance and sing and play our instruments; a lute, a trumpet, a drum, an accordion and a saw. We would tumble and balance, eat fire, juggle, play with knives and clown. And then, when we were all tired out, we would talk.

There were always some great stories to be told – high old tales of Russian aristocracy or wild romances of Romanian peasantry.

These nights were our luxury; a lot of hard work went into maintaining them. On the road, in between towns, in between shows, we were all up at five in the morning. The night before we would have erected a practice tent and for the three hours every morning we would rehearse. Well, those who needed to would rehearse – the rest of us would do the packing and cooking and see to the animals. As well as the elephant and the horses we had a python and a zebra.

My role in the performance itself was mainly to look pretty. I looked pretty around knives and I looked pretty handing burning torches to the fire-eater. On my first day Hans had smiled and said, 'Maybe a bit with fire? Maybe knives?'

And I had replied, 'Maybe not.'

But Hans just laughed and so, still protesting, I was put standing up against a board and told not to move as a very dainty little man flung knives at my outline. Once I got used to that the rest was easy. I stood beside the fire-eater pointing and smiling, prompting the crowd's applause and then, for my solo bit, between the animal parade and the trapeze act, I was Pierrot. I found the suit in the wardrobe trunk and insisted on wearing it; Hans had already chosen an Arabian two-piece for me.

'Seven veils, doll face,' he said, waving it before my eyes. 'Some very foxy dancing.'

'Pierrot.' I answered, producing my outfit, and this time I held firm.

Finally Hans agreed to let me try it and, despite the decorum of my costume, my act was a success, so I was allowed to continue with it. The act itself was charmingly simple. I would come out on to the ring in my loose, flopping costume; pure white with four black, soft balls about the size of my fist, hooked over the buttons of the jacket. I would start with a sorrowful little dance played out to the thin wail of the saw and then I would unhook the balls and juggle with them for a bit. Then, while still looking sorrowful, I would make one disappear up my sleeve, or toss one behind my back, or hook one back in place on my jacket. If you work your hands quickly enough that much is easy; the magic of my act was that the music, my expression and my introductory dance all worked to convince the crowd that I was moving the balls very slowly, that their suspension in the air, their disappearance and reappearance were all done in defiance of gravity.

So my act was more of a trick than anything else and everyone knew it. Not that they minded, they knew that showmanship demanded trickery, but the real circus people mixed trickery with talent.

I loved the trapeze in particular. A family, the Kubrikovs, three sisters and a brother, worked that act. They tossed themselves to and fro, twisted and turned somersaults, but what impressed me most about them was the casual way they launched themselves on to the air. Watching them perform I could never rid myself of the suspicion that they could actually fly. The tightrope walker, though, was different; she just terrified me. There was no confidence of movement in her high, unsteady wobble. She would stop every now and then to raise a leg, or lower herself onto her hands and it was part of her act, at some stage, to feign a near fall. No, I much preferred watching the easy confidence of the trapeze artists. Them and the clowns, but then everyone loves the clowns; just like everyone loves a parade.

Before we rolled into a town we would draw up and arrange ourselves into parade formation. I loved being part of this. This was the best part. This was when we polished up our magic into something brighter than the day, something tempting enough to pay for.

Our parade was led by Uri, a long, thin contortionist dressed in a tight, lozenged suit and thigh-high black boots. He was supposed to be the pied piper, but to me he was always Harlequin. He danced ahead of us all, piping out a shrill call to attention. He worked his body around his instrument, caved his shoulders in and drew his knees up high and, as he leapt along, he would roll his eyes from left to right and the all the children would squeal if he as much as glanced in their direction. Then, behind him, came Hans sitting astride his elephant; all dressed up in red and black, his head held high by the folds of his stock, his long whip cracking the road on either side of his beast. And Bessie, the beast, was a glory to behold. She wore a tasselled head-dress and her back was draped with an azure blue numnah trimmed with gold.

Behind Hans came the acrobats and the contortionist, four men dressed in red long johns and tight vests tumbling down the road, rolling over themselves, cart-wheeling, flicking themselves onto their hands and up onto each other's shoulders. Behind them, the girls led the performing animals. Zanya went first with Polly, her python, wrapped around her shoulders and trailing down her back. Then I came, along with three others, all of us wearing nothing much sewn with sequins, all of us leading an animal. I used to lead one of the horses, a high-stepping proud stallion with his fetlocks wrapped in white and feathers woven through his mane. One of the trapeze girls, the tightrope walker and the other half of the contortionist act led the two other performing horses and the zebra.

The two other trapeze girls came after us. The older sister, Lana, led the last performing horse, a white mare with a mane spun through with gold and an ivory horn attached to the centre of its forehead. Dressed in what was supposed to have been my seven-veils costume, Lana guided this animal by a jewel-studded rein while her sister, Anna, stood on its broad back and occasionally folded herself backwards, on to her hands and then around and back onto her feet.

Behind them came the clowns. Two of them would jostle each other for attention and the third, high and imperious on a pair of stilts, would wander off in to the crowd stepping over the heads of the children. Those three clowns combined all the skills of the acrobats and the contortionists with an understanding of the simplicity of theatre and a mastery of mime. Using just their expressions and a minimum of props, they could play out a complete tragic farce. They would pick on members of the crowd, a pretty girl or maybe a child, and work them into some kind of physical narrative. They would try to woo the girl and it would go wrong, or they would try to find a lost child's parents and end up in prison. They also had a very funny routine involving the elaborate pick-pocketing of a gentleman: between the three of them they would just succeed in switching around the contents of his pockets. And they had a host of other jokes as well, they were brilliant mimics, they could imitate any expression or any gesture and so they could perfectly recreate the impression of any famous person. They were always very popular with the crowd and a few people would keep pace with them for the length of the parade just to follow the action of their drama.

Behind the clowns came the fire-eater, Ilya, and the knife-thrower, Georgi. They both wore long black robes buttoned at the neck over bare chests and they both stepped in time, stopping every few yards to perform. Ilya would kneel under his lighted torch and quench it in his mouth, and Georgi would clash the hard metal of two swords together before flinging both high in the air and catching them firmly by their handles.

Behind them came the strong man: a giant, bald peasant with tattoos covering both his arms and his scalp. He wore a loincloth tied in a knot over one shoulder and falling to just where it had to. He brought up the rear of the parade and would usually walk in between the shafts of a caravan, pulling it in place of a horse. Sometimes he would just walk with his dumb-bells, but every now and then he would drop whatever he was holding and, with a roar, run into the crowd, grab a child and hold him, or her, high above his head. Once the children knew that this could happen they would run by his side pleading with him to toss them, and later they would hang around our camp daring each other to provoke him into action.

The caravans followed the strong man. Mama's first; it was Mama's that he would pull, with Mama herself sitting up in the seat throwing sweets out to the crowd. The other caravans would creak along behind, every one driven by a member of the troupe all dressed up in colours and throwing treats. The musicians – the lute-player, drummer, trumpeter and accordionist – would wander through the crowds by our side playing their instruments as loudly as they could, carrying the charm of our spectacle further than the visual, spreading it out into the air, seducing those who were disinterested enough to stay indoors. And finally the circus children, and the rest of the troupe not directly involved with the parade, would run up and down the length of it throwing glitter, ribbons, streamers and petals high into the air, covering us all in colours. And under our feet firecrackers would spark our path; little flashes of magic carrying us along.

The necessities of the show came later: the tent, the lighting, the bench seats and the generator all followed at a distance folded into the back of our one battered old van.

Hans had his route well worked out and, by the time I joined him, he had worked it into a groove. He was well known in a few towns and was welcomed, but maybe he was better known in the others that he avoided. His tour took a full year to complete. He left Germany in February and travelled down to France, through Switzerland, down the west coast of Italy, almost as far as Rome, and then he would cut across to San Marino and from there lead us up the east coast of Italy, into Austria and on back to Germany.

Perhaps Hans found some comfort in spending his winters travelling home. Perhaps he had an economical or a social reason for working his way south during the warm months and heading north as the weather got colder. But whatever his reasons we never questioned them; his charm was such that all of us were just happy to accept his authority.

We travelled by road and rail. We would take a train to a region, then tour a cluster of maybe four or five towns before moving on again. I loved those train rides. We would chain the caravans on to flat cars and berth the animals down in caged cars with plenty of straw and water, then we would berth ourselves down in much the same way, with plenty of straw and enough to eat and drink.

In wintertime those prickly nests of straw were positively cosy but, during the summer, we would keep the doors of our carriages open and sit with our legs dangling down into that rush of movement, just watching the night fly by. We would sing to each other, passing old folk songs up and down the length of the train, spilling those old words out over the landscapes that had inspired them. I remember spending one night alone on one of the flat cars. I sat up against the wheel of a caravan, with my back to the engine, on the last car of the train and so, when I looked straight ahead, into the black gradations of shadow and form, I got the impression that I was being sucked out of the night. It was beautiful but disturbing. I never did it again; I much preferred the prickly comfort of the straw and the warmer comfort of company.

It may sound strange but during those nights, when I lay forgotten, lost in that ethnic mixture, rushing through a foreign country, I felt very much at home. I think I was at home in the universal humanity of it all. That was 1928. Ten years later and that spirit of humanity was to be wiped clean from a generation's consciousness.

CHAPTER 25

I was with Kaufman's circus for about seven months. Not that it was called Kaufman's; Hans's circus had no name. Painted on the sides of our caravans were illustrations of the wonders we had on offer: fierce men breaking chains and tossing fire balls; beautiful women with impossible curves writhing with snakes; dashes of brilliant forms flying from swings; enormous beasts baring their sharpened fangs. And above all of this, there was some elaborate, curved lettering proclaiming us to be 'The Greatest Show on Earth'.

I didn't make any lasting friendship with any of the circus people. I suppose I didn't really have the time – language was very often a barrier, though physically we became very close. You can't wash, eat, curse and sleep around the same tight group of people for seven months without getting close but, beneath all that forced intimacy, I didn't really have anything in common with any of them.

There were about thirty people in Hans's troupe. A good deal more if you counted the children, but I never did. Since my abortion I had trained myself to ignore children but, even if I had stopped to count, I think I would have found it difficult to separate and distinguish that hairy bundle of enthusiasm that fought, and raced, and squealed around our work. One little girl helped with the trapeze act and one little boy helped with the Zebra; the others ran wild. I never knew who they belonged to, it didn't seem to matter. The circus as a whole offered them a haphazard upbringing and they thrived on it. I'm sure that Mama would have spat up a sand castle on all of their upturned little hands.

After my first night with Mama she more or less dismissed me. She had tested me and had given me the benefit of her company for a full night; she had done her bit. All that I remember of my night in her caravan was the noise and the smell of her; a deep, green smell that she snored out into that poky little space. Then, in the morning, she gave me a small, yellow flower.

'Keep it,' she said roughly, 'and chew on it the moment you discover that you are pregnant. It will change your body's mind for you.'

My second night, and most other nights I spent on the road were spent with the trapeze family, the Kubrikovs. It wasn't an ideal arrangement, but I had no choice. Their caravan was the only one that had room for me and that 'room' amounted to a narrow bench with a seat that lifted up. That was the only space I had to store my things in and, because my bench was in the communal area of the van, I had to be the last to bed and the first up.

That caravan was terribly cramped. Alik slept on a bed that folded down over the table and the girls slept across the back wall in bunk beds stacked three high, but still it was the Kubrikov's home and they had decorated it with pride. There were embroidered cushions on all the seats, coloured glass bowls over the candles, silk curtains over the windows and a variety of lacquered screens, which were folded away during the day, but which provided us with a semblance of privacy at night.

The thin walls of the van were completely covered with photographs and pictures. Most of the photographs were of the four siblings in various costumes but, interspersed with these, were pictures of them as children; pictures of them wrapped in furs, fat little versions of themselves perched on ponies, a smiling Mama holding them in soft focus, a proud Papa standing poker stiff with a watch chain straining across his stomach. There were pictures of buildings as well: fine public buildings and some grand family villas. Outside these, families were arranged in tiers on steps, or in groups around chairs. And then there were newspaper clippings: pictures of the Tzar and his family, pictures and descriptions of social events and even some dress designs for gowns.

We were never really friendly, the Kubrikovs and I, although I did like them and we were always smilingly polite to each other. Still, I only ever got close enough to share a space with them; they were siblings and they were Russian, I was always the odd one out.

I preferred to spend my time with the clowns Ilya and Georgi. I would ride with them during the days and we did have some good fun. Ilya was Bulgarian, and Georgi was Greek, two of the clowns were from Yugoslavia and one from Albania. They were all good friends, though, and had obviously been touring together for years, since long before Hans found them. They had been together long enough to develop a sort of hybrid language. It was based on a combination of English and German and was coloured with idioms and expressions from each of their national languages.

Even when the two Yugoslavs were talking together they spoke in this strange dialect. And why not? They were happy with it, they had good friends to share it with and good things to say in it.

Every second spent with Kaufman's circus is worth recording. Every shower, every storm, every dusty road, every wild growth of flowers, every song and every story, every flaming row and every passionate reconciliation. Every meal was an event; every bottle of whisky a party. Sometimes I wish I had recorded it all at the time. It's not that the memory of it has faded. I can still see it in vibrant colour, but that's the problem. It couldn't always have been that vibrant; I must have lost some of the more mundane details in the drama of the whole. But then maybe my memory is right; maybe the whole of the adventure was dramatic.

I remember the pride I felt parading down the main street of so many little towns. I remember the flurry of having to pitch our camp before the dark or the cold settled in on us and I remember the way people would look at me with a lustful envy as I floated from shop to shop, from bar to bar, giving out fliers, flaunting a glimpse of absolute freedom.

Our performances always started at dusk and so the times varied with the seasons. I don't know what reasoning dictated this, when I asked I was just told that it was tradition. But then 'tradition' was the answer given to most of my questions. 'Tradition' was why we couldn't work thirteen shows running, why we could never put a hat on a bed, why we couldn't wish each other good luck, why some of us threw coal at a new moon and why others spat whenever they said their own names.

Our show usually lasted a little longer than two hours. We would start our programme by racing, all of us, out on to the ring. Hans would stand in the middle of our whirl of activity cracking his whip and we would tumble, and clown, and juggle, and balance, and swing all about him with drums a-drumming and pipes a-fluting. Eventually he would gain control of the situation and herd us all back into the wings of the tent. From there he would call us out one by one, thrilling the crowd with descriptions of our talents.

The show always went down well; we were a good circus. What we lacked in skill we made up for in charm, and we were a charming lot. We were young and good-looking, and people are always willing to pay for quality flesh. The women, wrapped in black and aged with drudgery, smiled at the breadth of the strong man's chest, while their men stared at our legs, busts and tightly nipped waists. The children were happy with the elephant, the clowns, the night and, of course, Olaf, the strong man. He played up to them just as much as he posed for their mothers, and that's what Olaf did best, pose. It wasn't that he was a fraud, he really was a very strong man. Maybe it was just that he was lazy, or bored, or plain tired out but, whatever his reasons, he was the only one of us who actually cheated.

His dumb-bells weren't real; they were hollow, made of wood, I could lift them easily. How he got away with it was simple enough, though. He would roar and snarl at the crowd, advancing on one bench of them and then, pretending an animal distraction, turn, and, as if following a scent advance, roaring, towards another bench. A few minutes of doing this had the crowd quaking with the joy of fear. Children would cling a little tighter to their mothers, and fathers would start squaring themselves against the fabricated threat.

Then, when things were nice and tense, Olaf would reach out for two children and snatch them into the ring. Some parents protested, some children cried, but mostly people were too scared, or too embarrassed, to make too much of a fuss. Olaf would then mime to the children that they were to try and lift his weights, one on either side of his dumb-bells. The children, once they realised that they weren't going to be eaten, usually relaxed enough to do what they were told. If they had tried at all they could have lifted those hollow blocks of wood, but they were never given the chance. Once they had positioned themselves, one on either end, their little arms straining around the pretend weights, Olaf would sweep them into the air. For all the world it looked as if he was carrying two stupendous blocks of lead along with two squealing, dangling children. No one ever thought to question him.

CHAPTER 26

Once we left Italy the road got harder, colder. I knew then that one season would do me. Sometimes I thought it would do for me, but I knew not to complain, I had to learn to live with it; I had no choice but to. I had nowhere to go and not enough money left to take me there. My only option was to stay on with the circus until we reached Berlin where, I assumed, I'd be able to find work.

During that hard, cold slog up north, Hans was the only one of us who managed to maintain his good humour. Every night he'd try to rally us together with a bottle and a few songs. He had always been the first one to sing, and now, very often, he was the only one. Sometimes we weren't even bothered to stay up to listen to him. We would all crawl away to our caravans as soon as our meal was eaten, but Hans would still sing. Whatever the weather, he would always sit down by one of our fires and sing to whoever stayed by him and, when no one did, he would sing to himself.

I used to listen to him, wrapped up in my gold coverlet, stretched out on my narrow, stiff bench – I would listen and marvel at his durability. Night after night he could keep up a stream of verse that would, eventually, lose itself in alcohol. He sang in German mostly, and those nights, when I fell asleep listening to the lilt and tone of his songs, proved to be a great help to me later on. By the time it was necessary for me to learn German I already loved it and knew what it sounded like; all I had to do was find the words to fit the tune.

But, despite his late nights and his drinking, Hans was always the first one up in the morning. It was always Hans who called us to work and the further north we travelled the harder that work became. It was the rain that did it. The rain weighted our tents and lodged our caravans in pools of mud. In a continually damp atmosphere our costumes steamed instead of dried, our fires spat instead of sparkled. My feet swelled and blistered from being wrapped in wet stockings and buckled into too-tight shoes. And still we rose at five to practise, and still we rolled on from town to town, and still we lined up in parade formation, but something bigger than our enthusiasm was missing.

We worked our way up to Berlin from Munich to Nürnberg and then on to Leipzig, stopping in a host or more of little towns in between. This was Hans's homeland. In certain towns, in certain bars, he called to people by name and some reacted well, but there were others who just scowled. Hans was too much of a universal creature to recognise what was happening, but the swarthy members of our troupe must have had some sense of what was in the air. Those among us with black hair or Slavic features tramped through the parade with their heads lowered and, during the show, something made them throw their tricks out into the crowd in anger. Hans saw this and tried to stop it. He pleaded with us and then he threatened us, but one man's innocence wasn't enough to change the atmosphere of a country.

We weren't drawing any crowds. Hans couldn't understand it. He said that business had been better during inflation times and he shook his head, but the rest of us understood that it wasn't just a lack of money that was keeping our numbers down. At that time Germany was awash with politics, and every German was called on to flow one way or the other. Those on the right shied away from our ethnic mixture, but those on the left had no time for us either. They were busy plotting their way out of the inevitable. There were always rallies to organise, arguments to start and fights to finish. There was always something more important than the circus to attend to.

In one town, near Munich, our parade clashed with a Nazi demonstration. Nothing happened; we stood back to let them pass. But they looked at us, twenty or thirty young men burning with hate. It was then that I think Hans broke. Sitting high up on Bessie he was made to feel ridiculous, and his reality of charm and magic crumbled. The circus was knocked out of him. After that Hans didn't sing so much at night, but he still drank.

By the time we reached Berlin we were a silent lot, cold and hungry from too much weathering and too many empty houses. We rode the last length of the trip by rail, huddled together and, for the first time, muttering against Hans.

Some said that he should have stayed out the season in Italy. Some said that he should have taken more notice of the omens we had witnessed, the strange cloud formations and the deviations in the flight paths of migrating flocks, but then Mama said that Hans should never have toured his usual route that year, and we believed her.

'The ages of man are counted in sevens,' she explained. 'And a man must change his road to suit his skin. He cannot walk his old path in his new skin or else he calls upon calamity.'

We all nodded when we were told this. We were all happy to accept that the length of time Hans had spent touring Europe was the only reason for our troubles. We all preferred Mama's story to any other, especially those among us with black hair or Slavic features.

Once we reached Berlin, Hans told us exactly what those empty houses had done. They had ruined him. He told us that he was sorry. And then he said it again, and then again. I don't know what response he was expecting but none came.

'The animals will have to go to the zoo,' he said and there was no reaction.

'The equipment will be offset against debts.' Still no movement.

'Your caravans are listed as company property.' At that I went and fetched my things, packed up quickly and rolled up my coverlet. When I returned Hans was still trying to break the news to the troupe. The words he was using were harsher and his tone was firmer; he was trying to hammer his meaning home.

'They'll be coming for everything tomorrow or the next day. I can only pay you a part of what I owe you. We won't be performing tonight…or ever again.'

And all around him his people stood in silence, just staring at him. They stood in the rain dressed in satin, and ribbons, and long, drooping feathers. They stood staring a new reality straight in the face and it killed Hans that he was the one forcing them to look at it. I stepped up to him and kissed his cheek.

'*Auf wiedersehen,*' I said, and he smiled, 'Goodbye, doll face; sorry.'

He handed me a few notes, a fraction of what I was due, but I refused them. I had a little money and I knew that Hans had lost far too much already.

And then there was Berlin.

CHAPTER 27

Ruth and Deirdre sat in Dr Delaney's consulting room, two middle-aged children braced against the inevitable.

'We've had to increase her morphine intake,' he was saying. 'I doubt she will regain consciousness again.' And there he paused, looking from sister to sister. 'At this stage it may be hours or it may be days. We will of course ensure that she is kept as comfortable as possible.'

The two women nodded obediently in acceptance and gratitude.

'It may be a good idea to let any family members know, especially those who may have to travel.' They nodded again and allowed themselves be politely hand-shook from the office.

Once outside they relaxed a little. It's hard to know what expression to wear when being told that you're terminally ill mother is finally reaching her end. Relief seems heartless but everything else seems dishonest, and so the strain of the interview, and so the immediate shifting of shoulders and exhaling of air as they wandered on down the corridor.

'I'd like to stay with her,' Ruth said.

'We both will,' Deirdre said, and they did.

They stopped to make some coffee at the station by the nurses' desk and then slowly carried it with them into their mother's quiet, overheated room. They sat either side of the bed and they talked about logistics. Ellen was still at home; she would stay on for the funeral. Deirdre would ring James that night. They would post the death notice in both *The Times* and the *Independent*, and then they were quiet. Their mother's breathing filled the void, still in, still out, a life exhaling.

'I wonder what she's thinking now?' Deirdre asked.

'God knows,' Ruth answered, emphasising the words. 'Could be anything, anything everything and nothing.' She paused, tried to keep her tone level, but the hurt was still palpable when she added. 'She didn't seem to think of us at all this last while.'

'Ah, what harm?' Deirdre answered. 'Sure she thought of us and only us for far too long. I don't mean it badly, but we were all she had; it was a burden to put on us, wasn't it? Like she had no friends, nothing to interest her outside of the family.'

'I never felt that…'

'Sure? Are you sure there was nothing you ever wanted to do but didn't because pleasing her was more important?'

'Like Holland?'

'Yeah.' Ruth sat silent after that, listening to the light gasps of breath coming from the bed. It seemed such a betrayal.

'I'd have liked to have worn my hair long and to have gone to one of those festivals, at least one. I'd like to have seen Bob Dylan play, or Jimi Hendrix.' Deirdre laughed softly, an incongruous sound in that room, but a heartening one.

'You still can see Dylan; 'fraid you've missed Hendrix.'
They finished their coffee. Ruth left to ring the family, tell
them that if they wanted to visit again now would be the
time. She walked slowly back from the phone. Surprisingly
she felt the need for a cigarette. Deirdre waited until her
sister sat down again before speaking, and then she did so
slowly, carefully, choosing her words.

'I've been thinking about what you asked me the other
day, about why you think your family don't love you the
same way we did Mam, about how you think you went
wrong. I've been thinking that you did it right, did it better
than me. I was so set on not being Mam I lost sight of James
a bit. You did it the hard way, the way neither me nor Mam
could. You really loved your lot unconditionally, loved them
so they didn't have to do anything like mind you, or work
to make you happy. Real love like that really hurts because it
expects nothing back; you just really want them to be happy.
Mam always wanted us to make her happy and I think we
let her down.

'She was scared of everything. Scared of the whole world
and us going into it, but I think she wanted us to do stuff
and bring it back to her. To get us to take her new places, tell
her new things, she just never equipped us for that.'

'Like Holland?'

'Yeah, like Holland, and maybe like Hendrix.'

Brigit Egan groaned in the bed, heartfelt, stomach-
clenching groans. She steadied under Ruth's soothing hands
and then Brian came in. He nodded at Deirdre and crossed
over to Ruth's chair. For the first time in ages she leaned
against his bulk and felt the full comfort of it.

CHAPTER 28

I was right. My death breath is bloating flesh-filled images, too real now. And I have the feeling of London with the drugs and the drink too loud in my ears. But I don't want to die here, not on the streets of Berlin, drowned in the blood of a civilian war. Even in the beginning that option was there, even though, as I walked away from Kaufman's, I felt quite excited. After all those brown, muck-sodden months it felt good to walk through a city again. And Berlin looked good with its richly ornate Prussian architecture, the weight of it is pressing down on me now. It's hard to breathe. But Berlin did look good with its colourful advertising pillars plastered with layers of posters.

I expected some good things from Berlin. I had been told about it often enough; about nights bright enough to eclipse Paris, about the cabarets and the uncensored cinema, about the crazy legacy of Dadaism and the splendour of Max Reinhardt's spectaculars, and all of this heaving under the Berliner Luft, the atmosphere of the city. I had a few dollars in my purse, a great confidence in my street smarts, and I was happy that that was enough.

I knew nothing.

I knew nothing about the reality of Berlin; about the foot-fetish girls cracking whips on street corners or about the boys who rented out themselves, and their sisters and sometimes their mothers. I knew nothing about the slums filled with the displaced, about the true effects of opium, about the indignity of tired nudity touring the tables in the bars, or the crudeness of sex so casual it barely suspended a conversation. And I knew nothing about politics. I couldn't read the defaced, torn, overlapping posters that papered every wall. I didn't know why some boys had to avoid some bars, why groups suddenly ran together in the streets punching and kicking, fit to kill, why sometimes the police just stood back and watched it all play out. I knew nothing.

My dollars went quick enough. I spent my first couple of weeks in a hotel on Augsburger Strasse; a horrible place that expected no luggage and asked no questions, but it was cheap. Back then I had a plan. I thought that I would tour the clubs and the *Lokals* (the bars), get myself a job, work hard for about six months and earn enough to head home to Paris in style. I imagined myself welcomed by all my friends, regaling them with some good stories of wild success.

For two weeks I was naïve enough to think that this plan was feasible. Christmas was in the air and that may have helped. The Salvation Army had erected a huge, illuminated tree on the Wittenbergplatz, and so nothing seemed hopeless. But after New Year's Eve, even those small graces disappeared and so did my money. And still I toured the clubs and the *Lokals*. I told them I could sing. I shook my breasts about to show them I could dance and I hinted that I was willing to do more, but I still hadn't learned to drop my pretty-girl act and so, again and again, I was refused.

I had to leave my hotel and I had to leave without paying. The fat old desk clerk was waiting for me one evening. My bill was overdue and he threatened to take my belongings in lieu. I hadn't enough money left to settle what I owed, and so I pouted a little and told that great big greasy lump of a man that he had to be nicer to me, that I was just a helpless little girl all alone in a big city. He smiled at me then and waddled his way around to my side of his counter. He ran his hand down over my waist and around my buttocks, pressed his greasy, bristling mouth close to mine and his warm, onion breath blew gently onto my face. He whispered that we might come to an arrangement and I licked my lips, glancing my tongue off his as I did, and agreed that we might.

That evening, an hour before he was to come calling on me, I threw my case out of my window, into the back alley, and then crept around to retrieve it. I spent that night walking to keep off the cold and, as soon as it was morning, I went looking for a room. When I first arrived in Berlin I had imagined myself living in a nice apartment in Charlottenborg, I liked the *Schloss*. I also liked the area around Nollendorfplatz and all those tree-lined avenues to the west of the city. But when the time came for me to rent a place I had no choice but to go straight to Kreuzburg, to the slum district.

I found a room with a family who had advertised in their local tobac.

'A room for rent on Simeonstrasse'. I forget how much it was but it must have been going for next to nothing if I could afford it, and it came with the option of added extras: 'breakfast and washing facilities included'.

It sounded perfect. I remember hurrying down the road worrying that it was gone, that something so good would have to be snapped up. And then I worried that I might put them off, that my nail varnish was too garish or my coat was too old. I was still worrying when I stepped through the huge street doors of number ten. Too worried to notice the stench, the graffiti, the dark brown death of that stairwell. I don't know how, but I was still enthusiastic when I pushed the bell of the Muellers' flat.

Frau Mueller, Frieda, opened the door to me. She flung it open, stood in front of me with her hands on her hips and her face flushed, and started in on what sounded like a tirade of abuse. It took me a moment to realise that she had mistaken me for someone else. Initially I thought she was giving out to me for the way I was dressed, but then I realised that she thought that I had come to collect some money from her. She was shouting '*Kein geld*!' at me over and over again. 'No money! No money!' And then she pulled a purse out of her apron pocket, turned it inside out and shoved it in my face. I laughed and shook my head.

'*Zimmer*!' I shouted over her continuing rant, and I showed her my money, what little I had left of it. This had a sudden and great effect on her. Her features bounced into a smile and she started nodding, nodding almost as low as a bow.

'Most delighted,' she said in perfect, radio English, and that was all the English she had. She was proud of it, though, and said it quite frequently.

For the length of time I stayed with the Muellers I was treated like royalty. Frieda, her husband Klaus and their teenage daughter Anna constantly referred to my privileged past and apologised for my present, lowly surroundings. This may have been my fault though because, from the start, I gave them a wrong impression of myself. As soon as I had introduced myself as a potential lodger I was shown around the flat and I saw that Anna kept a picture of Rudolph Valentino pinned up over her bed. I suppose I was feeling a little nervous and I wanted to sound impressive, so I told her that I had met him. After that all the Muellers would point to the pictures in their illustrated papers – pictures of society ladies, of minor royals, or first nights at the opera and ask, 'Is she really an opium addict?'

'Does he really have five swimming pools?'

'Does his wife really bathe in milk?'

They would ask me about balls in Vienna, fashion shows in New York or parties in Hollywood and, in the beginning, I did keep saying that I didn't know anything about any of it. But they would just smile, and nod, and tell me that my German would soon improve. When it did I told them what they wanted to hear, it was easier that way, and then Anna would tell me how she longed to be a dancer, and Klaus would tell me how he once managed to pay for private lessons for her, and then they would both insist on showing me what she had learned.

They would clear a space in their crowded kitchen and Anna would talk me through her image of herself.

'Now, you will imagine me in a long, white robe. I will be a little taller maybe and of course very thin. You will imagine us all outside, with trees in blossom behind me and, in my hair, maybe lilies. Now this (a dishcloth) will be a long scarlet scarf and there will be beautiful music.'

Then, swinging her cloth, she would bounce around the room, humming a little, her eyes glazed over, lost in the beauty of her imagination. She was a big girl and it was hard to meet her eye when she finally stopped and looked for my reaction. But, after the first time, I got good at pretending. I would flutter my brightly coloured nails and tell her that she was 'just too, too talented' before bolting for the door. I knew that they hoped that I would come home one night with the likes of Max Reinhardt in tow, singing their praises and changing their lives. I may have constantly disappointed them, that's one way of looking at it, but I also offered them constant hope and, in those times, in that place, that was something.

I wasn't the only lodger the Muellers managed to squash into their tiny little flat. Two boys, young men, shared a room only a little larger than mine, Rudi and Gerhardt. They called themselves Bill and Gerry; English nicknames were very fashionable at the time. Bill and Gerry were very rarely at home; like mine, their room was far too small for comfort and, like me, their money was to be made on the streets. But, unlike me, they must have spent every penny they earned on their clothes. They dressed like a couple of sharps: double-breasted suits and Brylcreemed hair, gold signet rings and soft, open-topped shirts. They mostly worked in the west-end bars, where the tourists drank and where good-looking boys could name their price.

My room was beside theirs and had once been part of it, we were only separated by a flimsy partition and so, just like in the circus, we were forced to be at least superficially intimate. I heard all about their happy union and they heard all about my loneliness and so, sometimes, they asked me to go out with them and, whenever they did, I went. They were nice boys and always good company.

My room was tiny. There was just space for a narrow bed, a clothes rail and a stool. My grubby little window looked out into the box-tight courtyard and so very little light ever reached me. The boys' room was only slightly bigger than mine. Theirs could fit a double bed, a wardrobe and a chair. The rest of the flat was made up of only two other rooms, the Muellers' bedroom and the kitchen, Both were small and filthy, although some effort had been made with the kitchen.

Frieda, a heavy woman in her forties from Bavaria, had enough of the *Hausfrau* in her to know that a woman's kitchen should reflect a woman's pride in her home, and so she tried. Trouble was, I suspect, Frieda didn't have much pride in her home and so her attempts at the kitchen were only ever surface deep. She put paper doilies everywhere and then left them to soak up the dirt that belched out of the greasy central stove; they left patterns behind them whenever they were moved.

The large, square kitchen sink served as 'the washing facilities' that Frieda had proudly advertised, and the shared toilet was one floor up.

I never ate with the Muellers. I knocked a few marks off the rent, offered to pay two weeks up front and told Frieda that I never ate breakfast. Frieda shook my hand, then hugged me and then kissed me. I cursed myself. I could have got away with paying even less than the pittance I had negotiated.

After paying Frieda I only had a few marks left and I was hungry. For the first time since I had left home I was scared. This was real. I really had no money, no friends and not even the words to ask for help. For the first time since London it was just me, just me and the streets.

CHAPTER 29

It's an old story, Mother dear, and here's how it goes. You don't let anyone see what you're wearing when you leave your house because there are certain types of shit you just don't need to drag home. You go to where you've seen a few others work and you hide your coat in a bush. You tell yourself that it's not so cold. You make some noise with your heels when you walk and you try to hide the darns in your stockings. You start by trying to catch their eye. You think a smile will get them going, and when that's not enough you start whispering.

'You like it?' you whisper.

'Hey mister, you want it?'

'You wanna tell me what you like, what you want?'

And still they walk on by and so you get to calling. I soon got to calling. My pretty-girl act was gone now and I was left wild and raw, crawling my way through the streets, calling out for survival.

'You come with me, mister, and I'll tell you what you want. I'll give you a taste of what you've never got before.' That worked and so the next day I ate.

I didn't know it then, but I was lucky. For one full week I worked up and down Unter den Linden, and for one full week no one stopped me. I had expected trouble; I was on the lookout for it and I had already decided to go with it. I was so lost that a pimp's protection seemed almost attractive. But no one stopped me; perhaps they thought I was someone else.

And that was my second piece of luck. I did look like someone else, like Garbo and like Berlin's home-grown version, Marlene Dietrich. It was a fashionable look, one that men were willing to pay for and for a full week I let them. They pawed me down alleys, they pulled me into their cars, they used me worse than they had in London, or maybe it was just that now I was sober.

After a week I managed to break free. I got a job. It was the usual interview, in the usual looking cellar club, just off Nollendorfplatz, not quite in the west end. I followed the owner around listing my talents in English, throwing in the occasional German word, batting my eyelids, wriggling and pouting, but he barely looked at my routine and then he yawned.

'*Mensch aber*! *Kanst du etwas anders?*' he said and I just stared back at him; I didn't understand.

'Can you not do something else?' he shouted in rough English. 'All the girls do this.' And he started pushing me towards the door.

'Yeah?' I shouted back, right into his face. 'Yeah, but I can do it on… rollerskates.' And I turned and marched away. He caught up with me outside.

'*Wirklich?*' he asked. 'Really?'

And so there I was. Me and my great break! Touring the tables of the Kabaret Keller, topless and on roller skates. It wasn't at all bad though, really, it was a friendly enough place to work in, but I knew never to tell the other girls that the skates were my idea.

And that, more or less, was how things stayed for the length of my stay in Berlin. I had my little back room, I always managed to keep a job on the go and I gathered up a few friends. I never went back to Paris. I made excuses not to, and my first excuse was Phil Anderson Junior.

He came into the club one night and sat at one of my tables. It was a busy night and he was just another guy, slumped into the shadows, hunched over a drink. He didn't look up at all, didn't look at me and didn't look at the show, just every now and again he would knock his empty glass off his table and then I'd know to wheel by with another drink. His behaviour wasn't that odd, though, I was well used to worse, and so I didn't pay him much attention. He was quiet and that was all that mattered to me.

But he didn't stay quiet. After his fourth drink he started muttering and, with every other drink, those mutterings grew louder and louder.

'Piss poor spirits,' he spat out. 'Call this a drink? Can't get a fucking straight shot in this town. Fucking whores running the show. Fucking bitches! Can't get a square drink 'less you're willin' to pay for some old cunt. Fuck that and fuck you!'

He was shouting now and the force of his words had pushed his head right back. I was standing over him ready to pour him out his eighth shot and, behind me, the management were squaring up for a fight.

'Phil?' I asked. I had to ask because, although I knew I was looking down on Phil's body, I didn't know who I was talking to.

'Yeah,' he said and then he had to think. Eventually he added, 'JoJo', my working name, and he even said that aggressively. 'You gonna give me that drink?'

I did, with a warning to keep it down. Maybe the shock of seeing me had knocked some of the fight out of him, or maybe he was still sober enough to know how to avoid another beating – either way, he did as he was told and kept more or less quiet for the rest of the evening.

As soon as my shift was over I joined him at his table. He didn't say a word, didn't even seem to notice me. For a long while I just sat opposite him, watching him. Watching the shakes in his hand, the scars on his face, the bloody, pulpy swelling over his left ear, the grey, ingrained filth of his flesh, the dirty, frayed state of his clothes and the hard line of his mouth. He wouldn't look at me, he was still drinking and he kept his eyes fixed on his glass. Eventually he spoke,

'You want something?' he asked, and wheezed out a thick, mucus-sodden laugh. ''Cos I got nothin' left to give you, babe.'

'I don't need anything,' I said, and that was wrong thing to say.

'You got it all, have you?' he muttered, still staring at his glass. 'So what you still doin' here? Want to give me a bit of pity maybe? Want to make yourself feel good by doin' the right thing by an old friend? But you're not listening, babe. I told you I got nothin' to give you, an' that includes the satisfaction of doin' a bit of charity work.' And then he stood up, drained his glass and stumbled away from the table. As a parting shot he called over his shoulder. 'You got some good tits though, JoJo, always knew you'd make me proud someday.' And he coughed out another laugh.

I followed him home that night. Kept a little behind him, ignoring all the insults and later, early the following afternoon, I crouched under his uncoordinated punches and tried ignoring them too.

Phil was dying and he was dying in squalor, in a filthy room maybe eight foot square, on a urine-soaked mattress.

'We all find our level, babe,' was how he explained his surroundings, maybe he couldn't afford better or maybe he just didn't care.

I stayed by him until the end, for almost three months, but I did him no good. I got him a better bed to sleep on, fed him cleaner drugs and good, strong liquor, managed to wash out the worst of his sores and tried talking him out of the hell that had clogged up his senses.

I talked to him about good days, sunny skies and parks filled with children. I reminded him of his old tastes, of how he used to love soft cheeses, strawberries, well-roasted pork and sharply chilled champagne. I told him that I still had my gold coverlet, that Paris was still missing him, that good friends still gathered to talk about him. I looked out of his window at the rain drumming down on the grubby terraces and described the view as mist settling over the cosy warmth of community. I told him that I loved him.

But I did him no good; all he ever did was laugh at me. All he ever saw was a whore tending to a dope-fiend, in the squalor of a ghetto, in a country filled with hate and bristling to fight. His bright optimism had long since been flushed out of him, spat into the gutter, vomited up on street corners and beaten out by dealers and pimps. All that was in him now was the drugs and the streets and I knew that all the money and all the time I was spending on him could make no difference to that. In the end all I could do for Phil Anderson Junior was make sure that he died between clean sheets.

I called to him one afternoon and found the door to his room wide open. The place had been stripped bare and there was a strong smell of bleach. I didn't cry; isn't that the saddest thing, Mother? I never cried for Phil.

Once he was gone, so was my excuse for staying in Berlin, but still I stayed on. At first I told myself that I couldn't afford to go back to Paris, but I could. Once I started making money I made enough. My week on the street had taught me a new act and that new act could make me a lot of money when I bothered to work it right.

Then I told myself that the timing was wrong. That there was no point in going home in the summer because everyone would be away, and it was no good going home in the winter because Christmas tended to just busy everyone up.

Truth was I didn't want to go back. Every now and again I'd hear from the old crowd and the news was always the same; things were changing. The beautiful people had moved south, taking their glamour and their dollars with them, and that wasn't news I wanted to hear.

Truth was I needed the dream of my Paris to keep me going. I was living with jackboots and riots and the promise of something worse and so, like the circus people, I had to create a reality for myself. And my reality was a Paris night in 1923, sitting in the Dôme, watching the door, waiting for whoever would bring on the night. Waiting for Kiki or Flossie, McAlmon, Phil or Claudette and always hoping for Pablo. Later there would be The Jockey, later still maybe Bricktop's and some good sweaty dancing with Robert before breakfast, and then one more gin fizz before bed.

So, even while I was actively saving my money and planning to go back to Paris, in my heart I always knew that I never would for fear of hearing even an echo of jackboots on the Boulevard Raspail. I wasn't brave enough to risk witnessing that, and then, sometimes, Berlin wasn't so bad.

Kaffee and Kuchen was always good. Kaffee and Kuchen served in one of those high-class cafés that were always muted and warm, and that usually had a quartet playing discreetly from behind the palms. And the Tiergarten was always good, and the Grünewald, and the breadth of Unter den Linden and those long summer evenings by the See or at the fairground on Potsdamer Strasse. And then there was the novelty of those flamboyantly camp clubs up west, or that huge cinema by Zoo station where a forty-five-piece orchestra accompanied the silent movies and, of course, there were always the movies.

All the girls dreamed of being in the movies. They all queued for hours hoping to get picked for crowd scenes or screen tests, and they all spent their money on cosmetics that promised to cream up their complexions, or diet regimes that promised to firm up their stomachs while skimming pounds off their hips. But I never bothered with any of that, I just applied myself to the job in hand and, just like in Paris, the job improved.

I used the fact that I looked like Dietrich and it worked. She had built herself quite a reputation before moving on and so, all I had to do was step into the void her leaving had created. I dressed a little like her with a boa, a monocle on a ribbon, a short skirt and no underwear, but I added to the image. I darkened my eyebrows, painted my lips into a tight red bow and varnished my nails in outrageous colours, just like Kiki used to do and, just like Kiki, I got myself a little pet rat. I chained him to my wrist and he sat happily on my shoulder. This was my new act.

I hung out in the Keller Kabaret mostly, but I'd often tour the clubs around the Ku'damm and I soon got known. One of the girls taught me how to crack a whip and sometimes, even in quite crowded clubs, I would stand, legs spread, my rat on my shoulder and my whip sparking off the floor. I no longer looked at the world through my pretty-girl eyes, I no longer fooled my men into thinking they were the first. This time I was in charge. I cracked the whip and that told them that I had seen it all, done it all, been bored by it all before. Sad little men came to me with their sad little perversions and I never laughed, never as much as raised an eyebrow. Sometimes all they wanted was for me to shout at them, sometimes they wanted a little more, but it was always my choice and they always agreed to my price.

I didn't know it at the time but I had stumbled upon a very popular form of prostitution. At that time men from all over Europe came to Berlin wanting to be educated in sex, and they took their education seriously. Among the non-fetish heterosexuals, middle-aged women were the most popular types of prostitutes, well-seasoned women who could tell a man what was expected of him and show him how to live up to those expectations. The gay men went for the working-class street boys who asked no questions and were in no position to pass judgement, and the fetishists went to us, any girl with a whip and an authoritative manner. Mostly these poor men were just desperate to be led and I got good at leading them, I'd use my street cry,

'You come with me, mister, and I'll tell you what you want. I'll give you a taste of what you've never got before.'

The money was good. The money was so good that I told the owner of the Kabaret Keller, a Herr Voeller, that I was putting on some clothes and taking off my skates, and he didn't argue. He knew that I was good for business, that I attracted a good type of customer, men who were willing to sit and drink for the night, and so he told me that I could have a part in his cabaret.

The stage in the Kabaret Keller was a small, box affair with a moth-eaten backdrop behind it, a worn velvet curtain in front of it and a lot of tiny coloured bulbs surrounding it. It looked good, though. The acts weren't always good but that didn't matter; the acts were only part of the show. A moth-eaten backdrop, lit from behind, could look like the night sky, a ventriloquist could look as if his lips were sealed; the dancers could wriggle even if they couldn't dance; I could look like Marlene Dietrich; and sparkling wine could fizz like champagne.

I wore a classy type of dress – silver and spangled with a high feather in my hair and some glass beads down my back. I sang in German with an English accent and in English with a French accent and all the men, especially those who knew me in leather, applauded my multiple talents. Some nights I would close the show. I would sing the finale and, from the wings, the dancers would high kick their way on to the stage. They'd step and kick forwards and backwards a few times, throwing kisses out into the crowd, hitching their skirts up a little higher, slapping each others thighs, throwing their eyes up to the heavens and hinting that they were preparing to throw caution to the wind. The crowd, usually the non-regulars, would stand, and clap, and shout, 'Off! Off! Off!'

And over it all I would be singing fit to bust, waving my arms up high and acting the proper diva. The dancers and I would reach our dramatic pitch together. I would hold that penultimate note, the one I had held so often in Paris, and the dancers would toss their wigs off and whip the stuffing out of their bras. Then they'd thump off the stage, walking like the lads they were and, just as the curtain fell, I'd sweep into a bow. Sometimes the applause was slow in coming, but it always came; it was a good show.

CHAPTER 30

I stayed in Berlin for too long. I stayed with the Muellers for too long. I was there for years, five, or six, or was it seven? I lost count, and I never even unpacked fully. I suppose I thought that if I did I would be admitting that Kreuzberg was my home, and if I bothered to find a better place to live I would be admitting that Berlin was my home. And so I stayed put, living out of a suitcase.

Although I may have been static, the world around me wasn't; it was whipping itself up into a frenzy. There were elections, and debates, and riots, and fear – and though everyone was faced with the worst, no one quite believed it would happen. I knew homosexuals who thought that Hitler's brand of authority might be good for the country; they never thought that he would gain a majority. And I knew Jews who firmly believed in the humanity of civilisation. I knew one softly spoken, kindly man, Levi, who showed me his medals from the First World War. He shook his head and told me that the Germans were always good to their heroes. I knew a young Jewish boy who swore he'd stay to fight. He died in a street brawl in 1931, before the proper fight had even started.

But there were always fights of some kind. In the mornings there would be pools of blood on the streets. People began disappearing from quite early on. And over all the terror, over all the beatings and the killings, over all the rhetoric of hatred and the policy of division, there stood that ideal of superior beauty.

First they were on the posters, those blonde girls and boys smiling into the future, smiling down on our grey, grit-bound lives. Then they were in the beer gardens still smiling, rattling their collection boxes. Later they were on the streets stamping after their red and black flags singing, '*Deutschland, Deutschland über alles.*'

Late in 1929 the world economy collapsed. It started in New York, but it spread quickly, and by 1930 the delicate fabric of the Weimar Republic was unravelling. Unemployment rose and rose, the threat of inflation returned and those smiling girls and boys gained in popularity. They sang, '*Deutschland Erwache*'.

And a lot of people sang along with them. They seemed to believe that it could be that easy to claim a stable future for themselves.

In the cabarets we mocked them; him in his lederhosen with his foolish, staring eyes, her with her false innocence hiding a wealth of sexual experience but, as the years rolled on, fewer and fewer people laughed.

And still I stayed on. Others did too. I think we were immobilised by it all; we felt that to react to the horror would be to admit to it. I waited until I was forced to realise my circumstances before I reacted and I think that that's what a lot of us did. Some of us reacted on time, some of us didn't.

And of those of us who didn't, the more optimistic amongst us, the more trusting, the kinder people – these were the ones who suffered. Bill and Gerry for instance.

They were both good boys. They both saw good lives stretching out before them. They were popular on the streets, in the bars and at home. They only expected good things from people and so they honestly offered themselves to casual friendships. They were too honest. Everyone knew of their sexual preferences and everyone knew that Bill's grandmother was Jewish. They were never political, though sometimes they felt a little guilty about that. Sometimes they would shake their heads and say that things were getting to be very bad. And then, when things got worse, Bill would frequently shake his head and say, 'For me now things are getting to be very bad.'

They flirted briefly with Communism, thinking that an organisation based on equality would be able to offer them a little protection but, after only a few meetings, they realised that there was no equating their concerns with those of the common worker. They were on their own.

They had their plans though. They told me that they were going to go to Frankfurt. They thought that they would be able to start over there.

I like to remember them looking their best, all spruced up for a night on the town; gleaming, white shirt collars framing strong, brown necks; bright round faces shining with aftershave and expectations. Sometimes I went with them, to those tourist places up west, and watched them work. They were tame clubs really; they offered a lot to see but precious little to touch. Cross-dressers, lesbians and homosexual men would dance together, simulate sex together and sometimes cruise the tourists tables just to tease. It was wonderful to see what a reaction Bill and Gerry got; they were almost applauded as they strutted along, and rightly so. Their brand of eroticism reminded me very much of Rudolph Valentino's tango, far from being effeminate, it was exclusively masculine.

They called each other 'my man' in English; an intentional pun as *Mann* in German means 'husband'. They introduced each other to wealthy-looking men as 'My man Bill', 'My man Gerry', 'Maybe we will sit with you?'

They were never refused.

My time in Berlin ended quite abruptly. As they say in stories, it happened one night. I was on my way home when I met Bill and Gerry on the street. I hadn't seen either of them in a while and I remember being very glad of their bright expectant faces on that cold, grim evening. They were cruising the *Lokals* around Kreuzberg. This was quite a fashionable thing for the braver tourists to do. This was where you could get some real action, where boys like Bill and Gerry could make some easy money. The Cosy Bar was one of the more popular dumps and that's where they were headed. I had nothing to do, it was my night off, the Muellers were home and the streets were cold, so I happily agreed to go with them for a drink.

Things happen, but more often places and people happen. London happened, Paris, Kaufman's, and Berlin – they all happened. And Phil Anderson Junior and McAlmon, Pablo, Flossie, Claudette, the Hemingways, Zelda and Scott – they all happened to me and, I suppose, I must have happened to them. But sometimes things just do happen, sometimes events just take control, like on that spring night when I decided to join Bill and Gerry for a drink.

I hurried back to the Muellers, shouting out to them.

'I will need some money and I should bring a scarf – it's freezing. I'll follow you.'

And so I got my scarf, and my money, and I followed my friends.

Sometimes things can happen that easily.

The bar was quiet when I burst in through the door, the cold propelling me forward. I expected conversation, laughter and music, and the silence momentarily confused me. It seemed to take me an age to see what was going on. The usual clientele were standing by the back wall. That straggle of cheerful decadence knocked grim and passive. A man wrapped round with a boa, lipstick smeared across his chin, a delicately built man in an expensive suit, the affectation of his cane limp by his side. A few others, and Gerry. I was reminded of Hans Kaufman astride his elephant gazing into the unfolding of an alien future.

Blank faces, undirected stares, thoughts focused on someplace, anyplace else. Two men stood in front of this line of defeat, nightsticks idly slapping off thighs and, in the centre of the bar, Bill, blood blurring features, hair clotted to his scalp, was struggling onto all fours. A boot kicked him sideways and a voice barked at him to stand up. He tried again.

Four men were standing around him, laughing, casually throwing comments at each other. The next time Bill lifted himself onto his arms they aimed for his head. The blood hit the side of the bar and I shouted.

'No!' I ran forward and grabbed at the man nearest me. I knew what I was doing, I had taken the time to rationalise the situation and thought that perhaps they wouldn't hit a semi-respectable-looking woman. Or if they did they wouldn't hit her too hard and I figured, after a split-second weigh-up, that a bust eye or a broken limb was better than a broken spirit.

So I shouted out 'No!' as authoratively as I could and I ran forward and pushed and tore at the men. But they weren't about to surrender control of the situation to some meddling foreigner. Instead, with clinical cruelty and professional politeness, they showed me just how little I and my actions meant to them.

'Excuse us, miss,' they said, gently sidestepping me to plant another kick.

'Perhaps the lady would like a drink?' they asked the barman.

'We're almost finished miss; take a seat, we won't be much longer.'

They left Bill when he stopped moving. He should have done that much earlier, but maybe his fighting to stay conscious was him fighting to retain some kind of dignity. As the men left they each took the time to bow politely to me. One asked would I like to join them for something to eat. I said nothing. And I did nothing as Bill's friends closed around him; soothed him, managed him into a car and off to a doctor who was known to be sympathetic towards these types of cases.

The bar was more or less empty and I was still sitting, stung and humiliated. The barman had the decency to look shame-faced when he set an expensive bottle of wine down in front of me.

'Compliments of the gentlemen,' he said.

I left the bottle there and walked outside where I belonged.

All Gods Dead

I was an outsider. Since stepping up to Phil's car, I had accepted that role. Living on the fringes of other people's art, their lives, their loves, their passions. I hadn't been able to gain any real access to any of it, any of them. What had made me think I would be able to claim their fight?

It was time to go home. And that no longer meant Paris. Maybe it does now.

But home first meant my parents' house. A well-timed arrival, a sick mother, a dying father and a fiction to walk straight into.

Later, home meant the solidity of William Egan's respectability. Children, a dog, a big garden. Coffee in the morning and someone else's thoughts to fill your head with, inform your conversation with.

You tell yourselves stories as you grow older. Your favourite stories, the ones you play over and over in your head, blend into the telling. Soon the memory is eclipsed by the recall. Not this story. I never told this story to myself. Not until now and so the memory is fresh, and my bones are sore and my breath is weighed down and I wonder what good the rest of my life did. I hid these memories behind a smile of conformity, left them fresh to claw death bloated real into this room. And I have a feeling of London with the drugs and the drink too loud in my ears. I don't want to, don't need to remember any more.

CHAPTER 31

Ruth and Deirdre stood side by side at the open grave. There was a good turnout, especially considering their mother's age. Ruth was surprised by how much this meant to her, that her mother's passing was an event. The undertakers lowered the coffin, heads bent. The mourners, battling with unsuitable shoes, respectfully picked their way around neighbouring graves. Under the muffled chant of the rosary being led by the priest, Deirdre slipped her arm around her younger sister's shoulders.

'Once there were two middle-aged women, both very beautiful and both very kind,' she whispered and Ruth, unbearably, wanted to laugh.

Afterwards they went to a hotel and spoke to cousins and friends. 'It was very pleasant,' everybody said. 'We mustn't just wait for funerals to meet up.'

And everyone promised to make more of an effort to stay in touch.

Afterwards, the immediate family, a few friends and the favourite cousins went back to Ruth's house where she had thoughtfully ordered some catered food and a case of wine. The evening stretched into night and Ruth stretched with it, taut and tired.

At one stage Ellen, a little bleary from drink, cornered her in the kitchen, slipped an arm around her waist and kissed her cheek.

'I'm so sorry, Mum,' she said. 'I just hope you live as long. I couldn't bear it if you died. I'm not going back to London,' she continued. 'Do you mind if I move back in for a while? Just till I get sorted?'

'You're always welcome, love,' Ruth said, and for the first time she had no interest in the whys behind the story. If Ellen wanted to tell her she would.

Much later, weeks later, Ruth cleared out the storage unit where herself and Deirdre had left the pieces of furniture they were going to bring to the cottage in Kerry. Quite a lot of it fitted into the car, the rest she organised to have collected by a delivery company. She added the box of her mother's books that she had taken from the house with a mind to read. She never had. *Being Geniuses Together* was still balanced on top. She was going to drive down to Kerry and stay there for a week, maybe more, maybe much more. She was physically yearning for solitude, for somewhere to let her thoughts settle.

It was a long drive. Past Dingle and on. Down bad roads, through rain and thick, drenching mist. She arrived late, turned up the boreen and bumped along for the last quarter of a mile. She left everything in the car, just bringing in the bag of shopping she had stopped off to buy. The place smelled of damp, green damp and camphor.

The smell hit Ruth square back to childhood, summers run ragged over fields and stone walls, splashing and squealing through the breaking waves of the Atlantic. She hadn't visited the place for a long time. Since her mother's fall the cottage hadn't been used much at all and it showed. Despite the man who came to keep an eye on things, it had the look of neglect, it seemed to be dissolving into its surrounding shrubbery. Ruth made a mental note to have words with O'Connor, if she could find him at all that was; he was usually very elusive when any of them were down.

She unpacked her food, switched on the heating, made up her bed in the slightly bigger bedroom, plugged in an electric blanket to air it and did her best to coax a fire out of the grate in the sitting-room. 'Sitting-room' was a bit of an exaggeration, though, it was basically the only room aside from two tiny bedrooms and a badly tacked-on bathroom. In the corner a sink, pine table and a bulging, crammed dresser described a kitchen and, in the centre, a heavy, sagging, battered settee did for everything else. Ruth sat on that and felt the damp rise through her. It would be cosy in a while, smelly-damp cosy, but until then she took the top blanket off one of the beds and wrapped herself up in it – a worn, tatty gold thing with some kind of faded purple motif on it.

Later, warmed by wine and a too scalding shower, Ruth wrapped herself naked in it and lay on the bed.

'Lay lady lay…' she hummed to herself and then laughed because she had forgotten that she was, actually, laying on a big brass bed. Brigit Egan's box of books lay on the floor beside her. Ruth had dropped McAlmon for the comfort of Fitzgerald, but was finding *Tender is the Night* a bit plodding. She delved back in looking for *The Great Gatsby* and came across her mother's flip book, the one that showed a middle-aged man's face melt into that of a young girl. Deirdre and herself had always found it creepy, but their Mam had loved it. 'From me to you' was inscribed on its battered cover.